By ELYSE SPRINGER

World Turned Upside Down

HOCKEY GODS AND MONSTERS
Suckerpunch

Published by DREAMSPINNER PRESS
www.dreamspinnerpress.com

FOAL

ELYSE SPRINGER

SUCKERPUNCH

Published by
DREAMSPINNER PRESS

5032 Capital Circle SW, Suite 2, PMB# 279, Tallahassee, FL 32305-7886 USA
www.dreamspinnerpress.com

This is a work of fiction. Names, characters, places, and incidents either are the product of author imagination or are used fictitiously, and any resemblance to actual persons, living or dead, business establishments, events, or locales is entirely coincidental.

Suckerpunch
© 2019 Elyse Springer

Cover Art
© 2019 Aaron Anderson
aaronbydesign55@gmail.com
Cover content is for illustrative purposes only and any person depicted on the cover is a model.

All rights reserved. This book is licensed to the original purchaser only. Duplication or distribution via any means is illegal and a violation of international copyright law, subject to criminal prosecution and upon conviction, fines, and/or imprisonment. Any eBook format cannot be legally loaned or given to others. No part of this book may be reproduced or transmitted in any form or by any means, electronic or mechanical, including photocopying, recording, or by any information storage and retrieval system, without the written permission of the Publisher, except where permitted by law. To request permission and all other inquiries, contact Dreamspinner Press, 5032 Capital Circle SW, Suite 2, PMB# 279, Tallahassee, FL 32305-7886, USA, or www.dreamspinnerpress.com.

Trade Paperback ISBN: 978-1-64405-431-4
Digital ISBN: 978-1-64405-430-7
Library of Congress Control Number: 2019904443
Trade Paperback published October 2019
v. 1.0

Printed in the United States of America
∞
This paper meets the requirements of
ANSI/NISO Z39.48-1992 (Permanence of Paper).

This book is for Claire,
who somehow convinced me to go to a hockey game back in
2016 and then tricked me into falling in love with the sport.
This is all your fault.
Thank you.

Author's Note

I STARTED writing *Suckerpunch* in the spring of 2017. When I outlined the "Hockey Gods and Monsters" universe, the NHL looked pretty different; there was no hockey team announced in Seattle, and Vegas hadn't even played their first game yet. The Seattle Cascades were created on Day 1 of the writing process, and I didn't feel the need to change that once the Seattle expansion team was officially announced in December 2018. But since there is now officially an NHL team coming to Seattle, a disclaimer: I do not lay any claim to the Seattle NHL team or any other real-life hockey things that you may recognize in this book.

Okay? Okay.

(If the NHL ends up naming their new team the Seattle Cascades, then… uh, let's just hope they don't?)

That said, I've done my best to write all of the hockey scenes in this book as accurately as possible. If I've made any mistakes, well… this is a sport where even the referees don't know what goaltender interference is.

I hired two brilliant translators to help with the Russian and French dialogue in this book. Thank you to Elena Kazachenkova and Gabrielle P-B for all of wonderful translation work!

A few more thanks: my parents, as always, for supporting me in everything I do. Hannah, for sending me hockey gifs when I'm sad. Anna, for being the best hockey game seat buddy on earth. And Sarah, for picking me up from the airport at 2:30 a.m. in exchange for getting thanked in this book.

And finally, thanks to the Dallas Stars because I love them and I'm writing these acknowledgments the day after they were eliminated from the playoffs. Hockey is heartbreaking, y'all. (But this book totally isn't, promise.)

Roster for the Seattle Cascades

Player	Number	Position	Birthplace
Seth Bayer	22	C	USA
Shawn Cartier	3	D	USA
Theo Eklund	14	LW	Sweden
Johan Engel	55	RW	Germany
Avery Johnson	2	D	USA
Luca Klausman (A)	34	RW	Switzerland
Pierre Leduc	70	LW	Canada
Akseli Mäkelä	38	LW	Finland
Derick Merkley (C)	96	C	Canada
Tyler Morgan	6	D	Canada
Luke Oettenger (A)	7	D	USA
Alexander Petrov	12	D	Russia
Braiden Rager	18	C	Canada
Andrej Rybár	26	RW	Slovakia
Oliver Sjöberg	5	D	Sweden
Brad Thompson	88	RW	USA
Mikhail Volkov	42	LW	Russia
Noah Wilson	23	C	Canada
Matthias Hertzog	30	G	Germany
Alexander Fanning	31	G	USA
Eduard Despres	29	G	Canada

Chapter One

Goaltender Alex Fanning might not be the most recognizable face in the Portland Loggers franchise, but his name is certainly on everyone's tongue after the incredible save he made in the remaining few seconds of last season's playoff final. That save brought the Calder Cup to Portland for the first time in franchise history, and made Fanning's #30 jersey a fan favorite.
—Jason Rawlins, PortlandHockeyBlog.com

THE DOOR creaked when Alex pushed it open, and he winced, freezing in the doorway and watching for movement. The hotel room was completely still apart from the steady deep breathing that emerged from beneath a lump of blankets. With a silent exhale, Alex nudged the door open the rest of the way and slid inside, then closed it behind him as quietly as possible.

His roommate didn't budge.

Success.

The clock on the nightstand between the two beds glowed an angry, accusing red, letting Alex know that it was well after midnight, and *well* after curfew. But they'd played a game earlier that evening, and the hard loss against San Diego had sent everyone back to the hotel early—which meant no one had been around to see Alex sneak out shortly after ten, or return hours later.

He pulled his phone out of his pocket and tossed it on the bed before starting to strip out of his jeans and hoodie. The display lit up, obnoxiously bright in the dark room, and revealed a missed text message.

Meg: Sorry again for being so late, man. I owe you one.

Alex rolled his eyes and let the screen go black again without replying. His team, the Portland Loggers, weren't in San Diego more than three or four times a season, but he'd met up with Meg every time they'd come through town for the last three years now. She'd never once been on time. Tonight hadn't been just ten or fifteen minutes, though;

she'd shown up almost an hour late, flustered and sweating despite the early January chill.

"Beggars can't be choosers," his dad had always said, and Alex was definitely not in a position to be choosy. Besides, once Meg showed up, she was always extremely professional, which was more than Alex could say for some of his contacts in other cities.

Tonight's visit had been much needed, or he wouldn't have waited so long for Meg and risked getting caught returning after curfew. The Loggers were in the middle of a road trip, and it would be another three days before he was back in Portland. They'd left Phoenix a couple of days prior, riding high on a victory, but back-to-back losses against San Diego had combined with a growing ache in his chest, and driven Alex to text Meg before he'd gotten in the shower in the locker room after tonight's game.

At least Meg was always broke, which meant she was willing to help him out, even on short notice.

He balled up his shirt and tossed it on top of his suitcase in the corner. A flash of movement out of the corner of his eye caught his attention, and he glanced over to see his reflection staring back at him from the mirror above the TV.

Thank goodness that myth isn't real, he thought. He fit the stereotypes to a T otherwise—too pale, nocturnal, and too fond of red meat. *But, hey, that describes almost every other hockey player I know too.* Mirrors and garlic were useless superstitions, and these days only the dumbest humans believed in them. But the sunshine myth... that one was true enough, and it was pretty much the only reason he'd been able to hide in plain sight from the anti-Para nutjobs.

He was a professional athlete in a sport that played mostly night games during winter, and he lived in a city where the cloudy days outnumbered the sunny ones four to one. At this rate, he was hopeful no one would find out that he was a vampire unless he got traded to Florida or something.

Half vampire, he mentally corrected himself. The half part was important for two reasons: One, it meant that he didn't combust on the walk from his car to the arena during daytime practices. And two, it meant that he could cling to that 50 percent of humanity and try to forget about the rest.

Nights like this were harder, though. Staring at himself in the mirror, the taste of blood still lingering on the back of his tongue, Alex couldn't help but see exactly how *inhuman* he was—how he was, in fact, a Para, even if he tried to ignore it.

The pale white skin was the most obvious sign, though a faint pink flush highlighted his cheeks and chest now that he was recently fed. A face that was a bit too young—he was twenty-two, but the guys in the locker room teased him for being popular with their teenage fans, calling him *babyface* and *jailbait*. A sense of smell that meant he could sniff out a bar of dark chocolate from across the room, but also made him want to breathe through his mouth when entering a locker room. And an ability to see better than average in the dark, which only ever helped him when sneaking into a shared hotel room in the middle of the night.

Unfortunately, the human half of him needed sleep. They'd have to be up early to get on the bus and head north to Bakersfield, so Alex pulled his gaze away from the mirror and crawled into bed, collapsing face-first against the pillow.

Seattle Police Dispatch (@SPD_Dispatch)
AUTO ACCIDENT/INJURY
EMS NEEDED, 84TH AVE NE, MEDINA
04 JANUARY, 12:05 AM

HIGH PRIORITY

SASHA STEPPED out of his car and exhaled, breath forming a white cloud in front of him. Seattle never got truly *cold*—not like Russia did—but the early-January front that had moved in was wreaking havoc across the city. Given the rarity of nights like this, where the temperatures dropped to the 20s, it was no surprise that drivers were vastly unprepared for the icy roads that had appeared.

Case in point—

The vehicle in front of him had once been a sleek black sports car, the kind that turned heads as it cruised down the road. Now it was scrap metal. From what Sasha could tell, the car had slid out of control until the front had hit a telephone pole, crumpling the metal frame like it was a piece of paper. Now, lit up by flashing red lights, it looked like something out of a nightmare.

He tucked his hands into the pocket of his coat and jogged across the road to the nearest police car.

"Hey, officer?" It was late, and he had to struggle to remember his English. "What happened here?"

A tired-looking police officer glanced up. "Car skidded out on a patch of ice. But you can't hang around here, sir."

"Wait, пожалуйста." Sasha shook his head. Going on six years in North America, but sometimes even the simplest words escaped him. "Please. This is my friend, I think. My teammate, Ed Despres. He called me, said he was in car accident. I tell him to call 9-1-1 and I will come find him."

The officer hesitated, then pulled out a notepad from her back pocket. "Well, you're in the right place. You said he called you first?"

Sasha nodded. "He sounded very out of it, you know? Like he was in pain, but also like…." He thought for a second. "Like concussion. He got concussion three years ago, after bad hit to head during a game. Sounded like this tonight, confused."

"That fits reports from the emergency dispatcher." The driver frowned. "Your friend was almost incoherent when EMTs arrived. We managed to get a name, but not a lot more. You said he's your teammate?"

"Yes. We play hockey, Seattle Cascades. My name is Alexander Petrov." A glimmer of recognition sparked in the officer's eyes, so Sasha continued. "Please, he is injured badly? I need to call other people from team."

Sasha's English was fading fast, a combination of the late hour, the cold, and the fear for Ed. He had no idea why his friend had been out so late, especially the night before a game, but he'd been woken up by the call just after midnight and hadn't hesitated to rush to the road that Ed had described.

Before the officer could respond—or feed him some kind of bullshit line about patient privacy—someone called his name. When he looked up, Ed was being wheeled by on a stretcher.

"Officer—"

The woman nodded. "Yeah, you can go over. I'm sure the EMTs will have some questions for you, and they'll need emergency contact information if you can provide it. Then I'll need to talk to you and get some information as well, okay?"

Sasha quickly ducked around her and rushed toward the ambulance. Ed looked horrible: a bloody cut stood out on his jaw, and livid bruise was already forming across his cheek—possibly from the airbag. His eyes were glazed too, though he smiled unevenly when Sasha approached. But what concerned Sasha the most was the brace around his friend's neck, and the sling holding his arm against his chest.

"Ed," he said as soon as he was close enough. "Eddie. What happened?"

Eduard Despres, starting goaltender for the Seattle Cascades, blinked slowly. "Sasha."

"Yes, Старина, I'm here."

"Hurts." Ed winced, then groaned when the movement pulled at the injuries on his face.

He was speaking quietly, and Sasha had to bend over to hear him. When he got closer, he could smell beer and the sharp tang of alcohol on Ed's breath and clothes. It was enough for him to put the pieces together and figure out what had happened.

Not again. "You been drinking, Eddie?"

Ed scowled. "Just a couple. To unwind, y'know? 'M not drunk."

The presence of the police, combined with the hundred-thousand-dollar sports car currently wrapped around a pole, told Sasha otherwise.

"Oh, Eddie. We got a game tonight. Why were you drinking so late?"

Eddie tried to sit up, and an EMT had to rush over to haul him back down. "I'm fine. I can play tonight."

Sasha met the eyes of one of the medical technicians, who shook their head. "Okay, Eddie. But right now you gotta go to the hospital and get checked over. I'll call Denis and other trainers, okay?"

Two of the EMTs moved to load the stretcher into the back of the ambulance, leaving Sasha alone with the third. He sighed and wished he could get some of whatever painkillers the EMTs were putting Eddie on; he had a monster headache building.

"So, how bad is it really?" he asked.

The EMT shook his head. "Hard to tell without X-rays, but probable dislocated shoulder, maybe a broken arm. He's not passing concussion protocol, but we can't tell if that's because of the adrenaline and alcohol or not."

"Shit."

"Yeah. Look, Mr. Despres isn't answering any of our questions. We need to know if he has any allergies or prior medical conditions that we need to be aware of."

Sasha thought for a second. "Not sure about allergies. Not for food, I don't think? I need to—I can call team trainer; they will know all this."

"Okay. Why don't you make some calls, and we're going to get your friend to the hospital so doctors can start running some tests. Tell your trainers he'll be at Virginia Mason."

The EMTs finished securing Ed's stretcher, and then the ambulance pulled away with a burst of siren. The police officer from before was still waiting for him, looking just as cold as he felt and increasingly impatient. Sasha clenched his hand around his phone in his pocket and thought longingly about his nice, warm bed.

Police, paramedics, and one drunk-driving goalie. *It's going to be a long night*, Sasha thought.

Seattle Cascades (@CascadesNHL)
#BreakingNews Goalie Eduard Despres out with upper body injury, estimated 3-6 months. Cascades recall goaltender Alex Fanning from AHL's @PortlandLoggers. https://t.co/vebMUVp1AZ

Seattle Sports News (@SeattleSportsNews)
Cascades' Despres (G) out 3-6 months after late-night car accident. Police suspect alcohol may have been involved. More details as we get them.

IT FELT like Alex had been asleep for only minutes when his phone rang. He jerked awake, heart pounding. The alarm clock said it wasn't even four o'clock; he'd managed only a couple hours of sleep.

"Shut it off!" The mumbled command drifted out of the lump of blankets on the other bed, as Alex's roommate Cory shifted and buried his head beneath his pillow.

Alex groaned and rolled onto his side, hunting for the phone in the mess of sheets and blankets. He found it a moment later and jabbed the Accept button.

"'Lo?"

There was a long silence before a man spoke. "Is this Alexander Fanning?"

"Yeah." Alex yawned and closed his eyes. It was too early for a telemarketer, but the number hadn't been one that he recognized.

"Mr. Fanning, this is Martin Dubois."

What? Alex sat up straight, clutching the phone to his ear. He knew that name. Everyone in the NHL knew that name. Former three-time MVP, two-time Stanley Cup champion, current general manager of the Seattle Cascades… and apparently calling Alex. At 4:00 a.m.

"Sorry for the late hour," Dubois continued, seemingly unaware of the shock racing through Alex. "I know you played a game last night, but we need you to come up to Seattle first thing this morning. We'll be emailing you an e-ticket shortly for a flight in four hours out of San Diego International."

It was way too early, and Alex definitely hadn't had enough sleep. "I'm sorry… what now?"

Dubois paused again. "Fanning, get your gear and get to the airport. You're dressing for the Cascades tonight."

Alex was vaguely aware that Dubois was still speaking, passing along information that he'd probably need to remember later. But he was too busy trying to process, blinking as Cory appeared from beneath his pillow to send Alex a concerned look.

He must have responded to Dubois, because the call ended a moment later with a reminder to get moving and get to the airport. Alex let the phone fall to his lap, the light from the screen illuminating his face.

"What the hell was that?" Cory asked.

Alex swallowed hard. "I'm playing in the NHL tonight." The words still didn't seem real, spoken aloud like that. He'd been dreaming of the NHL since he was a kid, had hoped the day would come when he was called up. And now that day had finally come. *Holy shit.* He swiped a hand through his hair. "I've gotta pack."

Chapter Two

POLICE REPORT
Defendant: Eduard Despres
Age: 29
Date of Birth: 06/02/XXXX
Date and Time of Arrest: 01/04/XXXX, 12:47 a.m.
Driver's License #: DESPREJ11LB
Observations: Officer responded to a 911 call at 12:05 a.m. for a single-vehicle incident at the intersection of....

SASHA STUMBLED into his house an hour later, more exhausted than he'd ever been in his life. He'd spoken with the EMTs and explained what he knew about Ed's previous injuries. He'd spoken with the police, who had informed him firmly but politely that his friend had almost definitely been drinking, and he was going to be charged pending a blood test.

And then, while he'd navigated his own car through the quiet streets of suburban Seattle, he'd had the honor of waking up his coach and explaining the entire situation to him.

Coach Henrique had ordered him to go back home instead of heading to the hospital.

"He's my best friend," Sasha had protested. "Like my brother. I need to be there for him."

But Coach had stood firm. "He'll be in testing and possibly surgery for the next several hours, if what you told me is accurate. You won't do him a damn lick of good sitting in a waiting room. Go home; get some sleep. Play your heart out tonight against Houston. Despres wouldn't want you missing a game because of this."

That last comment had rung true, at least. He'd been assigned as Eddie's rookie when he had first come over from Russia, even though Sasha was a defenseman and not a goalie. But Eddie was the kind of guy who knew everything about Seattle, and he'd taken Sasha under his wing and helped ease him into life in the States. The goalie had spoken about four words of Russian—and none of them fit for polite company—but that had been four words more than anyone else in the locker room. And even though neither of them spoke English as a first language, they'd realized pretty quickly that they understood each other just fine.

"There are only two important things you need to know," Ed had told him. "The first is that team comes before anything else. The second is that you should always keep your head up."

They'd become friends almost immediately. At one point Sasha had wondered if they might be *more*—he'd looked up to Eddie, worshipped him with all the naivety a nineteen-year-old could possess. But Ed was straighter than a goal post, and eventually some of that hero worship had worn off. Now, five and a half seasons later, there were other Russians on the team—including Sasha's own rookie, Mikhail, who had managed to stay sound asleep in the guest room down the hall through the early-morning phone call and Sasha rushing out the door. That didn't mean Ed wasn't his best friend, though.

And Eddie *would* be furious if Sasha missed a game for no reason.

Not 'no reason,' he told himself, grumbling as he kicked his shoes off inside the front door. *But maybe Coach is right. No point in sitting in a waiting room.*

He had to be at the arena in twelve hours to start getting ready for a game, although his game-day schedule was already a disaster. Sasha had always stuck to a strict routine on days where they were playing at home, but there was no way he was getting up when his alarm went off in a couple of hours.

"Why don't you go ahead and skip practice today," Coach had said. "Come by a little earlier this afternoon and stop by my office to talk. I need to go make some calls now, but you get home safe."

Now he was home and eager to face-plant in his bed and sleep until late morning. Sasha lumbered into the bedroom, shedding layers as he went. He crawled into bed, barely remembering to send a text to Mikhail so he wouldn't be woken up for practice, and threw his phone on the nightstand before collapsing into his pillow. Then he closed his eyes and waited for sleep to come.

Except his brain wouldn't stop working.

Ну, блять. Sasha rolled over onto his back and stared up at the ceiling.

He didn't worship Ed anymore, but he did love him, the way he loved his little sister and his parents back in Moscow. He'd been honest when he told Coach that Ed was like his brother. Still, he knew that Ed had his faults: he loved partying a little too much, loved women and expensive things and being one of the faces of the Cascades franchise. But now those faults were catching up to him; this would be Ed's second drunk-driving charge in the last year. He'd been given a DUI last May after drinking too much when the Cascades were kicked out of the playoffs in the first round. And this time he'd hurt himself pretty badly.

Broken arm, maybe concussion. Four months, maybe more. That meant the rest of the season, probably even into playoffs—assuming they made it. Sasha tried to imagine playing the rest of the season in front of Hertzog, or whatever complete stranger they found to fill the open spot on the roster.

Shit, they're probably gonna give Ed's stall to the new goalie. The thought rankled him. Thinking about walking into the locker room that afternoon and seeing some new guy sitting where Eddie had sat for the last five seasons? Sasha made a face. *No, thank you.* There had been illnesses and minor injuries over the years, but this would be the first time since Sasha was a teenager that Ed wouldn't be on his team.

The sky outside his window was starting to turn gray when Sasha finally managed to stop tossing and turning and let sleep catch up to him. He closed his eyes, and hoped that when he woke up again this would all just be a bad dream.

@SCartier3 on Instagram: #TBT to when me and this kid won gold at World Juniors. Can't wait to be wearing the same jersey once again! Welcome to the Cascades, @goaliefanning! #TeamUSA #beauties #goaliesareweird #phantom

Liked by cascadesnhl, akselimakela38 and 1,616 others
View all 182 comments

THE FLIGHT from San Diego to Seattle wasn't a long one. Alex dozed fitfully with the window shade closed, his hoodie tugged up over his head and baseball hat pulled low. Exhaustion was the only thing keeping him from having a panic attack—and it wasn't the turbulence at 32,000 feet that was freaking him out. The phone call from Dubois kept replaying in his head, interspersed with the thoughts, *I'm playing in the NHL. Tonight.*

They want me to suit up for an NHL game. Tonight. Even knowing that he was just going to be riding the bench for the full sixty minutes didn't matter… because he'd be riding the bench in *an NHL arena*—holy shit.

It didn't help that the cabin was too bright, and he could feel the sun against his arm as he slumped back in his seat. Thankfully by the time they landed at Sea-Tac, a thick layer of clouds had rolled through. He slid on his sunglasses anyway and followed his fellow passengers to the baggage claim.

His duffel, leg pads, and suitcase came out with no problem, but his sticks took longer to appear on the oversized baggage ramp. Alex was relieved when they finally rolled down—undamaged thankfully—and he propped them on top of his luggage cart. Then he turned, ready to find a cab or shuttle to take him to the hotel that the Cascades had booked.

A shout stopped him.

"Fanning!"

Alex turned just in time for a six-foot-six wall of muscle to tackle him in a hug.

"Dude! I heard the news this morning when I woke up, and told the front office that I'd grab you from the airport." Shawn Cartier pulled back, flashing a wide grin. He was missing another tooth, and his nose had been broken since the last time they'd seen each other, but right then he looked like the best thing Alex had ever seen.

Not that Alex was going to admit that. "If the Cascades wanted me to feel welcome, they shouldn't have sent your ugly mug to greet me."

Shawn just laughed and knocked Alex's hat off to ruffle his hair. "Weak, Phantom. Man, it's good to see you, though!"

Hearing his old nickname helped to drain some of the tension in Alex's shoulders. He pulled Shawn back in for another hug, burying his nose in the other man's shoulder. Shawn still smelled bright and fresh, like sunshine, the same scent he'd had since Alex had met him. *God, I've missed this.*

"It's really good to see you too, Carts. Do I have time to drop my stuff at the hotel and take a nap before I need to be at the arena?" His entire body ached, a combination of the daylight and the sixty minutes he'd played the night before.

It wasn't like Alex was short or skinny, but Shawn muscled him out of the way easily, claiming the luggage cart so he could push it toward the parking lot. "You're not staying in a hotel, Phantom. Coach said you're here at least three months, maybe longer. That's probably the rest of the season. No way you're getting stuck in a hotel for that long."

Alex trailed after his friend, bemused and too tired to put up a protest. He'd checked the news while waiting to board his flight that morning, and knew the Cascades' starting goalie was out for several months. But he hadn't thought through what that actually meant for him.

"Uh. Where am I staying, then?"

The question earned him an eye roll and an exasperated sigh over Shawn's shoulder. "With me, duh. I got a guest room, a PlayStation, and a housekeeper who comes once a week. Plus we can carpool to the arena until you can get your car up from Portland."

Alex was quiet while they walked through the parking garage. Shawn filled the silence, chattering easily about Seattle, the weather, their game that night, and whatever else crossed his mind. It was soothing, in a strange way. But Alex couldn't help but think about what staying at Shawn's house would entail. It was hard enough hiding his Para nature living alone in Portland; frequent road trips and hotel roommates meant someone was always at risk of noticing his strange behavior, late-night meetings, and his sometimes-unusual diet. Most of the guys on the Loggers brushed his quirks off as "goalie weirdness," but Shawn knew him way too well for that.

And he had no idea if Shawn knew his biggest secret. Just thinking about it sent an icy tendril of fear down his spine.

Alex had told him the truth, back when they were teenagers. They'd been drunk one night, sharing a bottle of cheap rum that Shawn's billet brother had smuggled in for them, and Alex had let slip that it sucked how alcohol didn't affect him the way it did everyone else... and why. Shawn hadn't said anything at the time, and he'd acted normal the next day, but they'd never talked about it again.

Whether his best friend remembered that conversation or not could change how Alex's new living arrangements were going to work. *If he forgot, then I need to make sure he never finds out. And if he remembers... well, either he didn't care or he'll use it against me some day.* It was painful to assume that about his best friend, but Alex had learned over the years that his genetics had to stay secret if he wanted to keep playing hockey.

Shawn led him to an expensive-looking SUV and loaded the bags into the trunk without allowing Alex to help. Alex waited until they were both in the car, doors closed, and Shawn was navigating to the airport exit before he finally spoke.

"Carts, hey." His voice was rough, and he had to clear his throat. "You remember the thing I told you back in Juniors?"

Shawn glanced over, then had to slam on his brakes when another car cut him off. "Watch it, asshole!" he yelled, his thick Minnesota accent coming through. He cursed under his breath and eased the SUV into an open lane. In a normal tone, he said, "You're going to have to clarify, man. You told me a lot of things in Juniors."

Alex exhaled. "Never mind." Either Shawn was being purposefully obtuse, or he honestly didn't remember. If it was the latter, Alex was more than happy not to remind him. Alex could be careful while he was staying at Shawn's house, and his secret would be safe.

But Shawn wasn't ready to let it go yet. "Wait, bro, is this about that time I caught you and Tomàs together at that party, and that talk we had after? Because I can promise you no one here will care about that. We've got a good locker room, and I know Coach and Merks would bag skate anyone who gave you shit."

Merks was probably Derick Merkley, the Cascades' captain. Alex filed that information away. "That's, uh, good to know," he managed. "But you know I'm not gonna be open about that while I'm up here."

Let him think this is about the "gay" thing, not the "Para" thing. It's safer.

"Sure, I get that. But you could be, if you wanted. Just sayin', you wouldn't be the only one in the room."

When Alex didn't respond, Shawn reached over to pat him on the shoulder, then turned the radio on to fill the silence.

Chapter Three

vampnutri:

Little known fact: vampires, alukah, draugar, and other Para of the undead variety can still consume human food! While a lot of these creatures prefer to feed on blood or human energy, a careful diet of iron-rich foods can be super beneficial. If you're having a vampire friend over, consider some of the following meal options.

#vampires #paranormals #paras #nutrition #food

SHAWN LIVED downtown in a luxury sky-rise building with floor-to-ceiling windows and a view overlooking the water.

"Damn." Alex whistled as he stepped inside. "So this is where the NHL gets you in life."

Shawn punched him in the arm and led him on a tour of the apartment. "I had the housekeeper come over first thing this morning to make sure the guest room had clean sheets and wasn't covered in dust," he said, stopping in front of a plain, undecorated bedroom. "Throw your stuff in here for now. I'll show you the rest of the place."

The kitchen was modern, all sleek chrome and granite countertops. Two large brown paper bags sat on the counter. "Oh, nice. Grocery delivery came too. I called on my way to the airport and asked them to send over some things I thought you might need until you can put your own order together."

Alex paused in the doorway. "Carts," he said, shocked and struggling to process. "You only found out about me coming up a few hours ago. How the hell did you get this much done so fast?"

His friend shrugged sheepishly. "Made some calls, you know? Like, what's the point in having millions of dollars if I can't help a friend out on short notice?"

"You didn't have to go through all this trouble for me." Alex stepped into the kitchen and wrapped an arm around Shawn's shoulders. "But thank you."

Shawn grinned. "Of course, man. I remember how freaked I was when I first made the Show. I was staying with Otter—that's Luke Oettenger, he wears one of the As—and he and his wife just made me feel so at home, you know? Helped a lot with the nerves."

He'd known Shawn for years, since they were skinny teenagers coming up in the US National Team Development Program, and Alex knew his friend wasn't the big dumb jock that he sometimes came off as. Times like this reminded him of why Shawn was his best friend, though.

"We should probably put everything in the fridge. I'll start clearing a shelf off for you."

Alex wandered over to the kitchen island and peered into the bags. At the top were bags of peanuts and pistachios, which he pulled out and set aside. They'd been a staple snack of his for years, and it meant a lot that Shawn remembered that. Then, curious, he dove deeper.

A paper-wrapped package with a label declaring it to be steak. That made sense, given the fact that they were hockey players who both hated cooking if it didn't involve a barbecue grill. But a twelve-pack of coconut water? Spinach and broccoli? A box of iron-enriched cereal? None of that was what he expected to find.

He could have passed them off as Shawn stocking up on his own food, except for a packet of chicken livers at the bottom of the bag.

"You hate liver," he said.

Shawn hummed in agreement from where he was standing in front of the fridge, playing Tetris to rearrange the contents. "Yep."

"*I* hate liver," Alex continued. "Neither of us eat it. Why would you buy it?"

"Well, I read that it's really iron-rich." Shawn made a triumphant noise as he managed to fit a bottle of vinaigrette into a shelf on the door. "I figured it'd be a good emergency backup, in case you can't find a blood source here quickly enough. And I read online that coconut water can be used as a blood transfusion substitute in an emergency, so I got some of that too!"

"You—I—*what*?" Alex's brain short-circuited, and terror flooded his body. *Oh fuck, he knows.*

"I know, shouldn't believe everything you read on the internet, but—" Shawn turned all the way and interrupted himself with a sudden laugh as he caught sight of Alex's face. "What the hell, man. You look like you saw a ghost. Or, well, a phantom. Get it?"

Alex opened his mouth, then closed it. His heart was pounding in his chest, hands shaking slightly. He clenched them into fists and resisted the urge to take a step backward, to put as much distance between himself and the potential threat as possible.

"The look on your face, bro." Shawn was still chuckling. "Did you think I didn't know? Wait, hold up, is this what you were trying to talk to me about in the car?"

Alex had to catch himself on the edge of the counter as he shook his head. He sucked in a deep breath, trying to calm his racing heartbeat. "I didn't think you remembered."

"That you're a vamp? Not exactly something I'd forget."

"Half vampire." Alex buried his face in his hands. "But—you never said anything." The bags of food suddenly made way more sense; they were all things that Alex turned to when he had to go an extra few days between feedings. In fact, the groceries read like Shawn had googled a list of iron-rich foods.

He could hear Shawn's footsteps, and then Alex felt a hand on his shoulder as his friend stopped in front of him. The touch made Alex jump, but nothing else came from it except the comforting warmth of Shawn's touch through the fabric of his shirt.

The laughter was gone from Shawn's voice when he spoke again. "I mean, it wasn't a thing, right? Like, you made it pretty obvious that it was a secret, and you didn't catch on fire the next day when we snuck out to eat away our hangovers at McDonald's. I just figured it was like the gay thing—you didn't mention it, I didn't mention it, and we pretended like it wasn't happening."

Peeking through his fingers revealed Shawn's concerned face, looking far more serious than he usually did. "And you're okay with that?"

"With the gay thing or the Para thing?"

Alex exhaled and dropped his hands to his side. "Both."

Shawn shrugged and reached past him to grab a bag of groceries. "Sure. Doesn't affect me either way. NHL doesn't care if you're gay, either."

"But they care if I'm Paranormal." Alex spoke the words to Shawn's back, voice low.

The flat of coconut water was shoved onto a shelf with a little more force than necessary. "It's not against the rules," Shawn said. "I looked it up after our draft. They can't kick you out of the league for being a Para. It's a protected class or whatever…. It'd be discrimination."

It was true, but neither of them seemed willing to say the next part: the rules didn't apply to sports, where there were always ways to work around them. Everyone knew the story about the fae who'd been a star pitcher for the Yankees... until his nonhuman status had been revealed, and the team had stopped playing him, pushed him out of the locker room, forced him to retire. The NHL, if anything, was even more intolerant than Major League Baseball. There had even been rumors buzzing for months about a proposal during the upcoming CBA negotiations that the league and owners wanted some way to know who was Para and who was human.

"Anyways, it doesn't matter." Shawn closed the fridge door hard and turned back around, crossing his arms. "Your secret is safe with me. You're here now, you made the Show, and no one's gonna stop you, okay?"

Alex closed the distance between them and wrapped Shawn in a fierce hug. "Thanks, man."

Shawn patted him on the back. "Of course. Now go crash for a few hours. I'll text management and let them know we'll be in around lunchtime."

NHL Stats: Alexander Fanning (#31)
G | 5' 11" | 170 lb | Age: 22 | Seattle Cascades
Born: April 30
Birthplace: Minneapolis, MN USA
Catches: Left

Seattle Cascades (@CascadesNHL)
Check out these new threads! Goalie Alex Fanning will wear #31 for the #TealAndWhite and will back up Matthias Hertzog in tonight's match against Vancouver. https://t.co/NyiQQvWCDS
(Retweeted by @goaliefanning)

Alex Fanning #31 (@goaliefanning)
Going from Portland green & orange to Seattle teal & white! Excited and honored to be wearing this jersey tonight.

ALEX SLID into the locker room unnoticed, hugging the wall until he found his stall at the end. He'd come in a few hours prior to sign paperwork and meet with the team doctor. He'd also turned his duffel and pads over to one of the equipment guys, and now he found his gear bag unpacked, pads and mask set out in his stall with his skates tucked neatly away. A jersey hung behind his seat, bright teal standing out against the dark wood. He ran a finger over the nameplate, FANNING stitched in bold white letters.

He'd been playing hockey for pretty much his entire life and had been in dozens of different locker rooms, but something about being in an NHL room took his breath away.

Changing out of his game-day suit and into his Under Armour was a comforting routine, and the familiar motions helped him relax. He pulled on his leggings and the tight spandex shirt he wore under his pads, then sank to the floor to start stretching.

Other players trickled in while he was bent into a butterfly, stretching his quads and thighs. He tilted his head up to watch, curious about his new teammates. Most of them were familiar from past tournaments or watching Cascades games on TV, but now he'd actually be playing with them.

A ball of nerves coiled up in the pit of his stomach.

Alex stretched his leg out straight in front of him and grabbed his foot as he observed the room. *That's Mikhail Volkov, the Cascades' first-round pick from this past summer*, he thought, watching the eighteen-year-old kid enter, followed by a shorter man with red hair. *And Tyler Morgan, who scored that crazy goal in Game 4 against Dallas last year.*

A tall blond man who Alex recognized as Akseli Mäkelä walked in, headphones on and bopping his head to whatever song was playing. He immediately unplugged his phone and docked it on a set of speakers on the opposite wall. Blaring music filled the room.

"Shit, dude, turn that garbage off. No one here wants to listen to your awful Finnish metal." That was Shawn, already tugging his tie loose as he walked in, carrying his refreshing bright scent with him. He looked around immediately, though it took him a second to spot Alex on the floor. "Fanning, hey!"

Alex reached up as Shawn approached, and let his friend pull him to his feet.

"You ready for tonight?"

"Ready to ride a bench, sure." But Alex was smiling as he spoke, Shawn's excitement contagious.

Shawn slapped him on the shoulder. "Give it time, man. You'll get your chance soon enough. Hey, you met the guys yet?"

"I was introduced to Matty earlier when I met with the goalie coach." Matthias Hertzog had been the backup goalie previously, and he'd been noticeably anxious about getting bumped up to starter so suddenly. Alex could definitely relate.

"Well, lemme introduce you to the team."

Shawn glanced around the room, taking stock of the guys in various states of undress, and finally spotted whoever he was looking for. "Merks, Mo, c'mere and meet Phantom."

Derick Merkley came over, looking every inch the responsible captain. Morgan followed a few steps behind him, eyes wide. "Hey, man," Merkley said when he was closer. He held a hand out for Alex to shake. "Sorry, didn't see you over there. You blend in, you know?"

Morgan caught the last part of that and nodded. "Had no idea you were here yet. Sorry, not exactly a great welcoming committee."

"That's why we called him Phantom in the NTDP," Shawn said. "Dude's quiet and practically invisible when he wants to be."

Introductions were made, and Alex allowed himself a single moment of glee at shaking Merkley's hand. The Cascades' captain was one of the best goal-scorers in the game, and Alex had spent hours poring over old game tape and imagining stopping Merkley's wicked slap shot. Morgan—"Call me Mo"—was another defenseman and seemed like a genuinely friendly guy.

What followed was a whirlwind tour of the locker room as the rest of the team trickled in. Shawn introduced him around to guys he'd watched on TV for years, and Alex nodded and shook hands and tried not to panic.

Locker room nicknames are about as sacred a hockey tradition as any, and even Head Coach Daniel Henrique of the Seattle Cascades can't escape the honor. "We call him Rico," confesses Cascades Captain Derick Merkley, or "Merks" to his teammates. As for some other nicknames that you might hear in the locker room? "[Johan] Engel gets called Angel a lot, because he's probably the nicest guy you'll ever meet. And I guess we have an animal theme going on—Seth Bayer, Pierre Leduc, and Luke Oettenger are Bear, Ducky, and Otter."

—Jamie Sinclair for Deadspin

SASHA WAS late and pissed off.

He'd come in earlier in the afternoon to recap the previous night's events for what felt like the hundredth time. First up had been Coach

Rico and GM Dubois, who had spent hours going over the events in excruciating detail. It hadn't just been Ed's injuries that they'd been worried about, but also everything from the police officer he'd spoken with to the phone call Ed had made to Sasha and how he'd sounded.

Next up had been the team's lawyer, who had asked all of the same questions that the coach had, but with way more intensity. He'd been noticeably nervous about the charges that had been filed against Ed... and the fact that it was his second DUI. Of course, that had been followed by Alyssa, the Cascades' PR rep, who had coached him on half a dozen talking points for the media after the game that night. Apparently Sasha's presence at the scene had been noticed, and the sports news sites were clamoring to know more.

The end result was that Sasha was running far behind in his usual game-day routines. He didn't think of himself as especially superstitious—not like Engel, who had an almost religious devotion to his playlist on game days, or Carts, who had been eating the same lunch before games for almost a decade. But he did have the timing of things down precisely, and watching the clock tick later and later was stressing him out.

When Sasha did finally burst through the locker room door, he was already half an hour behind schedule. Still, he couldn't help but pause as he walked inside, head turning automatically to stare at Ed's stall.

Where there was a kid sitting on the ground and stretching.

And it *was* a kid. The guy looked like a goddamn teenager, eighteen or nineteen at best. *This is our new backup? A literal child?* He was bent over his own legs and hadn't looked up when the locker room door opened, which gave Sasha a moment to study him unobserved.

Okay, the kid was honestly kind of cute. Floppy brown hair, pale skin, and lean muscle that flexed beneath his thin base layers. Under different circumstances he'd be exactly the kind of guy who would catch Sasha's eye in a club—not that he'd do anything about it, but he'd enjoy watching and fantasizing. The new goalie had an expression of absolute focus on his face as he went through his stretches, showing off flexibility that made Sasha's mouth go dry.

But circumstances were what they were, so it didn't matter how nice the kid looked. He wasn't Ed, which meant he didn't deserve to be sitting in that stall, with his name on top like he belonged there. Just the sight of him made Sasha want to yell and kick something.

"Sasha, hey!" That was Shawn, calling him over to joke about how late he was running.

His defense partner was enough of a distraction to pull Sasha's attention away from the child across the room.

"Long night last night. You heard?"

Shawn made a face. "Yeah. Is it as bad as social media is saying?"

Sasha resisted the urge to rub his temples where a headache was threatening to form. "Worse," he said shortly.

"Shit. Three to six months, huh?"

Sasha hadn't heard any confirmation, but with the injuries he'd seen, it wasn't a surprise at all.

But Shawn was the kind of guy who didn't linger on the negative. He balanced Sasha out that way—usually cheerful and energetic when Sasha was more dour and solemn. "But hey, man, at least there's some good news. You remember I told you about my best friend from Juniors? Alex Fanning? He's our new goalie!"

Before Sasha could respond, Shawn was already yelling across the room.

Sasha stiffened. *That* was Carts's best friend? The child who had been brought in to replace Ed? Impossible.

There wasn't any chance to digest this realization properly, however, because Shawn grabbed him by the arm and spun him around. And, sure enough, the man who shared his name, and who he'd heard so much about from Shawn over the years, was the new goalie.

Up close, the guy didn't look quite as young as Sasha had initially thought. His face was young, cheeks still a little soft, but his eyes were intelligent and bright, and showed far more maturity than the rest of his appearance.

And, somehow, he was even more attractive up close. Handsome wasn't the right word, or even cute. Fanning's brown eyes were fierce and bright, and his skin was flawless, like he'd look more fitting on a runway than in a locker room. *Прекрасен*, Sasha thought, then immediately banished the word from his thoughts with a sour taste in his mouth.

Beautiful or not, he didn't want anything to do with this temporary replacement, and he'd make sure this kid knew it.

NHL Stats: Alexander Petrov (#12)
D | 6' 6" | 245 lb | Age: 25 | Seattle Cascades
Born: November 12

Birthplace: Nizhny Novgorod, Russia
Shoots: Left

THE ROOM emptied out before too long, guys splitting off to the players' lounge for a pregame snack or to join in a round of two-touch in one of the back hallways. Alex finished his stretching on the floor, head down while he tried to get into his usual pregame mindset.

But something was keeping him from being able to focus. Locker rooms were always a miasma of weird smells to him: sweat, blood, the artificial tang of a sports drink, and sometimes even the rare, distinct scent of another Para—though most of them smelled just as human as they looked. But there was something different about the Cascades' room.

Between the usual layers of cologne and sweat, he kept catching a hint of something new, a scent that tickled at the back of his mind. Alex closed his eyes and inhaled deeply, trying to single it out. It was faint but enough to make saliva flood Alex's mouth.

Whatever it was, it smelled *delicious*.

Shawn's voice picked up from the other side of the room, where he'd been taping his sticks, at the same time the smell grew stronger.

"Sasha, hey! Was wondering if Coach was ever going to release you."

Alex opened his eyes in time to see Shawn reach out to bump fists with another man. From the back, Alex could make out shoulders and arms straining against the fabric of a dress shirt, and a pair of thick thighs inside pressed slacks.

Whoever Sasha was, he was built like a freakin' brick house.

"Alex!" Shawn called. "Stop meditating for a second and come here. I want you to meet someone."

Alex pushed himself up easily, stretching his arms above his head before following the command. Up close, it was obvious that Sasha was even bigger than Alex had thought. He was the same height as Shawn, but had at least thirty pounds more muscle on him. While most guys were struggling to maintain weight and muscle mass in the middle of the season, Sasha apparently had nothing to worry about.

"Sasha," Shawn said, yanking on the arm of the man and jolting Alex out of his thoughts, "this is my friend Alex Fanning. We played together as kids, and he's here as our backup goalie while Eddie is out.

Alex, meet Alexander Petrov, my D-partner. You're both Alexes, but thankfully he goes by Sasha or this would get confusing really fast."

The hulking defenseman turned around, and the polite greeting on Alex's tongue vanished.

Holy hell. Petrov was *hot*. Dark brown hair cropped short made his face look more angular than it actually was. Cheekbones sharp as knives jutted out from beneath a pair of icy blue eyes. He looked like he could hold Alex up against a wall without breaking a sweat. *And I'd let him too.*

The strange scent that Alex had caught before returned, stronger than ever, and Alex almost choked when he realized it was coming from Petrov. It was earthy and rich, and it overwhelmed everything else in the locker room.

After a second, Alex realized that he was standing there like an idiot. He inhaled more of that incredible scent, then opened his mouth to speak and introduce himself—and maybe test the waters a little with Sasha. But he was interrupted by Mikhail Volkov, who shouted across the room, "Hey, you're late, Паразло!"

Alex's mouth closed with an audible click. He didn't speak Russian, but he'd played in enough international tournaments to have heard that word before. North American teams usually penalized a player who used an anti-Para slur like that, but the Russians didn't seem to care.

Petrov just laughed and flipped his countryman the middle finger.

But the slur had been enough to jolt Alex back to reality. It didn't matter how attractive Sasha Petrov was, or how amazing he smelled; the fact was, Sasha was human. So was Shawn, and Mikhail, and probably everyone else on the team. And if Alex wanted to play with them, he needed to be a lot more careful.

Like, maybe don't sniff your teammates as though they're a bouquet of roses. And definitely don't think about flirting with humans… especially your human teammates, and especially *ones who laugh at slurs like that.* Two decades of playing hockey and creating rules to protect himself, and Alex had been about to throw them all away over a pair of pretty blue eyes and a jawline that would make Captain America envious.

By the time Sasha—*Petrov… I can't let myself get too close to him*— had turned back from Volkov and was paying attention to the introduction once again, Alex had managed to lock down his emotions and paste on a carefully neutral expression. He took a step back, almost subconsciously, then glanced up to find Petrov studying him with his lips pressed together.

He doesn't like me. The realization hit Alex suddenly. It was obvious in Petrov's expression, and the way he held his body, not bothering to extend a hand for Alex to shake. His blue eyes were narrowed as they took Alex in and clearly found him wanting.

"Nice to meet you," Alex said, but his tone said just the opposite. He folded his arms over his chest instead of offering his own hand to shake.

Either Shawn wasn't fazed by the rising tension, or he hadn't noticed it. He squeezed Petrov's arm playfully. "Sasha, smile and be nice to our new goalie."

Petrov bared his teeth in what could only charitably be called a smile. "I'm late," he said to Shawn, words lightly accented. "Gotta get dressed."

He pulled away from Shawn's grasp, stomping over to his locker. The decadent smell vanished with him.

"He takes a while to warm up to people," Shawn said with an apologetic smile.

Alex snorted. "Yeah, he seems like a real charmer."

At least the guy's a dick. It would make it easier to keep his distance going forward.

NHL Box Score (Final)
Seattle Cascades 2
Houston Cosmos 3
SEA: B. Thompson; B. Rager
HOU: T. Ford; S. Rabinowitz; M. Wronski

A LOSS always rankled Sasha more than it did most of the other guys, especially in a game they should have been able to win easily. Houston was one of the worst teams in the league right now, and yet the Cascades were the ones heading back to their locker room tonight in disappointment.

The only person on the team who didn't look upset, as a matter of fact, was the new goalie. He still had on his Loggers-themed mask and pads, making him stand out among the sea of blue, and he had a bounce in his step as he followed the team off the ice.

Why is he so excited? The kid was wide-eyed, the way he'd been since the game started. Not that Sasha had been looking, exactly, but it had been impossible to miss. *Who the hell does this kid think he is?*

Sasha fumed, stripping out of his sweaty gear and throwing it into the laundry bins.

"Bro, you okay?" Carts bumped against his arm companionably. "You look like we just lost a Game 7."

"Fine."

Carts laughed. "Man, you're in a bad mood today. It's all right. Houston had to win one eventually."

Of course Shawn didn't understand. Sasha's play had been sloppy from the exhaustion of the previous day, sure, but he hadn't played badly. And that was the problem—he'd played decently but still hadn't been able to make any difference in helping the team win.

Across the room, the kid had pulled his pads off but was still sitting in his stall without undressing further. He had his head tilted up, and looked like he was… meditating maybe? His chest expanded and contracted as though he was taking deep breaths.

Logically Sasha knew the new goalie wasn't a child. He had to be about the same age as Shawn, which made him only two or three years younger than Sasha himself. But he looked like one of the pop stars who Sasha's little sister had posters of hanging up on her wall, not like an NHL-caliber goalie.

Can he even play hockey? He was short and lanky, practically a beanpole. Eddie and Matty were both large men, well over six feet, and bulky enough to fill their nets and stop pucks. *Okay, maybe he's not that short,* Sasha mentally corrected. The kid—Fanning, he recalled—was only a hair below six feet. *And he's not as lanky as he looks, more compact muscle than bulk.*

But still.

Sasha turned around to his stall, purposefully putting his back between them.

"You know, if you stare hard enough, he will probably burst into flames." That was Mikhail, the brat, speaking in Russian as he sidled up to Sasha while he was deep in his thoughts. He had a shit-eating grin on his face as he invaded Sasha's space.

Sasha rolled his eyes. "I don't know what you're talking about."

"Sure, sure," Misha said easily. "But the way you were glaring just now, I figured I should come over here in case you are going to lunge across the room and stab him with a skate blade."

He laughed and threw his sweaty shoulder pads at Sasha, who batted them away in disgust.

"You are a child," Sasha said gravely, but his heart was racing. A glance around showed no one else was paying attention; no one else had seen him staring at Fanning so intently.

Misha didn't look even the slightest bit chastised. "Sorry, Sasha," he said, though he didn't sound anything of the sort.

"Go away. Shower. You stink." He shoved his rookie away so he could return to his own postgame routines.

But Misha's words stuck with him. Hate and lust, it was a thin line and one that Sasha wasn't sure he wanted to examine too closely.

Anyway, it didn't matter. The kid was cold as ice, had rejected Sasha from the start, so why should he even bother? Fanning would be up for a few more months, he'd play a couple of games to back up Hertzog, and then he'd go back to Oregon where he belonged.

Sasha could ignore him until then.

Chapter Four

> "Look, I'm just saying—the Cascades might be in trouble. Despres was the backbone of this team through the first three months of the season, and losing him is going to hurt. Hertzog has shown us so far that he's a serviceable replacement, but he's never played more than thirty games in a season and he has a history of injuries."
>
> "I don't disagree, Bob, but if you've been following the Loggers over the last few years, you'll know that Fanning has been absolutely spectacular. He's the reason Portland won the Calder Cup last year. If he can maintain that skill at the NHL level, I think the Cascades won't have any problem making playoffs again this year."
>
> —Bob Rousseau and Emily Burnwood, Seattle Cascades Intermission Report

IT TOOK six more days before Sasha was finally able to visit Ed in the hospital.

First they took a short road trip east to Winnipeg and Minnesota, where Hertzog managed to hold down the fort long enough for the Cascades to collect four valuable points. In between, Sasha tried calling the hospital half a dozen times, only to be told that Ed was with the doctor or undergoing another test or that he was sleeping.

So by the time they had two days off before their next home game, Sasha was getting desperate to see his best friend—and no nurse, doctor, or stupid hospital regulation was going to prevent him from doing so.

He had Ed's room number from one of the trainers, but Sasha still ducked his head as he walked down the hallway, shoulders up as though any second an orderly was going to lunge in front of him and stop him from going any farther. But no one said a word, and he arrived at the door to room 308 without any problems.

And, miracle of miracles, Ed was alone in the room and awake. There was a speaker next to the bed, and Sasha recognized a replay of a basketball game from the night before. Ed had never been a basketball fan, though, so Sasha didn't feel any guilt in clearing his throat and stepping into the room.

"Golden State wins by four, in case you were wondering," he said.

Ed's eyes widened, and he sat up straight in his hospital bed. He had a gown on, but a pair of sweatpants beneath them. The bruise on his cheek had turned a nauseating shade of purple and green.

"Sasha! You came!"

The smile that stretched across Ed's face sent relief through Sasha's body. "Sorry I couldn't come sooner. We were out of town the last few days."

"I heard." Ed held an arm out, and Sasha stepped forward to wrap him in a hug.

Until Ed hissed, and Sasha sprung back in panic.

It was then he noticed the plain white cast on Ed's arm, and the sling wrapped over the opposite shoulder. "Sorry, sorry."

Ed shook his head, but even that gesture was clearly painful. "It's fine. A couple of broken ribs, dislocated shoulder, and a clean fracture on the arm. They tell me it could have been way worse."

Sasha had seen the car. He had no doubt that Ed was lucky to be in the shape he was in.

"Anyway, tell me about the games. I listened to you guys beat Winnipeg, but they started me on a new antibiotic that's kicking my ass, so I was passed out for the Minnesota game."

Hooking a chair with his foot, Sasha dragged it over and sat down. He rested one hand on Ed's knee, relieved to see and feel proof that his friend was going to be okay. "The Minnesota game. It was… what's the phrase Bayer likes? 'Shit show.' We won, but only barely."

He launched into the game, pleased to see Ed grinning and laughing as he recapped the highlights.

The game had been one of those fast-paced, high-scoring barn-burners that fans and media loved but players absolutely hated. By the end of the sixty minutes, the entire Cascades roster had been sweating buckets and longing for the final buzzer. But the game hadn't been without its moments of fun, of course… and hilarity.

"And then the puck goes flying into the bench, almost hits Fanning right in the head! Look on his face, so startled." Sasha cracked up, remembering it.

It took him a second to realize that Ed wasn't laughing.

"Who's Fanning?"

Sasha sobered quickly. "Eddie—"

Ed shook his head, a quick jerking movement that had to hurt. "You're talking about Alex Fanning, from the Loggers, aren't you?" His lips pressed together and his nostrils flared. "My… replacement."

He said the last word as though it were something distasteful.

"No!" Sasha gripped Ed's knee. "Not replacement. Only playing a couple of games, just until you're recovered."

But Ed didn't look satisfied with that response. "Tell me about him."

Sasha twisted his lips. "He is… young. Looks like a child, but is same age as Carts. Very small, like strong wind will knock him over, you know?" *But he's also very handsome. And something about his eyes draws you in. Mama would say he has an old soul.* Sasha shoved those thoughts aside, and added aloud, "You know, they play together for US Juniors team."

Ed was still frowning. "But how does he play?"

"In practice he is good. Very fast." Seeing the way Ed's face darkened, Sasha hastened to add, "But he has not played in a real game yet. Practice is not everything. He will play Tuesday night, and I will come Wednesday and tell you how it goes, okay?"

That didn't seem to satisfy Ed, but he grumbled and rested back against his pillow nonetheless. "Don't get me wrong," he said, frowning deeply. "I never want to see you lose a game. But I can't help but want this Fanning kid to fail. If Coach thinks he's found a new young gun to fill my spot, then I hope they're proven wrong, is all."

It was a contract year for Ed, he recalled. Normally they'd have renewed his contract back in the summer or sometime during the year, but he remembered hearing that contract talks had stalled. Ed's agent was asking for one amount, and the team was hesitating to pay it. Of course it would all be wrapped up soon, Sasha assumed, but this injury couldn't be helping with the negotiations.

"There's no way Fanning is better than you, Ed. Don't worry; just rest and focus on getting better, okay?"

Ed smiled. "For sure. And hey, maybe next time you come, you can sneak me some real food? I wouldn't mind some Chinese from that place we always go to for lunch. Man, a container of sweet and sour chicken, and a nice beer… you sneak that in on Wednesday, okay, Sasha?"

Sasha laughed at the joke. "We'll see what I can do."

Oliver Marks (@OliverMarksESPN)
Hearing from sources that the NHL and Seattle Cascades are meeting to discuss potential investigation following arrest of G Eduard

Despres after car accident, including option of suspension. This is Despres's 2nd DUI charge in eight months.

Watching his first NHL game from the bench might not have sounded all that great, but the reality had been far more than Alex could have expected. The AHL was a great league to play in, but the NHL was on a whole different level. Everything moved faster, and the shots were harder. Television hadn't prepared him for this in the slightest.

He'd gotten to observe four games now in the last week and a half, and warming the bench gave him a chance to see the team in action. It was obvious that Merkley was the star player. Fans chanted his name, and his goal that evening caused the entire building to shake from the cheering. He also took the chance to watch Shawn—and with Shawn, Petrov, who landed big hits and skated in a way that utterly belied his size.

But the biggest takeaway of the last few games had been a simple revelation: *I'm better than Hertzog.* The Cascades' goalie was a journeyman with an impressive pedigree, and a Stanley Cup as the backup for New Jersey a few years before, but he was old and his reflexes weren't what they used to be. Alex wouldn't say it aloud, but he could take that realization and wrap it around himself the next time the nerves hit. *I can play in the NHL. I'm good enough for this.*

So when Coach called him into his office and told Alex that he'd be starting in a few days, Alex swallowed his fear and let those words wash over him. *I'm good enough for the NHL.*

Mrs. Merkley... a girl can dream! (@MerkleyFan96)
ohmygod the new guy? alex fanning? is *gorgeous*! here's a pic of him from when he was on the loggers last year. those eyes! pic.twitter.com/zEh3....

Emma (@Cascadiac)
@MerkleyFan96: damnnnnn, he looks like something off a boyband album cover. Are we sure he's really 22 though? He looks like he's barely 18.

Seattle Cascades (@CascadesNHL)
Last year @goaliefanning was the AHL Top Goaltender, and tonight he's starting in net for your Seattle Cascades! #TealAndWhite

Check out these stats from his last season with the @PortlandLoggers: GP: 48 | GAA: 2.02 | SV%: .927 https://t.co/y9eDacVxui

ALEX SAW his first NHL action three days later, on the second half of a back-to-back. The first game had been a shootout loss, leaving the team grouchy and frustrated. But the second was against a division rival, and nobody wanted to lose to Vancouver. Especially not Alex.

Matty tapped him on the leg with his stick as they were waiting in the hallway to go out to the ice. "You got this," he said confidently.

Alex pressed his lips together and nodded.

He found a place near the center red line to stretch, focusing on getting his muscles warm instead of on the movements of his teammates. When it was his turn to receive a few practice shots, Alex bumped shoulders with Hertzog as he skated to the net, and received a wide grin through his mask. Everyone seemed relaxed, but there was an undercurrent of excitement that was contagious.

But beneath the nerves and the anticipation was a ball of hunger that sat heavy in Alex's gut. He hadn't fed since that night in San Diego, and he was feeling it now. Two weeks wasn't the longest he'd ever gone, but it was close, and there was only so much that human food could do to bridge the gap. He'd gone out for dinner after the previous night's game with a group of guys from the team, and Shawn had given him a concerned frown when Alex had ordered his steak rare.

Hell, those chicken livers are starting to sound better and better.

He'd texted a few of his regulars in Portland to see if anyone could connect him with a source in Seattle, but hadn't heard back yet. Desperation was starting to gnaw at the back of his mind, and his entire body ached in a way that had nothing to do with muscle fatigue.

Still, it wasn't the first time he'd played hungry, and Alex knew it wouldn't be the last. The trick was to channel the hunger into focus, to ride the edge of the craving.

He licked his lips, grimaced, and forced himself to focus as the game began.

The Cascades' starting line was clicking well tonight, the three forwards getting a shot off on Vancouver's goal before turning the puck over. And then Vancouver was tearing down the ice toward Alex, forcing him to get his head back in the game.

He stopped his first shot, and caught the rebound neatly a split second later, hearing the approving roar of the crowd around him.

"Nice," Shawn said, smiling as he skated by to set up for the face-off. "Guess you're a real NHL goalie now, huh?"

The praise from his best friend, and the cheering of the crowd, washed away any lingering trace of nervousness.

It's just hockey, Alex reminded himself. He knew he was good enough to be there. Now he only had to prove it.

Chapter Five

Welcome back to KTCP Radio 102.7, home of your Seattle Cascades! We're past the halfway point in the second period. Derick Merkley wins the face-off and kicks the puck back to Mäkelä. Akseli Mäkelä is currently a Hart Trophy candidate, and he's been on fire this season so far. Mäkelä passes to Petrov, who sends the puck into the corner of Vancouver's zone and gives chase. Vancouver's Deleon gets there first, though, and tries to move the puck along the boards, but Petrov is on him and BOOM what a hit! Deleon is down and Petrov has the puck. Vancouver's bench is screaming for a penalty, but the refs are waving it aside as a clean hit, and now it's Petrov to Merkley, to Rybár, he takes the shot!—saved by goaltender J.T. Parker, and the score is still tied at zero with 5:31 remaining in the second.

LIKE ANY good Cascades player, Sasha hated Vancouver. It was practically a requirement of being on the team. Even one of their rookies, Braiden Rager, had accepted and given in to the pointed hostility, despite the fact that he was from the Vancouver area and had played in the WHL before being drafted. The rivalry was fierce, and more than a few games involved punches being thrown.

That animosity, Sasha told himself later, was the reason he reacted the way he did when that asshole Bilovsky skated toward the net fast and stopped on a dime just outside the blue paint, spraying Fanning with a thick wave of ice shavings.

Sasha was certain that it had been entirely on purpose, and the mean smirk on Bilovsky's face only confirmed it.

He couldn't help himself—he saw red. After the game he'd justify it to himself that Bilovsky was a thug and a bully, that he had no talent whatsoever and was only kept around by Vancouver so he could drop gloves. It had nothing to do with the way Fanning had looked afterward, shocked and furious. Sasha would do the same for any of his teammates, even the ones he didn't like.

So he skated forward and shoved Bilovsky in the chest.

Bilovsky pushed him back.

Distantly he was aware that Fanning was cursing at them both, and that play had continued to go on while the two of them tangled in front of the crease. He could hear a ref yelling at them to knock it off, but Bilovsky had one glove tangled in Sasha's jersey, and a look in his eyes that said he was ready to drop gloves and go.

One second Sasha was shaking his wrists and loosening his gloves—

The next, there was a siren going off, and the lights behind the goal were illuminated.

What the.... Sasha froze, not entirely sure what had happened. He looked over and saw Fanning on his knees, still hovering in the middle of the net. The puck sat behind him on the ice, accusingly.

The Vancouver players were celebrating. Bilovsky smirked, then untangled himself from Sasha and skated off to join in the celebration, leaving Sasha alone in his own crease with a dejected goalie at his side.

Oh no.

Sasha looked up at the clock. The score was now 2-1 Vancouver, with less than two minutes to go in the game. He looked back down at Fanning, and was almost taken aback by the icy look being leveled at him through the goalie's mask.

For a second, Sasha considered apologizing. But then Fanning looked away, his entire body stiff.

Whatever, Sasha told himself. *Not my problem.*

While the scrum in front of the net was almost certainly a response to Bilovsky spraying goaltender Fanning with a shower of ice, it's clear that Petrov once again let his temper run away from him. The defenseman has racked up an impressive 42 PIM at the halfway point in the regular season, including two fighting majors. But while tonight's overreaction didn't result in a trip to the penalty box, it did result in a goal and the loss of two points for the Cascades.

—Sharon Zurasky, CascadesFanReaction.net

THE FINAL buzzer sounded a few minutes later and dejected fans filed out of the arena. The Cascades looked equally upset as they made their way back to the locker room.

But Alex was too angry to be sad… and too hungry to rein his anger in.

"What the hell was that?" Alex stomped into the locker room and aimed straight for Petrov's stall like a heat-seeking missile. He was distantly aware that the rest of the locker room had gone quiet, even the muted buzz of conversation dying away. But his heartbeat was pounding in his ears, and Alex was hungry, and *he'd just lost his first ever NHL game because some* asshole *couldn't control his temper and had to start a kindergarten shoving match right in front of his net.*

"It's always the quiet ones who blow up when you least expect 'em to." Seth Bayer's words were amused but too loud in the dead silence that had filled the room.

Alex pulled back and realized abruptly that he'd said that entire last part aloud. He flushed but wasn't ready to let go of the anger yet. "I don't care if you want to drop gloves and brawl like it's the 1990s again," he said, staring up at Petrov and letting every ounce of disappointment and upset fill his glare, "But you keep that shit out of my crease. Got it?"

Petrov stared back, face unreadable.

When it became clear that he wasn't going to get an apology—or, hell, any reply at all—Alex let out a rushed, angry breath and turned to make his way back to his own stall.

He bent his head over, focusing on untying his pads and skates and stripping down as quickly as he could. Eventually, conversation picked back up again. Coach Henrique came in to talk to them, a short speech that was half "I'm disappointed" and half "You did a good job, though." Alex didn't pay much attention, just threw his dirty Under Armour in one of the laundry bins and rushed into the shower before the press came in to start their postgame interviews.

Shawn was waiting for him when he emerged, though.

"That was a bit harsh, eh?"

Alex paused in the process of pulling his shirt off its hanger, closing his eyes briefly. "Yeah, I know."

Shawn huffed a laugh. "But you weren't wrong."

"Yeah, I know that too." Alex pulled his shirt on, fingers numb as he tried to button it up. "Are the guys pissed at me?"

"Pissed? Nah." Shawn laughed, and Alex finally lifted his eyes to look at him. "Entertained maybe. You're so quiet normally, I don't think anyone expected that out of you."

Alex found his pants and finished getting dressed. "Sorry." He dug out his phone and exhaled an audible sigh of relief when he saw the text waiting for him on the lock screen.

Shawn leaned closer to take a look, and Alex tilted the screen to let him, inhaling deeply as he did so. The fresh scent from Shawn helped the last dregs of his anger to drain away. "Wait, have you not—" He cut himself off, looking around the room, then lowered his voice. "Phantom, bro, have you not fed since you got called up?"

"When would I have had time?" Alex glanced down at the text again, a message from Luis in Portland who had been one of his steady blood sources for a couple of years. *Found you someone. Call her. She said she's available tonight.* The name and number that followed were the best things Alex had seen in days. "I can't just go up to a random person and ask for a nibble. I had contacts in some AHL team cities, but that doesn't help much now that I'm not in the A."

His friend looked horrified. "But it's been *two weeks*." A pause, then, "I guess that explains the yelling before, though. Hangry, right?"

"Ha. Yeah, something like that." Alex rolled his shoulders, feeling his muscles protest. "I was starting to get pretty desperate. Look, I'm gonna rush out of here before I get roped into doing any media. If anyone is looking for me…."

"I'll cover for you." Shawn bumped fists with Alex. "Go, feed. Stop being a moody dick."

Alex grinned and escaped before anyone else could stop him.

HEATHER WAS tall, blonde, absolutely stunning, and surprisingly cheerful for a woman who was about to let someone bite her neck. She was also, Alex realized with a start, a succubus.

"And you're a vampire," she responded with a smile when he said that aloud.

Alex grimaced but didn't correct her. It didn't matter what percentage of him was Para or human tonight; for all intents and purposes, he was a vampire, and he was going to drink blood like one.

Feeding had always been something Alex enjoyed, and he knew it was equally appealing to the person he was feeding from. Normally he tried to savor the experience, like eating a decadent dessert, but tonight he just wanted to get it over and done with. He followed Heather into her lavish apartment, toeing his shoes off politely at the door even though he didn't plan to stay any longer than he had to.

"So," Alex began awkwardly. He tucked his hands into the pockets of his slacks and hunched his shoulders forward, feeling out of place in his suit. "Luis didn't mention how much—"

Heather interrupted, flashing pearly white teeth as she grinned. "Oh, I don't do this for human currency."

"What other currency is there?"

That earned him a laugh. "You feed on blood. I feed on… emotions."

Oh. Alex flushed, heat rushing to his face. "You mean sex."

Heather shook her head. "Not just sex. Any strong emotion will do. While you drink from me, I skim off the top of whatever recent emotions you've experienced. Mutually beneficial, and everyone goes home happy."

Alex twisted his hands in his pockets but nodded. "Yeah, all right." He trusted Luis, who had been his friend and feeding source for almost the full three years that he'd been in Portland, and he knew Luis wouldn't send him to someone who could hurt him. "Can I…?"

"Oh, sure! Let's move to the couch; it'll be more comfortable."

Heather led him into the living room, tying her hair up in a bun on her head while they walked. She was dressed like she'd been expecting him, wearing a tank top that left her long neck and tanned shoulders exposed.

Alex shrugged his suit jacket off and laid it over the back of the couch, then rolled his sleeves up to his elbows before joining her. "How do you want to do this?"

"Like this." Heather leaned back against the cushions and tilted her head to the side, drawing Alex to her with one arm around his waist. She smelled like saffron, dark and sweet. Usually the smell would have been appealing, but tonight….

He thought about the earthy scent that had plagued him for the last week every time he stepped foot into the arena, and scowled.

"Okay, yeah. Whatever you're thinking about right now?" Heather's eyes fluttered shut. "Damn, that's nice. Let's get this show on the road, vamp boy."

With the invitation hanging between them, Alex stopped resisting and gave in. Heather was warm and soft, and he brushed his lips over the pulse on her throat before moving down to the spot where her neck and shoulder came together and the veins sat just beneath the skin.

And then he bit in.

Feeding was one of his few pleasures in life, outside of hockey. It wasn't usually sexual, but there was a genuine satisfaction in sating the hunger that always lingered in the back of his mind. Heather gasped beneath him, and he knew she was enjoying it as well, could imagine the languid sensation that was settling over her.

One second he was thinking about saffron and spice, and the way her smaller body fit beneath his. And then Alex was thinking about how wrong it felt, how he'd rather have hard muscles leaning over him, pushing him down, the rich, tantalizing smell surrounding him while he drank from—

No. Alex shifted, swallowing and feeling Heather hum in contentment under him. *Don't think about him. Don't think about how incredible he smells, how he looks so damn good even when he's angry. Especially when he's angry.*

Heather moaned. It wasn't an erotic noise, but instead like someone taking a bite of an expensive dessert.

Would Sasha sound like that if I drank from him?

But as much as Petrov's scent called to him, the man himself left a sour taste in Alex's throat that even Heather's rich blood couldn't erase. Shawn had mentioned in passing that Petrov and Despres, the goalie who Alex was filling in for, were incredibly close friends. It was obvious that Petrov disliked Alex—*Because he thinks I'm not good enough to be here? Or because he thinks I'm taking over for his friend?* Either way, Petrov's mere existence was infuriating, driving Alex crazy every time he caught the defenseman glaring at him.

He finished drinking from Heather, pulling his fangs back and pressing his lips to her neck until the bleeding stopped. The wound closed up almost immediately, as it always did, leaving behind only a small bruise that would be gone by morning.

Heather's skin looked flushed when he pulled away, and her eyes were bright as they met his own.

"Did you get what you needed?" he asked.

"I did." Heather looked curious. "Whoever you were thinking about tonight…." She shook her head with a laugh. "Sweetie, you need to sort out what you're feeling there. Your emotions were all over the place."

Alex exhaled. "He's—it's complicated."

"It always is. But either hate him or fuck him, is all I'm saying."

Succubi. Alex rolled his eyes and huffed out a laugh of his own. "Yeah, I don't think the second one's going to happen. For one thing, he's a he. For another, he's human… and he hates me."

She winced. "You're an athlete, right? Luis mentioned. Hockey?"

"Yeah. With the Cascades. They can't know that I'm—"

"Gay?"

"Or Para."

Heather sat for a moment in silence. "Look, Alex, I like you. You're sweet. And you're a damn fine meal. I don't get to feed on other Paras often, you know? Mostly around Seattle you get nymphs or dryads, and they're like drinking milkshakes three meals a day."

"Too sweet?"

She made a face. "Tooth rotting. No depth at all." She tapped the spot on her neck where the bruise was already fading, clearly thinking. "But given who I am, feeding off humans is almost impossible."

Alex blinked. "Given who you are?"

Heather's lips twisted in amusement, and her eyes crinkled like she was holding back a laugh. "You have no idea who I am, do you?"

"Uh, no?"

She stretched slowly, then pushed herself off the couch and walked across the living room to a shelf full of books and magazines. She selected one at random and flipped through it until she found whatever she was looking for.

When she passed the magazine to Alex, he glanced down and was surprised to see an advertisement for a television show on the page, featuring Heather and a handsome blond man in police uniform.

"You're an actress."

"Yes." Heather tapped the page. "I have a good career. I enjoy what I do. But I can't feed as often as I'd like, because people know who I am. I don't want to get called out as a Para any more than you do."

Alex glanced back down at the page and waited.

"You need to feed every couple of days, right?" she asked.

"Yeah. Every three or four days would be ideal, but whenever I'm not on the road for sure."

"The same for me. So I'm thinking maybe we have a solution that covers all of our bases." Heather sat up straight. "Let's date."

Alex's brain skidded to a halt. "What? Look, you're gorgeous, but I don't… I mean, I'm gay. So."

Heather tilted her head in obvious amusement. "Yes, I gathered as much. I mean, we make it look like we're dating. We're both Para, so we can handle feedings even more regularly without negative side effects if needed, and an exclusive feeding arrangement when you're in town means neither of us risk getting outted. Plus, you can tell your teammates that you have a girlfriend. It's a win-win for both of us."

"I don't—" Alex paused, the words sinking in. It made sense and gave him a steady blood source. It wouldn't look suspicious if he met up with Heather once or twice a week, especially if they sometimes went out in public to have dinner, or if she came to one of his games.

"Yeah, okay," he finally said. "You have a deal."

Chapter Six

Seattle Cascades (@CascadesNHL)
Tonight it's #TealAndWhite versus #TealAndOrange here in Seattle as we take on San Jose. We're ready for another West Coast battle!

Chelsea in SEA (@ChelSEA_Scades)
Wish they'd give Fanning another chance in net tonight… feel so bad for the guy after that crappy goal against in the last game. I liked what I saw from him, I think he'll be a really good backup for us.

THEY HAD a day off after the Vancouver game, with a mandatory practice in the morning. Sasha kept his head down while they were on the ice and put himself through a solid workout in the gym after. No one said anything to him about what had happened the previous night, but he caught a few glances, especially from some of the younger guys who had already started to bond with Fanning.

It didn't help that Shawn was his usual self after practice, talking nonstop. Sasha tried to tune him out, especially once Shawn got on the subject of Fanning and their teenage exploits. Sasha rolled his eyes and pointedly taped a couple of new sticks while Shawn rambled on about their time rooming together in the USNTDP. If he screwed up the tape job because Shawn started talking about the time he dared Fanning to go skinny dipping, well… it was just because he was annoyed by the chatter. That was all.

There was an itch between Sasha's shoulder blades by the time he left the arena, and he was happy to escape for the day, a slow simmering anger resting right beneath his skin. *I've been on this team for five years; some kid who's been here for five* minutes *has no right to get pissy with me. The others will see soon enough that Fanning doesn't belong on this team, if he treats people that way all the time.* He drove straight to the hospital, bypassing the nurses' station once again to find Ed in his room.

"Sasha!" Ed greeted him with a wide smile as soon as he walked in. "I'm glad you came back."

At least someone is happy to see me. Sasha returned the smile. "Said I would." He pulled up the chair again and flopped down into it. "How're you feeling?"

Ed wrinkled his nose. "Better, and worse. I think they're going to let me out in a couple of days. Friday afternoon or Saturday morning."

Sasha pulled up his mental calendar. "We have a game Friday and Saturday. San Jose, then Anaheim. We fly down tomorrow morning and won't be back until Sunday."

"Yeah, I figured. Good division rivalry matchups, you all should have no problem winning either." Ed sounded pleased. "But I want to talk about that game last night."

"You saw?"

"Nah, listened again." Ed waved his hand at the speaker he had set up. "I can do short periods with a screen, but the doctor won't clear me for more yet. But look, Sasha, I wanted to say congrats."

Sasha blinked in confusion, feeling like he was missing something. "Congrats? But we didn't win."

That fact didn't seem to matter to Ed. If anything, his smile widened and he sat up straighter in his hospital bed. "Exactly."

What? Okay, Sasha realized, he was definitely missing something. Maybe a translation issue somewhere? Or maybe something more alarming—like that concussion or one of Ed's other injuries leaving him confused.

"Eddie," he said slowly, "the team does not get congratulations when we lose."

Ed rolled his eyes. "The team doesn't, but you do. Picking that fight with Bilovsky at the end of the game and screening the new guy so he let in that goal? Absolutely perfect."

The look on Ed's face was like the phrase the North Americans used sometimes about cats eating canaries. *Smug*, Sasha settled on, but in a mean way. It made Sasha frown uncomfortably.

"I didn't want a goal to happen," he explained.

"But it did. An experienced goalie could have stopped that. Rico will see that, and he'll know that they can't just throw me away."

"Throw you aw—Eddie, what are you saying?" Sasha put one hand on his friend's arm, worried. "You're talking nonsense."

And now that he looked closely, he could see that Ed didn't look so great. His pupils were enlarged even in the bright room, and there was a thin line of sweat on his forehead.

But Ed didn't seem to be in any pain. If anything, he looked like he was more than comfortable, despite the obvious injuries that had to be hurting.

"Sasha, we're best friends. I can trust you, right?"

"Of course." The answer was immediate, no hesitation.

Ed leaned forward. "The cops came by once I was moved to a regular room. They're gonna charge me with drunk driving, but you and I know that's ridiculous. I had, like, one beer. Maybe two. But the roads were slippery and I spun out."

Sasha sat back in his chair. "But the police would know if you were drunk."

"The cops don't know anything. They ran a blood test when I got to the hospital, but my lawyer said the results were close enough to the legal limit that we could fight it."

He cut off when a nurse came in. She smiled at Ed while checking the levels on his IV. Ed returned the smile with a flirtatious wink, and she blushed as she wrote something down in his chart before leaving without a word.

Once he was sure she gone, Ed continued. "My lawyer says it will look better if you'll come to the hearing and tell them what you saw. You know, explain that I wasn't drunk when you saw me, that you couldn't see any signs I'd been drinking. And maybe be a character witness. You could tell them I never have more than one drink when the team goes out."

Sasha's mouth parted, but he couldn't even begin to form a reply.... *Because nothing he just said is true.* He might have been tired and afraid for his friend when he arrived at the accident scene that night, but Sasha knew he'd smelled alcohol on Ed's breath. Maybe the glazed eyes could have been from the concussion or pain, but it had been more than obvious that Ed had been drinking.

And the other part—

Ed loved to go out with the team, any chance he could find. Making playoffs, of course, but also getting a shutout, winning a game against a rival, a teammates' birthday, whatever; any excuse Ed could find to throw a party, he'd be the first one proposing it. He would get spectacularly drunk each time, with the dedicated focus of a man who knew exactly how to go from sober to wasted in the most efficient way possible. Of course they were hockey players, so going out after a game wasn't exactly uncommon. But in the last few months, he'd noticed Ed going out other times too, often alone. And every time Sasha went by his house, there was always a drink on the table and a fully stocked bar on offer.

And this isn't the first time he's driven drunk.

Each thing on its own wasn't concerning. But putting it all together, with the accident as well, made Sasha frown with concern. There was something that he wasn't sure he wanted to examine too closely.

Ed was looking at him expectantly, so Sasha quickly searched for some way to stall on an answer. "You talked to the team lawyers and management about this?"

A scoff. "Management wants to throw me under the bus. I could tell when Dubois and Henrique were here, the way they were looking at me. It's why I'm glad that kid lost the game for you last night—shows them all that they'd be fools to get rid of me."

"Fanning," Sasha said.

"What?"

Sasha exhaled. "The kid, the goalie they called up. His name is Fanning."

Ed scowled. "I know, whatever. Point is, as soon as I'm healed up, I'll be back and he'll be gone. Until then we just need to keep showing the coach that the Fanning kid is useless, right? You can help with that, like you did last night. And I'll be back sooner if we can get these fuckin' charges to go away. So, what'd you say, *mon ami*?"

The question lingered in the air between them. Sasha would be the first to admit that he wasn't a fan of Alexander Fanning. The guy was cold, too quiet and too emotionless—except when he got close to Sasha, and then he'd wrinkle his nose in obvious dislike. He was untested at the NHL level, and Hertzog wasn't going to be able to hold the fort down by himself. They *needed* a starting goaltender, and that guy had to be Ed. If Ed was in prison, the team was screwed.

But....

But Ed was drunk that night. And it had only been pure luck and the late hour that resulted in the car hitting a telephone pole, instead of another driver.

"You know what, Ed? Let me get with your lawyer when we get back from California, and we'll talk then. Okay?"

Ed grinned as though he'd won something. Sasha tried to match it, but something inside him felt awful.

I would do anything for Eddie. He's been there for me since I got here. He's my brother in all but blood. But this.... Sasha swallowed. What Ed was asking him was something else entirely. To not only cheat his team and one of his teammates—because Fanning *was* a teammate, even if Sasha didn't like him—out of victories just to make Ed look more valuable... but also to cheat the legal system and lie for Ed.

I don't know if I can do this.

Seattle Sports News (@SeattleSportsNews)
Cascades goaltender Eduard Despres will appear in court today for an arraignment hearing on charges of aggravated DUI following his late-night accident on January 4. He's expected to plead not guilty. Follow us for the latest updates.

Emma (@Cascadiac)
I've been hearing rumors of Despres for years, not surprised that he was drunk driving and crashed his car. Glad he didn't permanently hurt himself or hit anyone else, but maybe this will force him to stop with the stupid behavior.

Mrs. Merkley... a girl can dream! (@MerkleyFan96)
@Cascadiac: I've honestly never liked Despres much, either on or off the ice. Maybe the Cascades will finally trade him!

Emma (@Cascadiac)
@MerkleyFan96: ha, doubtful. All we've got as a backup is Hertzog and the new baby!goalie from Portland. I may not like Despres either, but fact is he's a good goalie and the Cascades need him right now.

SIX GAMES into his NHL call-up, Alex was finally starting to feel comfortable about his place on the team, even though he'd sat on the bench for five of them. Hockey guys were hockey guys, no matter what league they played in, and it was easy enough to slide into the comfortable familiarity of the Cascades locker room. Most of his teammates treated him like he belonged, like he'd always been there, inviting him for lunch after practices or to join in a round of two-touch before a game.

The younger guys were immediately friendly. Rager was nineteen, a typical Dub kid with more energy than everyone else in the room combined, while Bayer was sarcastic and witty. Even Volkov, the team's youngest rookie, was polite enough—though he kept his distance more than the others, which Alex understood once he learned that the eighteen-year-old Russian was living with Petrov.

The older guys were welcoming too, offering advice and helping Alex navigate life in Seattle. Merkley had only been captain for a year, but he was always available to suggest restaurants or dry cleaners, or just stay late after practice to shoot pucks at Alex.

And now that he had a regular blood source, Alex was feeling a hell of a lot better about life in general.

The only thing he wasn't feeling good about was Petrov.

The guy was still glaring at him every time they were in the same room together.

"He's just upset that Despres is hurt," Shawn tried to explain.

But it was more than that. There was something else in Petrov's glare, a heat that Alex wasn't sure he wanted to examine too closely.

He's Russian, and possibly anti-Para, he reminded himself. And Volkov too, even though the rookie seemed cheerful enough. Alex kept his distance, trying to maintain a careful wall between them. *I don't want to be friends with guys like that, who would hate me if they knew what I was.* The fact that Petrov hated him regardless only made it easier.

Alex came in early the day before their home game against New York, planning to work out a little before they were due for on-ice practice. He expected to have the gym to himself, given the early hour and the fact that even Shawn had still been dozing into a cup of coffee when he left. Instead, he walked into the arena gym—and almost right back out again upon getting slammed with a wall of familiar, earthy scent. It took him only a second to spot Petrov lifting weights.

He stopped himself right inside the doorway, taking a moment before Petrov noticed him. It was obvious the defenseman had been working out for a while; his T-shirt clung to his body with sweat, and the water bottle at his side was almost empty.

I could leave and come back later. Alex immediately dismissed the idea, though. *No, I'm not going to let him push me out of a space that I'm allowed to be in, just because he's a dick.*

Head up and shoulders straight, Alex stepped into the gym and made his way to the treadmills against the wall. It was obvious when

Petrov noticed him; his steady reps on the machine stuttered, and weights hit the ground with a dull *clank*.

The plan was to put his music on, ignore Petrov, and focus on his own workout. But as Alex started his machine up, he realized he'd overlooked one very simple fact: the treadmills directly faced the weight machines. He was going to spend his entire run staring directly at Petrov and his stupid, angry face, and his hot, sweat-covered body. And every time he inhaled, Petrov's damn scent was impossible to escape.

Shit.

He tried to pay attention to the display screen on the treadmill. He forced himself to watch the ESPN highlights scrolling across one of the televisions. Alex even tried cranking his music up, as though jamming out to fast-paced rock would somehow erase the distraction in front of him. Nothing worked. Instead, his gaze kept drifting to Petrov as he moved from machine to machine, keeping his back to Alex whenever possible.

It's a damn nice back too. With the wet shirt clinging to his torso, Alex could make out every muscle of Petrov's shoulders. *God damn. He may be an asshole, but he's probably the most attractive asshole I've ever seen. It's not fair.*

The beeping of the treadmill a while later came as a relief, signaling that his run was over. Alex set the machine to cool down and wiped sweat off his face, spraying himself down with water like he would during a game.

When he opened his eyes and blinked the droplets away, it was to find Petrov watching him.

Petrov spun around and resumed his workout as soon as he realized Alex had spotted him, but the expression on his face lingered in Alex's mind. *He was looking at me the same way I had been looking at him before.*

It was that realization that made Alex turn the treadmill off, wipe his face off with a towel, and carry himself across the gym to where Petrov was now sitting on the edge of the bench press.

"You need a spotter if you want to lift."

Petrov gave him a withering glare. And because the universe had it out for Alex, the way Petrov's icy blue eyes narrowed only made him even sexier. "Yes. I know," he bit out.

Alex held both hands up defensively. "Okay, whatever. I was just saying, if you need a spotter, I could help."

"Waiting for Volkov" came the terse reply.

Alex had only chatted with Mikhail Volkov a couple of times since joining the Cascades. The rookie spoke English just fine, but he seemed more inclined to hang around Petrov and chatter in Russian when he could. But from what little he'd seen so far, Alex would be surprised if Volkov rolled out of bed a minute before he had to, let alone came to the gym early for an extra workout.

But Petrov had a stick up his ass, and he wasn't going to push it. "Cool. But I'll be here for another half hour or so. Let me know if I can help."

He turned to walk over to one of the thigh machines, bending over to set the weight. A movement out of the corner of his eye caught his attention—Petrov, standing up suddenly and turning to walk away.

Was he staring at my ass?

Alex shook his head. Petrov could watch all he wanted, but he'd have to get a personality transplant before Alex would give him the time of day.

Except the anger and resentment he'd felt toward Petrov from the start had mellowed out since Alex had met Heather. He was getting regular feedings now, and Heather was always more than happy to listen to him when he started ranting about Petrov.

Of course, she would laugh while she did so, and tell him how delicious his sexual tension was... but she still listened.

But the point was, Alex was well-fed. He was going to get another chance to start in goal on their upcoming East Coast road trip, and he'd get to prove himself there. So when Petrov glared at him or acted like an asshole, Alex was surprised to realize how little it bothered him.

And if Petrov *had* been staring at him earlier, then maybe there was something else to the hatred, other than Alex taking over for Despres.

It's worth watching him more closely, Alex reasoned. If Petrov was attracted to him, then it was definitely worth exploring. And if Petrov wasn't? *At the very least, I'll get something nice to fantasize about in my hotel room on this upcoming road trip.*

It was the first time he'd have a hotel room to himself since he started playing hockey on a traveling team... and with Petrov's glaring blue eyes fixed in his mind, he decided he was going to enjoy every second of it.

Chapter Seven

@SCartier3 on Instagram: bff time, just me & phantom & a truck named betsy. portland —> seattle. #roadtrip #movingday #butseriously #henamedhistruck http://bit.ly/2Iqn4VX

Liked by goaliefanning, cascadesnhl, and 896 others
View all 21 comments

January was scheduled to end with a ten-day, six-game trip to the East Coast. Alex was both excited and nervous, especially because he'd get his second start in one of the two back-to-back games they had to play.

But first they had two blessed days off, and that meant one thing:

"Road trip!"

Shawn kicked his shoes off and propped his feet up on the dashboard of Alex's pickup truck.

"No one needs those stinky things sitting right next to the air vents," Alex said, reaching over to shove them off.

The truck had been one of the first things he'd bought when he'd signed a pro contract, a vintage '68 Chevy in bright blue that he'd promptly named Betsy. He'd taken good care of it over the last three years, slowly replacing the old worn-out parts. It was a relief to have a chance to pick it up, along with more of his belongings from his apartment in Portland.

He'd woken up early that morning and hopped a quick flight from Seattle to Portland with Shawn in tow. They'd loaded up the truck bed with suitcases, more of Alex's gear, and whatever else he thought he might need for the next few months, and now they were heading north.

The drive wasn't a long one, and he had a feeling it would pass quickly enough with him and Shawn trading stories and chatting easily. They still saw each other every day, but with games, practices, workouts, and team events always going on, it felt like they didn't get a lot of time with just the two of them. Alex said as much.

"Yeah, that's one of the reasons I made you bring me along."

"What's the other reason?"

Shawn leaned forward and glanced up at the sky. It was gray and overcast, which Alex had hoped for. "Well, I know you checked the forecast carefully. But, y'know, if the sun does come out, I figured I could take over driving so you can get under some cover."

Alex glanced over, surprised by the admission. "I don't deserve you as a friend."

"Damn right you don't. But you could start by finding a drive-through and getting me a latte."

Laughing, Alex did so.

"So, we should talk about you and Sasha," Shawn said once they were on the road again and he had a coffee in hand.

"Uh, we definitely should not."

Shawn laughed. "Man, the look on your face when I said his name. You really like him, don't you?"

Alex swerved in his lane. "What?"

"At first I wasn't sure what was going on between you guys." Shawn took a sip of his coffee. "Like, were you gonna fight or fuck? Even the guys in the locker room picked up on the tension. They had a bet going on when you were finally going to punch Sasha in the face. But the more I watched you two, the more I realized how much you just want to fuck him."

Thankfully the road was pretty empty. Alex gripped the steering wheel and reminded himself that Coach would be pissed if he shoved Shawn out of a moving car.

"I don't even—Carts. What the hell, man?"

Alex had so many questions, and no idea where to start. He took a deep breath, then let it out. Shawn smelled bright and clean, the way he always did, and that familiarity was enough for Alex to latch on to so he could relax.

"Are you telling me," Alex said slowly, testing each word before speaking it, "that you bet the rest of the team that I was going to fuck Petrov?"

Shawn sat up straight. "No way, man!" He fumbled the coffee cup in his hands, turning to face Alex. "Dude, I wouldn't out you like that. Come on."

Alex exhaled. "Fucking hell, Carts. Don't scare me like that."

Shawn reached forward, resting his hand on Alex's arm. "I just meant that everyone could tell there was something going on between you two. I'm the only one who guessed that it's sexual tension, though. But, Phantom, you know they wouldn't judge you if they knew."

"They're not going to know." Alex swallowed around the sudden dryness in his throat. "Heather is going to let me feed from her on a regular basis, and she offered to pretend to be my girlfriend. And you're wrong about me and Petrov. He hates me, and I hate him, and that's that."

Shawn stayed silent beside him for the next few miles, moving only to adjust the air vents or skip a song. When he finally spoke again, his voice was soft. "Hey, I'm sorry, bro."

Alex reached over without looking to offer his fist, and Shawn bumped it gently.

"I only thought, y'know, it's obvious you like Sasha. I mean, you have a type, judging by the guys I walked in on you screwing back in the NTDP."

This time, Alex's "Fucking hell" was spoken with laughter. "I've been trying to forget about that for years."

"Man, I love you, but you were a terrible road roommate after you turned sixteen." Shawn stretched his legs out and rapped on the window, silent for a moment. "Sasha doesn't hate you, though. Just in case you were wondering."

"Uh, yeah. He does." Alex glanced over at his friend. "He won't even speak to me, let alone look at me. Even if I did have a crush—I said *if*, shut up—even if I did, it's definitely one-sided."

"Uh, Phantom," Shawn said, "I hate to break it to you, but I've played on a line with him for a couple of years now. I know the way he looks when he wants to punch someone. Hell, the entire NHL knows that look; he's kinda got a reputation for trying to hit people in the face when he gets pissed. But the way he looks at you? That is not a *punching* kinda stare, lemme tell you."

Interesting. But still. "Okay, so maybe he doesn't want to punch me, but he's still pretty clear about hating me."

"Nah, bro. He and Despres were really close, you know? Like you and me, only Sasha was Ed's rookie. I think he hates that you're replacing his best friend. He's talked about it a little."

And, okay, that was even more interesting. "Do you, uh, talk to him about me?"

"Yep. Mostly about the shit we got up to when we were teenagers. He pretends like he doesn't care, but it's obvious that he's listening."

Eventually Alex was able to steer the conversation back to safer topics, like catching up on gossip about their respective families and friends they'd kept in touch with from when they were younger. But Alex kept coming back to Shawn's words in his mind.

What if?

He'd seen the way Petrov had looked at him in the locker room, after all. And Shawn knew Petrov better than just about anyone else.

After a couple of hours, the Seattle skyline appeared. Alex let Shawn navigate them through the streets of downtown, and they pulled into the underground parking garage of Shawn's building only a little behind schedule.

"Thanks for coming with me, Carts."

Shawn grinned. "Anytime. It was fun to be on the road and not on a bus."

They managed to get everything up the elevator in a couple of trips, laughing and competing to see who could carry more as they did so.

Once everything was piled in the corner of Alex's room, Shawn leaned against the doorway.

"Hey," he said. "What I said at the beginning of the trip, about Sasha?"

Alex raised an eyebrow and waited.

"Just, give him a chance, okay? I don't know what's going through his head, but I can promise there's more to it than hate, okay?"

"Yeah, maybe."

And that was that. Shawn smiled and pulled out his phone, clearly done with the topic. "You got plans tonight? Want to grab dinner?"

Alex thought about it, then frowned. "Can't. I need to meet up with Heather and feed, but she'll probably drag me out to some restaurant first. We're leaving for the airport straight after practice tomorrow, so I won't have a chance otherwise."

Shawn nodded easily. "We can put a movie on when you get home later, then. Sjöberg got a care package filled with weird Swedish candy and he shared some with me, so I want to try it."

TMZ Exclusive

Seattle isn't known as a celebrity playground, but we spotted actress and model HEATHER BELL out and about with Seattle Cascades goalie

ALEXANDER FANNING! The two were seen having dinner at Le Renard Rouge. Could romance be in the air? Read more: bit.ly/xC4m....

FANNING WAS beginning to drive him absolutely insane.

Every time Sasha looked at him, Fanning was staring at him, brown eyes focused intently like they were taking Sasha in and judging him. It was unnerving, and he was certain that it was purposeful. Unfortunately, none of Sasha's useless friends would listen to him when he tried to bring it up.

It had started the day before they played New York at home, in the locker room. He'd been startled to see Fanning there so early, and furious to have his routine interrupted. But even though he'd tried to focus on his own workout and ignore the steady thump of footsteps on the treadmill behind him, he could feel Fanning's gaze fixed on him.

It had only gotten worse from there.

"I think he's trying to sabotage my game," Sasha told Wilson, halfway through the New York game. They were winning, but only barely.

Wilson rolled his eyes and chewed on his mouthguard. "What, by staring at you?" He glanced over Sasha's shoulder, to where Fanning was sitting on the bench. "He's a goalie, man. Goalies are weird. They stare at people; it's what they do."

But the staring wasn't just limited to when he was on the ice; no, every time Fanning was in the same room as him, Sasha would feel eyes on his back or glance over to find himself being studied by that intense gaze.

"He's doing it on purpose," he said to Andrej one afternoon while they were waiting for their turn to take a drill. The Slovakian forward spoke Russian well enough, which meant Sasha naturally gravitated to him.

Andrej patted him on the shoulder. "Who's doing what on purpose?"

"Fanning." Sasha practically spit the name out. "He's always around, getting in my way. Every time I turn a corner, he's there staring at me."

"Maybe he just thinks you're a handsome young man," Andrej said, patting his cheek.

Sasha pushed the hand off and frowned.

He tried Carts next. "Tell your friend to leave me alone."

Both of Shawn's eyebrows went up. "Who, Alex?"

"Yes. He is always staring at me like he's angry."

For some reason Shawn found that incredibly amusing. "Dude, I don't think it's anger that you're seeing."

Sasha shook his head. "He is still pissed at me for the Vancouver game."

"Nah," Shawn said. "Trust me. Phantom doesn't hold grudges like that. He just needed to vent after the game, and now he's fine. You should talk to him. I'm sure he'll say the same thing."

Sasha exhaled and walked away. *Useless.* Why wouldn't anyone listen to him?

His last attempt was the one that he was least looking forward to. He found Mikhail in the waiting area at the airport two days after they played New York at home. The team was getting ready to depart on one of their longest road trips of the season, heading east to play in Pennsylvania, Buffalo, and then up through eastern Canada.

"I hate him," Sasha said in Russian, flopping down in a chair next to his countryman.

Misha put his tabloid magazine down and turned to Sasha with narrowed eyes. "Alexander Vladimirovich, you are my good friend, and I am so thankful that you are letting me live with you during my first season in the NHL. But if you do not stop talking to me about how much you dislike Fanning, I will have to smother you in your sleep. Especially when it's obvious that you just really want to be his friend."

And this is why I didn't want to talk to him. Sasha sputtered. "I don't—I do not want to be his friend. I hate him, Misha."

Clearly no one had punished Misha enough as a child, because the brat had the nerve to roll his eyes at Sasha. "You watch him all the time, and you get grumpy when he ignores you. You hate that there's someone on this team that doesn't like you. You want to be BFFs." He dropped the last word into the sentence in English.

"I do not like Fanning," Sasha said firmly.

"Protest more, hm?" Misha laughed. "Maybe you should skip this road trip and go home to make friendship bracelets for you both."

Misha was a literal child, and Sasha said as much.

"Perhaps, but I'm not wrong." Misha was grinning smugly. Then the smile slipped away, replaced by a seriousness that seemed out of place on the younger man's face. "Sasha, I think he would be your friend if you talked to him."

Sasha sighed and gazed across the room toward the boarding door, forcing himself not to look around at his teammates. "I hate him."

"You do not."

"I do." Sasha sighed. "I hate that he's here instead of Eddie, and that everyone seems to like him even though he's cold and rude and stares all the time like he's judging people."

Misha tapped his fingers on the page he was looking at. "He's not cold at all. He's quiet, sure, but he's friendly. The only person he acts this way with is you," he said slowly. "Have you realized that?"

What? Sasha sat back in his chair hard and looked around the waiting lounge that the team was sitting in. It only took a second for him to find Fanning. The goalie was sitting cross-legged on the floor in the corner, with Bayer, Rager, and Hertzog in front of him. They had a card game going on, and everyone was laughing and shoving one another playfully... even Fanning, whose face looked far more open and beautiful when he smiled like that.

"*He* hates *me*, then," Sasha said.

He didn't see Misha roll his eyes again, but he could practically feel it. "He doesn't. He thinks that *you* hate *him*."

"I do."

Misha rolled up his magazine and whacked Sasha on the arm with it. "Go talk to him, idiot. Ask to join the card came they're playing. Maybe show him that you have an emotion other than *glaring*."

Could it be true? Misha spent more time with the younger guys on the team, and it made sense that he knew Fanning better than Sasha did. And it was tempting to go talk to Fanning. Maybe try to see the man beneath the icy exterior.

While Sasha was still trying to make up his mind, Alex detached himself from the group, standing up and dusting himself off before wandering off in the direction of the bathroom. The urge to go after him almost yanked Sasha from his chair. *I could talk to him. Now, alone. I could... apologize.*

He went to stand but was stopped by Misha's hand on his arm.

"Hey, Sasha." Misha's voice was amused. "Before you go, look!"

Turning, Sasha looked over at his friend. "What is it?"

Misha held up his magazine, flipping it around so Sasha could see. There, in color, was Fanning and a gorgeous blonde woman, arms linked together as they stood outside an expensive restaurant that Sasha recognized.

"Alex is in my magazine!" Misha sounded delighted. "He's dating the lead actress from that police detective show. He's famous!"

Sasha rolled his eyes. "You're famous, idiot boy." But the easy dismissal was only to cover the disappointment that flooded Sasha's entire body. *So, Fanning has a girlfriend. Of course.* Sasha slumped back into his seat as Alex walked out of sight.

So he has a girlfriend, he repeated to himself. It didn't mean anything. Clearly Fanning was doing well for himself, settling in easily and meeting lots of people. If he didn't want anything to do with Sasha, then that was his own damn problem.

He won't even be here long enough for any of this to matter.

For some reason, that thought made him feel worse than anything else.

Chapter Eight

Burn types differ between species, as seen in the case studies of Dr. Ritvik Patel, who proposes a fourth category with regards to vampires and other heliophobic Paranormals. Within his revised system, a first-degree burn results in superficial damage to the epidermis, specifically painful blistering and reddening. Second-degree burns affect the epidermis and dermis, with blackening tissue of the other layers of skin. Third-degree burns affect underlying musculature and can cause irreversible scarring and damage for the victim. Fourth-degree burns result in full charring of all layers, and possible loss of limb or life.

Müller, P. D. (2014). Reevaluating burn trauma in Paranormal beings. *Journal for Paranormal Medicine, 34*(2): 12-19.

THE DAY of Alex's second NHL start began badly and only got worse from there.

The sun was shining brightly through a gap in his hotel curtains when he awoke, the stripe of sunlight falling right over Alex's arm and leaving a painful sunburn in its wake. The pain yanked him out of bed and to the sink, where he cranked the faucet on as cold as he could and thrust his arm beneath it.

Alex stripped off the T-shirt that he'd slept in, soaking it and wrapping it around the burn while he dug one-handed through his toiletries case for the tube of burn ointment he always kept on hand.

The relief that washed over him when he rubbed the ointment in was incredible… and short-lived, because his phone rang a minute later.

Cradling his arm to his chest, Alex dodged the beam of sunlight and grabbed his phone off the nightstand.

"Hello?"

"Phantom, hey, you're awake!" Shawn sounded far too chipper for—Alex checked the clock on the nightstand—just after eight o'clock. "A couple of us are gonna go get breakfast outside the hotel. There's a place down the road that has the best pancakes I've ever had in my life.

I know, you wouldn't think Buffalo is the place to go for breakfast food, but I swear this restaurant will change your mind. You in?"

Alex winced. "I think I'll have to pass, sorry. I'm just going to order room service this morning." And take advantage of having a room to himself on the road so he could treat this damn burn without anyone noticing. Maybe it wasn't the way he'd prefer to be using the privacy this morning, but he'd take the silver lining where he could find it.

"All right, fair enough. Don't forget to meet for the bus to the arena at eleven for practice, 'kay?"

Shawn was a great friend, and he really seemed to care, but right then Alex wanted to get him off the phone because his arm was starting to sting again. "Sure, will do. Bye."

Maybe a little abrupt, he thought as he hung up the phone, but he needed to get some ice and another layer of burn cream stat.

Then the phone rang again.

"Carts, seriously, I said no," Alex growled.

There was a long pause on the other end. "Fanning? It's Daniel Henrique."

Well, fuck. "Coach. Sorry, I thought you were...." He trailed off, sitting down heavily on his bed.

Henrique hummed. "Well, at least you're already awake." His tone said he didn't particularly care if he'd woken Alex up anyway. "We're set up downstairs in the conference room right now, reviewing some tape, and I was wondering if you could stop by before we leave for the arena. Maybe ten thirty or so?"

Alex's mouth went dry. The words weren't a request; they were a clear command. "Yeah. I mean, yes. Of course."

"Excellent, I'll see you then." Coach hung up, leaving Alex to stare down at his phone with nausea rising in his gut.

What on earth could he possibly want? Is he going to pull me as the starter tonight? Alex slumped backward. Coach hadn't sounded pleased, and he could already picture the conversation to come. *Maybe they found someone better, someone who's actually won an NHL game, and they're sending me back to the AHL.* A sick, twisted feeling grew in his stomach. He'd been looking forward to this game since it was announced that he'd be getting the start; it was a second chance for him to prove himself and show the Cascades management that he deserved to be there. The fear that he was about to lose that chance made him want to curl up and cry.

And to make a shitty situation even worse, he had to be injured. The burn on his arm wasn't so bad, but it was a vivid, angry dark red that sat exactly where one of his arm pad straps would rest. Normally he'd just call Heather and get a quick feeding in, which would help accelerate the healing. But they were in Buffalo right now, not Seattle, and there were another five days after this one before he'd be back in Washington. He was, as Shawn would say, "totally outta luck, bro."

First things first—he put in a call for breakfast to be brought up, running through the mental list he kept of appropriate foods. As sick as he felt, he knew he'd have to eat something, if only to give his body energy to try to heal; oatmeal, eggs, and turkey bacon were all iron-rich, and would help at least a tiny bit. The burn throbbed as he ate, showered, and got dressed, and even a couple of painkillers and more burn cream didn't help to dull it much. He wrapped a bandage around it reluctantly, gritting his teeth and hoping for the best.

Time dragged on until the clock finally read 10:25. Alex tugged the sleeves of his shirt down until the bandage was hidden, ran a hand nervously through his hair, and left his hotel room with dread pooling in his gut.

Seattle Cascades (@CascadesNHL)
Tonight's starting line-up for your Seattle Cascades:
LW Akseli Mäkelä (#38) / C Derick Merkley (#96) / RW Brad Thompson (#88)
D Alexander Petrov (#12) / D Shawn Cartier (#3)
G Alexander Fanning (#31)
#TealAndWhite #LetsGoCascades

ONE-ON-ONE MEETINGS with Coach Rico weren't rare, but it was uncommon enough that Sasha pushed the door of the conference room open with mild trepidation. It was most likely that Coach wanted to talk to him further about the incident with Ed, but after three and a half weeks of radio silence from the team's management it seemed odd to be bringing it up now. Sasha rarely checked sports media sites, but he'd caught glimpses of a few articles about the accident and Ed's recovery... and the police charges against him. After seeing that headline, Sasha had stopped looking.

It was bad enough that he hadn't been to see Ed since the last visit to the hospital a week before, but Ed had finally been released and sent home, and now he was texting Sasha nonstop. Guilt made him ignore some of the texts, especially the ones about Ed's arraignment and upcoming trial.

So he was expecting a quick, informal meeting before boarding the bus for practice. He was not expecting to walk into the conference room and see Fanning sitting comfortably in one of the plush chairs, cradling a mug of coffee in both hands. He froze, meeting Fanning's dark brown eyes and seeing identical shock reflected in them. *Well, at least he's just as surprised as I am.*

"Come in, Petrov." Coach motioned him forward, and Sasha slunk inside and took a seat at the opposite end of the table. "Coffee? There's one of those single-serve machines against the wall."

Sasha shook his head silently.

"All right, then. I'm sure you both can figure out why I've called you in here today."

Uh, no. Sasha didn't have a clue, and a glance across the table told him that Fanning was in the same position, though he was trying to hide his confusion behind his drink.

"It's come to my attention that there was some tension a couple of weeks ago, after the Vancouver game. Words were exchanged."

Sasha went absolutely still, fisting his hands against his thighs.

"Sir." Fanning sat up straight, eyes wide. "I'm so sorry about that. It was entirely my fault, and—"

Coach waved a hand and Fanning fell silent. "No one is at fault here. It was a rough game, with a lot of emotion on the line. I understand that it was a tough situation for Sasha to be in, and a frustrating loss for you, Alex." He tapped the table in front of him. "But whatever issues are lingering between the two of you need to stop. Now."

Sasha bristled. "Coach, just because he throws a tantrum—"

"A *tantrum?*" Fanning turned to look at him, eyes blazing. "Are you serious, after your stupid little argument with that Vancouver player—"

Coach slammed his hand down on the table, hard enough to shock them both to silence. "Enough. This isn't an elementary school playground where the two of you can bicker about who's the bigger bully. This is the NHL, and your tension is putting a strain on my locker room."

Sasha crossed his arms and leaned back in his seat.

"Here's what's going to happen. For the rest of this road trip, the two of you are best friends. You eat together; you sit next to each other on the bus or the plane. You work through whatever the hell is going on between you, or else."

Fanning opened his mouth to protest, then shut it when Coach leveled a glare at him.

"Push me, and you'll be rooming together as well."

The rest of the road trip… that was three more games, each with a day in between. Five days, plus the entire six-hour flight back to Seattle. And he'd be spending almost every waking minute stuck with Fanning.

Coach dismissed them shortly after that, leaving Sasha and Fanning to eye each other warily as they walked through the hotel hallways to where the bus was parked. Fanning fidgeted for a second, staring at Sasha. He took a deep breath, and something on his face changed before he quickly turned away and started walking.

Sasha reacted without thinking, grabbing Fanning's arm. The reaction he got was not what he expected; Fanning jerked, hissing, and yanked his arm away with a strength that belied his smaller form. Sasha's eyes narrowed; that was the reaction of someone who was injured… but Fanning wouldn't be stupid enough to play with an injury, would he? *No, surely not.*

"Sorry," he said, studying Fanning's body language from behind. "Мне не стоило этого делать."

Fanning didn't move, not even to look behind him. "I don't speak *asshole*," he said.

God damn, like he was one to talk. Asshole? Fanning needed to take a long look in a mirror. Still, Coach's threats rang in his ears, so Sasha exhaled slowly and tried to get a grasp on his anger. "It's Russian," he said. "Means I shouldn't have done that."

That caught Fanning's attention, at least. He turned around, wary. "Done what? Grabbed me?"

"Yes." Sasha tucked his hands in his sweatpants pockets. "And also the fight, with Bilovsky. I'm sorry."

Fanning looked surprised. His brown eyes were round as he looked up at Sasha. "Are you serious?"

Sasha shrugged. "I messed up. I know this. Merks, he yelled at me after the game too, once media left."

"Oh." Fanning appeared to be at a loss for words. "Look, Petrov, I—"

"Sasha."

Fanning stopped midsentence. "What?"

"Coach says we must be friendly, yes? So, you should call me Sasha, and I will call you Phantom, okay? It's your nickname?"

Fanning laughed, a short, surprised noise. "Yeah, okay. You're Sasha. But you can call me Alex… only Carts calls me Phantom, like he thinks we're still back in Juniors or something."

"Good, then. Alex." Sasha rolled the name over his tongue. "We should go catch the bus. Coach will yell again if we're late."

Alex took another deep breath. He still seemed hesitant, but at least he wasn't glaring at Sasha any longer. "All right. Lead the way."

Maybe this next week of games and flights wouldn't be so bad, Sasha thought.

"We believe these proposed changes will help to preserve the sanctity of the game. The fact is that there haven't been sufficient studies on Paranormal athletes to determine what advantages, if any, are afforded by their nonhuman nature. By instituting required genetic testing for all players in the National Hockey League, we can ensure parity and equality for all."

—NHL Commissioner George Heatly

ALEX TRAILED after Sasha, resisting the urge to cradle his arm against his stomach. The defenseman had managed to grab right over the burn, and it radiated pain all the way up his arm. But there was nothing he could do about it, and no way to explain the injury to any of his teammates or the trainers, so he gritted his teeth and put one foot in front of the other.

But walking just behind Sasha introduced a new issue that he hadn't planned on. The scent that clung to Sasha wafted in the air behind him and flooded Alex's senses with every breath he took. He ducked his head, trying to breathe around it, but embarrassingly he could feel his fangs start to extend with every inhalation.

What the hell? He'd fed a few nights prior, before heading to the airport to fly out with the team. And he'd been fine for their first few games in Philadelphia and Pittsburgh. *It must be the injury. My body wants to heal the burn, and it's making me hungrier than I should be.* And Sasha smelled so ridiculously good.

Alex pressed his lips together and hoped no one would notice.

They entered the lobby, and Sasha stopped abruptly. Alex, head still down, almost ran into him and managed to stop only at the last second.

"Look, Fanning," Sasha said, turning around. He froze, staring down.

Alex was suddenly aware of how close they were standing. He inhaled sharply and gazed up into pale blue eyes.

"Alex," Sasha said, softer this time. "I meant to say, before...."

Heat rose between them. Alex wanted to lick his lips, to go up on his toes and see if the look in Sasha's eyes meant what he thought it meant. The way Sasha was looking at him right now, the bare emotions that Alex could see there.... *God, tell me I'm not reading this wrong.*

A burst of noise sliced through the tension as a group of their teammates emerged, heading outside to the bus. It was enough to break the spell, though it took everything in Alex's power to pull his eyes away from Sasha's before he could embarrass himself.

What the hell am I doing? Ten minutes ago this guy hated me, and now I'm standing here about to kiss him? No matter what Shawn seems to think, I'd probably get a punch to the face for my troubles, and another tabloid report to boot. Alex turned his head, breathing like he'd run a marathon, but every time he breathed in, his lungs filled with that decadent smell that was so unique to Sasha.

He looked to the side and caught sight of one of the lobby televisions, which was set to a sports network, NHL news scrolling by in the background as reporters talked. He could just make out the words from across the room.

"Commissioner Heatly's proposal has pro-Para groups in an uproar, with many claiming the new regulations would be discriminatory to any Paranormal players in the league. But NHL team owners claim the testing would stop cheating and remove any unfair advantages that a nonhuman player might have."

Liquid ice flooded Alex's veins, and the heated tension that had filled the lobby before evaporated in an instant.

The news anchor continued to speak, but Alex couldn't hear it over the pounding of blood in his ears.

"Alex," Sasha said again.

"Petrov—Sasha, sorry." Alex licked his lips. "We should go. We need to get on the bus."

He glanced back up to see those stunning blue eyes shutter with disappointment, replaced a split second later by that emotionless wall that Sasha was so good at. "Yes, of course."

Guilt chewed at Alex's stomach, but there was relief there too. *You're straight. You're human. And that's all you can be.*

Chapter Nine

The bus ride to practice hadn't been terrible, if Sasha was being honest. He'd climbed on the bus first and taken his usual seat near the back against the window. It had only been when Fanning—Alex, rather—had paused in the aisle that Sasha had realized his mistake. He'd been about to offer to trade or sit somewhere else when Alex had slid into the other seat silently.

"What's this?" Mäkelä had called out upon spotting them. "Are you two over your bitter feud now? Is this the start of a beautiful new friendship in the Cascades locker room?"

Sasha had flipped the Finn off while rolling his eyes. "Coach is making us." They'd gotten teasing from the other guys as well, but things had died down quickly enough.

And through it all, Alex hadn't said a single word.

Thankfully by the time they'd reached the arena, Alex had thawed out a bit. He was carefully relaxed, talking with the guys around them as the bus pulled into the underground parking garage. He'd even talked to Sasha a little, though with the same guarded reserve that he'd used around everyone else.

Something changed in the hotel lobby.

For a second, he'd thought Alex might kiss him. It was a fool's thought, of course, but they'd locked eyes for a moment and there had been something in that molten brown gaze that had made Sasha's heart pound in his chest.

But then it had been gone, leaving Sasha to wonder if he'd imagined it.

They were both greeted by another surprise when they walked into the locker room to change for practice: their stalls had been moved so they were side by side.

"I guess Coach is serious," Alex said, stopping a few feet away to stare at the nameplates above the lockers. "Damn. Looks like we're not going to get out of this so easily."

Sasha glanced over at him. Alex didn't sound upset; in fact, he sounded amused, and there was a bit of a grin on his face.

"Guess not," Sasha said. "You think he's gonna tie our wrists together, like parents do with naughty children who can't stop fighting?"

Now Alex laughed. "You sound like you're talking from experience."

Sasha smiled as well, relaxing slightly. "I have a sister. Natasha. She is three years younger than me. Now, we get along. When we were children? Eh, it's a miracle my mother does not strangle us both, you know?"

They started changing, ignoring the laughs they got from their teammates as they passed by. Bayer, who normally sat beside Alex, was across the room next to Shawn now and grumbling about it.

"I'm an only child," Alex said, taping up his socks. "I used to wish I had a sibling, but stories like that make me glad I didn't."

They continued to chat during practice and after, on the bus ride back. Gradually, Sasha started to relax.

Maybe he doesn't hate me after all.

In fact, he was beginning to see why the rest of his friends on the team had dismissed his complaints about Alex so easily. Alex was often quiet, preferring to watch instead of interact, but when he smiled and opened his mouth, he was absolutely charming.

It was more than enough to make Sasha reconsider his initial impression of their new goalie.

Maybe we can be friends after all.

Seattle Sports & Stats (@SeaTacSportsNerd)
CASCADES WIN! Final score: Seattle—4, Buffalo—1. Points spread:
Makela (1 G, 2 A)
Petrov (1 G, 1 A)
Eklund (1 G, 1 A)
Rybar (1 G)
Sjoberg (2 A)
Merkley (1 A)
Bayer (1 A)

"Hell yeah!" Bayer walked into the room and tossed his gloves into a bin before unsnapping his helmet. He went straight to Alex, who had just set his mask down on the shelf above his bench, and ran a hand through Alex's sweaty hair. "Look at this beauty, bringing us a sweet W tonight!"

Across the room, Leduc shouted an offer to buy Alex a drink when they went out that night. Soon enough, plans were being thrown around. Alex sat down in his stall, leaned back, and soaked it in while sweat cooled on the back of his neck.

First NHL win. It felt damn good.

Oettenger slid onto the bench beside Bayer and bent over to untie his skates and unwrap the tape from his socks. "Man, that save you made on Richards at the end of the second when he got that breakaway? Helluva save."

Alex nodded his thanks.

Shawn passed by and threw him a towel, then handed him something else: a puck with a piece of white tape wrapped around the outside edge. "Nice job, Phantom."

There was writing on the tape, and Alex turned it over to read it. Someone had taken a Sharpie and carefully written out the date and "First NHL Win" in block letters. Alex clenched it in his fist and glanced up to meet Shawn's eyes in thanks.

"Seriously"—Bayer kept talking, stripping out of his jersey and pads—"the way you snatched that puck out of midair. Fuckin' sweet, man."

Merkley walked by, tossing his own sweaty jersey into the laundry bin. "Dammit, Bear, leave the kid alone."

Part of Alex wanted to protest that he wasn't a kid, but he knew they wouldn't listen. Merkley was practically ancient in hockey terms, already having passed the thirty-year-old mark, and Seth Bayer wasn't far behind him. To the two of them, he *was* a kid.

Bayer wasn't done, though. "C'mon, Merks. You saw it, right? That save in the second?" He balled up his sock tape, shot it toward the trash can, and made a *swish* noise when it went in. "That was some Para-level shit there. Kid moved so fast I couldn't even see him."

Alex's heart stopped in his chest.

"Hey." Merkley sounded angry now, voice dropping low. "Shut the fuck up, Seth. I don't want to hear any of that crap in my locker room, okay? And the kid doesn't deserve to have you insulting him like that, either."

He'd spoken quietly enough that his words slid beneath the loud noise of the locker room, but Oettenger, sitting on the other side of Bayer, gave them a sidelong look.

None of them glanced at Alex, who took a deep breath, held it, and didn't move. He thought about the documentaries he'd seen in hotel rooms sometimes, when Animal Planet was the only thing worth watching on the TV: *If I hold perfectly still, they won't notice me and they'll forget that I'm here.*

"Shit, you're right." Bayer laughed, cutting through the tense atmosphere. He did turn to Alex then, but only to pat him on the shoulder. "Sorry, Phantom. Didn't mean to imply that you're anything other than pure human."

Merkley scoffed but nodded as his expression faded back to neutral. "Good. Just remember, I don't put up with any of that Para crap. Those creatures"—he spit the word like it was offensive—"shouldn't be allowed to live around normal humans, let alone play hockey. I sure as hell don't want them in my locker room."

He finally finished tossing his dirty clothes in the bin and took off. Bayer trailed after him, leaving Alex to finish undressing.

Alex didn't move for another minute, holding his breath until his lungs burned and he had to exhale shakily. When he worked up the nerve to look around the room, he was almost surprised to find that no one was paying attention. Even Shawn was grabbing a towel and heading to the showers, blissfully unaware of the conversation that had just taken place.

Dammit. Alex sank back into his stall and let the cool wood at his back help to center him. It was several minutes before his fingers stopped trembling enough to undo the straps on his pads so he could get them off.

What Merkley had said wasn't anything new. Alex had heard that kind of talk over and over—from coaches, from fans, even from other teammates. But something about the way his captain had sneered the words made hot tears prickle in Alex's eyes.

He managed to flee to the showers without anyone noticing, where Alex cranked the water on and quickly shoved his face beneath the spray, washing away any evidence of his little breakdown. He soaped up and rinsed off, the actions mechanical while he was deep in thought. First it had been Petrov laughing about anti-Para slurs. Alex had always known to be careful around Russian players, who came from a culture where anti-Para and anti-gay rhetoric was common. But Merkley was Canadian.

Canada had announced stronger Paranormal rights bills a couple of years ago, making it one of the safest places for Paras to live and work.

Just proves that nowhere is safe. Shawn might be okay with it, but most people probably won't be.

He needed to be more careful and blend in better. If Merkley or someone else on the team found out, Alex's NHL dream might be over before it even really started.

Seattle Cascades (@CascadesNHL)
The Cascades are 2-2 on their East Coast road trip going in to tonight's game against Montreal. Let's see if #TealAndWhite can triumph over #BleuBlancRouge! #WestCoastBestCoast

Montreal NHL/LNH (@MontrealLNH)
@CascadesNHL We'll buy you a plate of poutine to cry into when you lose. // On vous achètera une poutine pour vous consoler quand vous allez perdre.

Seattle Cascades (@CascadesNHL)
@MontrealLNH thanks, but we already had our celebratory poutine after crushing Toronto two nights ago.

Montreal NHL/LNH (@MontrealLNH)
@CascadesNHL We might owe you dinner just for that. Thanks! // Juste pour ça, on devrait vous payer le souper. Merci!

THE GAME against Buffalo had been the kind of spectacular win that put Sasha in an equally spectacular mood. The team had played out of their minds, everybody doing their job perfectly, passes connecting crisply and plays working exactly as intended.

And their goalie… well, the game had shown Sasha that maybe he'd been too hard on Alex from the start. Because Alex wasn't just an okay backup… he was breathtaking.

Forty saves on forty-one shots, and the only goal a fluke bounce off Mo's skate that had been impossible to stop under any circumstances. *Even Eddie couldn't have done better*, Sasha had to admit.

He'd skated up to the net toward the end of the third period to tap his stick on Alex's leg pad, and the smile he'd received in return had been blinding, like sunshine.

"Go score a goal for me," Alex had said, laughing.

The way Alex had looked at him, so full of pure joy, was enough to buoy Sasha for the rest of the game. And he could all but feel Alex's pride and excitement when, in the dying seconds of the game, Sasha was able to tap the puck in for the empty net to help bring Alex his first ever NHL victory.

Afterward the entire team had lined up on the ice to give Alex celebratory head-taps. Shawn had pulled the goalie into a huge hug, spinning him around while laughing loudly. And when it had been Sasha's turn....

"Поздравляю," he'd said, bumping his helmet against Alex's. "Congratulations."

And Alex had smiled at him, eyes glowing with such pure joy that Sasha's breath had caught in his throat.

But then, within the span of an hour, everything had gone wrong, and Sasha had no idea why.

Alex had been gone when Carts went to find him after showering and getting dressed. A bunch of guys wanted to go out for drinks, to celebrate the win and Alex's achievement. But the goalie had been nowhere to be found, and a trainer had eventually revealed that Alex had gone back to the hotel, not feeling well.

Maybe he was hiding an injury after all. Sasha's mind flashed back to their interaction in the hallway and the way Alex had reacted.

But if it was an injury, that didn't explain why Alex had completely withdrawn. He still rode the bus next to Sasha, sat next to him on the drive up to Toronto. But while they'd been friendly earlier in the day, the Alex after the game had been the same cold statue he'd encountered in the previous weeks. If Coach had wanted them to become friends… well, Sasha couldn't be friends with a brick wall, and that was about as much response and emotion as he was getting from Alex.

And nothing changed in the following days either.

They won against Toronto, Hertzog in net, then had a day off before facing Montreal. Alex dutifully spent their travel time with Sasha as required, but while before he'd seemed chatty and willing to open up, now he was withdrawn, distant.

"What the hell is wrong with Fanning?" he asked Shawn in the locker room, after losing to Montreal in overtime.

Shawn frowned. "I don't know. He's not talking to me. I'm getting worried, you know? Maybe it's the road trip; he's probably—" He cut himself off, guilt flashing over his face. "Actually, yeah, no. I'm sure it's nothing. Just leave him be, man. I know Coach wanted you two to bond on this trip, but I think it's best if you wait until we're back home."

With a friendly punch to the shoulder, Carts took off, leaving Sasha even more confused.

What does Shawn know that I don't?

Sasha left the locker room to find the visitor's gym so he could cool down on the bike for a few minutes. As he turned the corner, though, he heard a voice. Alex's voice, sounding happier than he'd heard him since Buffalo.

"Yeah, for sure," Alex said. When Sasha peered around another corner, he saw the familiar lanky form tucked into a back hallway, holding a phone up to his ear. He was, Sasha realized, holding his arm against his chest like it was in a sling. *So he is injured, then.* "No, seriously! Uh-huh. Fine, I'll take you out, somewhere fancy. You pick the restaurant, though; you're the famous one." He laughed, tilting his head back. "Well, a boy can dream. Okay. Yeah, we're flying in late after the Quebec City game on Saturday. Meet me at the airport? I'll text you the arrival time."

He listened for a second to whoever was on the other end.

"Thanks, Heather. I mean it. Can't wait to see you." Alex turned slightly, and Sasha could see that he was smiling, the same wide grin he'd given to Sasha after his win. "Okay, bye."

Sasha whirled around and hurried down the hallway before he could get caught, heart racing.

So that's why he's been so sad, then. He misses his girlfriend, and Shawn probably knew too. Sasha swallowed around the lump in his throat.

If Alex was too busy missing his girlfriend to pay attention to Sasha, then that wasn't Sasha's problem. It just proved to him that Alex wasn't interested in being his friend… and even Coach's orders couldn't change that.

Chapter Ten

cascadian-not-canadian
Photos from the Cascades 4-3 win over Quebec City on February 3.

see-me-in-sea-tac
does anyone else think the new goalie, fanning, looks a little under the weather? you can see him in the background of the third picture. god please tell me we haven't already broken our backup's backup! we're gonna need him in the next few weeks, so hopefully he's well enough to play!

By the time they boarded the plane for the long overnight flight back to Seattle, Alex felt like curling up and crying.

It wasn't just the hunger, though having not fed properly in eleven days made every inch of his body ache. Even if he'd wanted to try to find someone to feed on, he'd been stuck with Sasha the whole trip and hadn't been able to slip away without risking being caught. Playing a game in the middle hadn't helped, certainly, and the win over Buffalo had been a massive exertion. But he'd gone longer without feeding his vampire side before, even with being in net in between.

Instead, it was the fear that kept creeping up his spine every time he walked by a group of his teammates or suited up for practice. Merkley's harsh words had terrified him; combined with the television report he'd caught in the hotel lobby in Buffalo, Alex felt like he hadn't slept properly in a week.

If anyone finds out, I'm done.

All Alex had ever wanted to do was play hockey. It had been his dream since his dad had first strapped skates on his feet at age three. He'd done everything in his power to get to where he was today, playing in the NHL. And he'd done it all while hiding half of himself, feeding in the middle of the night and sneaking around teammates, always paranoid that someone might notice something. "He's too pale" or "Do his incisors look a little long to you?" were phrases that he couldn't risk.

Being a vampire didn't give him better reflexes or more speed. Hell, even full-blooded Paras didn't see extra benefits like that when they were in a human form. But humans like Merkley and the NHL commissioner believed what they wanted to.

And humans like Sasha see us, at best, as insults to laugh about.

So when Alex dragged his tired body onto the plane, the last thing he wanted to do was get stuck sitting next to a human for the next six and a half hours—especially not a human who smelled like everything Alex wanted and could never have.

But a look from Coach Henrique told him to suck it up, so Alex slid into the aisle seat beside Sasha without a word of protest.

"Hey."

Alex glanced over at the Russian. "Hey."

Sasha looked surprised at the simple response, and Alex was hit with the realization that he'd been kind of a dick for the last few days.

"Sorry," he said, "for icing you out. I haven't been feeling great."

The plane was dark and quiet as most of their teammates dropped off quickly to sleep. Still, Sasha looked around and lowered his voice. "It's the injury on your arm, yes?"

Alex blinked, adrenaline yanking him out of his exhaustion. "What?"

Gentle fingers touched his arm, where the bandage still rested. Six days without blood since he'd been injured meant it hadn't healed any faster than a human burn would have, and the skin was still an angry red beneath his sleeve.

"How'd you know?"

The fingers moved down, skirting the cuff of Alex's dress shirt. "May I?"

When Alex didn't protest, Sasha began to unbutton the cuff. Alex held his breath as Sasha rolled the sleeve up, fingers brushing against the soft skin on the inside of Alex's wrist.

Sasha hissed quietly when the bandage came into view. "How bad?"

"It's fine," Alex said.

Clearly Sasha didn't believe him, because he went to peel the bandage off, teasing the edge of the adhesive carefully before pulling it back.

"Alex." Sasha exhaled the word, eyes fixed on the wide burn as it was revealed. It was easily visible even in the dimmed lights, a dark line almost three inches wide that ran just below Alex's elbow. "You didn't see a trainer about this."

"They might have pulled me from the game," Alex said quickly. "I couldn't—you wouldn't understand."

Sasha pressed his lips together and replaced the bandage, sealing the tape down with his fingertips before rolling the sleeve back over Alex's arm. "No, I don't understand why you would hide this. It's just one game."

"It's not!"

Someone kicked Alex's seat and hissed, "Shut up, man!"

Alex lowered his voice again, ducking his head. "It's not," he repeated more quietly. "You've been playing in the NHL for, what, five years? You get to have this every single day, playing your heart out with the best in the world. But I've been dreaming about the NHL for two decades, and now I've finally made it here."

Sasha was still holding his wrist, Alex realized. He narrowed his focus on the point where their skin touched, the heat of Sasha's fingers a different type of burning than the one farther up his arm.

"I have to prove myself. Right now, people look at me and they see an AHL goalie. I need the chance to play, to make them see an NHL goalie instead."

Sasha opened his mouth, then closed it. After a minute he said, "I'm sorry."

"For what?"

The fingers on his wrist slipped away, and Alex almost moaned at the loss. He was cold suddenly, feeling all eleven days without fresh blood.

"Because I thought of you like this, before. An AHL goalie, who does not belong in the NHL. Ed—Eduard Despres, he is one of my best friends. I thought, *This new goalie, he can never replace Eddie.* So I look at you with hate, instead of giving you a chance."

That was what Shawn had said, on the drive up from Portland before they'd left on this trip. Hearing it from Sasha's mouth, however, meant more.

"I don't want to replace your friend," Alex said. "I just want to play."

Sasha nodded. "I understand. In Buffalo, you played amazing."

Alex had heard those words from his teammates after the game. Coming from Sasha now, however, they felt more meaningful. "Thank you."

They lapsed into silence, exhaustion pulling both of them closer to sleep. Alex shifted his arm back into his lap reluctantly, then tried to curl up in his seat to sleep.

"Hey. Alex." Sasha's hand was back, this time on his upper arm. "You can lean against me, if you need. Better for your arm, so it doesn't get bumped."

Alex stared at him for a long moment. Sasha's eyes were soft, tender. It made Alex long for things he couldn't have, and he swallowed hard. "Yeah," he whispered. "Thanks. I appreciate it."

Sasha's shoulder wasn't exactly a pillow, but it was warm and his shirt was soft, and he smelled incredible as Alex inhaled his scent. Alex closed his eyes, feeling safe and relaxed for the first time since Buffalo.

"Hey, Sasha?" he whispered as he dozed off. "I forgive you."

He fell asleep to the sensation of fingers carding through his hair.

Seattle Cascades (@CascadesNHL)
The Cascades head home after a long East Coast trip, which they split 3-3 with wins against Buffalo, Toronto, and Quebec City. Looking forward to a day off tomorrow, and then we're back Monday to take on Nashville at home.

SASHA SLEPT better on the flight home than he could ever remember sleeping on a plane. It was as though he could feel the pain draining from Alex's body as the goalie fell asleep, and that was enough to let him close his eyes and sleep as well.

He woke up when the plane started to descend hours later, groggy but pleasantly warm along his side where Alex was resting on him. Waking Alex up was almost as nice; he brushed strands of dark brown hair from Alex's forehead and watched those dark eyes flutter open, sleep-hazed and relaxed.

"We're landing soon," he whispered.

Alex smiled softly and pulled away, to Sasha's disappointment.

But that minor displeasure was nothing compared to what Sasha felt when they got off the plane soon after… and Alex walked straight across the tarmac and into the waiting arms of a stunning blonde.

That must be Heather. Sourness balled up in Sasha's stomach as he watched. They didn't kiss or even hug beyond a sleepy one-armed greeting, but it was obvious they were close. Heather opened the trunk of her luxury sedan, Alex loaded his suitcase in, and then they were gone.

"Damn," Engel said from behind Sasha. "Wish my wife would wake up at 2:00 a.m. to get me from the airport. How'd Fanning manage to get a girl like that so quickly after arriving?"

Some of the others laughed, though everyone was tired due to the late hour, but Sasha couldn't find any humor in it.

Instead, he dragged himself to his car, Misha barely awake beside him. "I can drive," Misha mumbled.

Sasha gave him a look. "Get your license first and then we'll talk."

"The test is stupid, and it's all in English." Misha made a face but didn't object any further as he climbed into the passenger seat.

Sasha navigated the almost empty roads of Seattle with ease. Late-night arrivals were, unfortunately, one of the least appealing parts of his job, but he'd gotten used to them over the years. Besides, he'd slept for most of the flight and felt surprisingly well-rested as a result.

He pulled into the garage half an hour later, relieved to be home.

"Gonna crash," Misha said through a yawn. "I'll get my suitcase in the morning."

He stomped inside, eyes barely open as he headed straight up the stairs. Sasha heard his door close a few seconds later. Rolling his eyes, he grabbed both of their suitcases, leaving them at the foot of the staircase before moving into the kitchen for a bottle of water.

He froze in the doorway to the kitchen, terrified.

The light was on, and there was a person sitting at his kitchen table.

A familiar person, he realized a moment later. "Ed, hey." Sasha swallowed, fear at seeing an unexpected person in his house slowly fading away. "It's late. What are you doing here?"

He'd given Ed a key to his house years ago, but his friend only rarely used it.

"Hadn't seen you in over two weeks," Ed replied. "I still get the travel notifications in my email, even though I'm injured. Figured you'd be home by about now and we could catch up."

Sasha took in the scene. Ed looked wide-awake despite the late hour. His arm was still in a sling, and he had his feet kicked up on another one of Sasha's kitchen chairs. On the table in front of him was an empty glass and the bottle of Sasha's expensive vodka.

The bottle was half-empty. It had been almost full when Sasha had left the week prior.

"It's late," Sasha repeated. "Why don't you crash here and we can have breakfast and catch up in the morning."

"Or," Eddie said, sitting up straight and kicking his feet off the chair with loud thumps, "we can talk now. You've been ignoring me, Sasha."

"I haven't." Sasha's response was immediate. "We were on a road trip for eleven days, Ed. On the East Coast, with the crazy time difference. And things were hectic, playing so many games and traveling so much. I'm sorry that I didn't respond to your texts, but I was honestly just so busy."

Ed twisted the cap off the bottle and poured himself another one. His hand was unsteady, a sure sign that he'd had more than a couple.

He must still be on painkillers too, Sasha realized with a start. That much alcohol, combined with the medication, couldn't possibly be a healthy combination.

"Or maybe you were too busy making a new friend."

Fuck. Someone must have told Ed about Coach's decision to force him and Alex to get along. Or maybe he'd seen it in the team's group chat, which Sasha rarely looked at. Either way, it was clear that Ed was displeased.

His mind raced to defuse the situation. "It was just Rico trying to force team bonding. You know how he is. Honestly, Fanning barely even talked to me the entire trip. He spent most of the time on the phone with his girlfriend, or with Carts."

Ed threw back the shot he'd poured, like it was water. Sasha hid a wince at the sight of his expensive imported vodka being wasted.

"I saw that he won his game too." Ed sneered, setting the empty glass down. "He got lucky. Buffalo had a bad night."

"Yeah, Ed, I know," Sasha said. "Everyone knows this. It means nothing."

Of course, Coach hadn't agreed. He'd been so pleased with Alex's play against Buffalo that rumor had it he was considering starting Alex again sooner rather than later. But Ed clearly didn't know that yet, and Sasha wasn't about to volunteer that bit of information.

"Look, Eddie, I really need to go to sleep. And you do as well, I think. The guest room downstairs is made up; why don't you crash here instead of driving home tonight."

"Can't drive home," Ed responded. He poured himself yet another drink. "They took my license, Sasha. Fuckers won't even let me drive anymore. I had to take a goddamn Uber to get here."

Now that he thought about it, Sasha hadn't seen any car parked out front. And it made sense, but of course it would piss Ed off. *No surprise that they would take away his license after a second DUI.*

"Even more reason for you to stay here, then," he said calmly. "We'll go to that breakfast place you like in the morning, my treat, okay?"

Ed stared down into his glass but didn't drink it yet. "Yeah, fine. And we gotta talk about the trial soon."

"Sure, Eddie," Sasha said. "But sleep first."

Finally, Eddie knocked back the drink and stood up, abandoning the almost-empty bottle and glass as he walked unsteadily toward the kitchen door. He brushed past Sasha, heading for the guest room where he'd crashed several times before over the last few years. Sasha watched him go, making sure he got all the way to the bedroom, then sighed and stepped into the kitchen to clean up the mess. It wouldn't do to have Misha see the vodka bottle in the morning and start asking questions.

Then, finally, he could give in to his own exhaustion. Sasha glanced at the guest room door one last time, then carried himself up the stairs and to his own bed.

Chapter Eleven

Seattle Sports News (@SeattleSportsNews)
Very optional practice for the Cascades this afternoon. On the ice are Engel, Klausman, Volkov, Oettenger, Merkley, Petrov, Johnson, and Fanning.

Sasha hadn't planned to go to practice less than twelve hours after arriving back in Seattle, especially since Coach had informed them that the practice was completely optional. But, then, he hadn't expected to be stuck with Ed's booze-heavy snores drifting out across the ground floor of his house all morning as his friend slept well past any semblance of a breakfast hour.

Knowing that Ed was sleeping off the better half of a bottle of expensive vodka made guilt pool in Sasha's stomach. There was something wrong with the man currently passed out in his guest room, but examining it too closely wasn't something he was emotionally prepared to handle.

So by the time noon rolled around, Sasha was desperate to get out of the house. He left a note on the counter, then dragged a sleepy, protesting Misha out the door.

And if he hid the vodka and the last of a twelve-pack of beer in the back of the pantry, well… it was only reasonable. С глаз долой, из сердца вон, as his mother always said; if Ed couldn't find it, maybe he wouldn't think about it.

Misha fled as soon as they got to the arena, heading straight for the player's lounge and the coffee machine located there. Sasha watched him go with amusement—and not a little sympathy—before heading in the opposite direction to the locker room.

The few guys present were mostly older, the ones who were married and had kids who would have woken them up early regardless of their 2:00 a.m. arrival.

But there was one man Sasha hadn't expected to see.

"Hey, you're here." Alex was already dressed in full pads, looking more awake and cheerful than everyone else in the room put together. "Didn't think you'd be coming in."

"I could say the same about you," Sasha replied.

But the Alex before him right now was not the man who had slept on his shoulder only the night before, looking frail and exhausted. The difference was startling. Now Alex was bursting with energy, clearly well-rested, and flushed a healthy shade of pink as he looked up at Sasha. His smile was bright, expression open and eager. He was practically glowing, and Sasha couldn't tear his eyes away from the sight.

Like sunlight. It wasn't the first time he'd made the comparison, but never had it been truer than now.

They separated for practice, Sasha working with Otter and Johnson, but he couldn't stop looking over at Alex every time he paused for a drink of water or to regroup on a drill.

This was the Alex from the Buffalo game: a brick wall in net, laughter and chirps carrying across the ice as he stopped pucks and showed off with big, flashy saves.

How did I not see this before? He'd spent so much time trying to hate Alex that he'd ignored the raw talent and incredible energy contained in the lanky, muscular body.

Alex found him after practice, both of them showered and changed back into comfortable sweats. Misha had escaped earlier, scowling at Sasha over another cup of coffee and declaring that he was done practicing for the day and was going to play video games with Bayer all afternoon. So it was just the two of them, Sasha following Alex to the parking garage.

He paused when he caught sight of a gorgeous blue truck ahead of them.

"That's yours?"

Alex turned to follow his line of sight. "The Chevy? Yeah, that's Betsy." He blushed a little, delightfully embarrassed as he ducked his head. It made Sasha want to do incredibly inappropriate things to him, possibly in the flatbed of that truck.

"It's beautiful. You restore her yourself?"

"Yeah. I mean, she was already in really good condition when I bought her a few years ago. I've tried to stick to factory original parts where I could, but some things had to get upgraded, like the radio and air-conditioning." Alex looked at the truck with pride, beaming.

Alex was charming, lit up with excitement as he talked about his truck. Sasha nudged him on the shoulder. "Come, I'll show you something."

He turned to the ramp that led down one floor. The garage was mostly empty, but he'd parked in his usual spot in a back corner that was mostly out of the way. Alex gasped behind him as they turned a corner.

"No way." He pushed past Sasha, approaching the car with obvious delight on his face. "What is this, a '68?"

"No, '69." It was Sasha's turn to stare at his car with pride. The Camaro had been one of his impulse purchases a couple of years ago, black with red racing stripes and a soft top that he could retract on the rare sunny Seattle day. He'd reupholstered the seats to be a buttery black leather, and took it out when he needed a pick-me-up after a rough game.

Alex was bent over, peering into the windows, practically vibrating with excitement. "Do you collect classics? I always figured if I made the Show for real I'd want to buy a house somewhere with a big garage, and spend my free time restoring old cars."

Sasha crossed the parking garage to join him. He rested his hand on Alex's back for a moment, caressing the warm skin he could feel beneath his thin T-shirt, then reluctantly let go so he could nudge the smaller man over and unlock the car.

"I don't collect," he said. "Someday, maybe I'll get another one. A Shelby or GTO."

Growing up in Russia, his family hadn't been wealthy at all. They'd struggled to put him through basic hockey programs. He'd watched old movies on their small television, American action films with fast cars and explosions, and dreamed of having one just like it when he was older. For him, the Camaro was a physical symbol that he'd finally made it.

Alex slid into the driver's seat, running his hand over the steering wheel. "You'll have to take me out in this someday. I bet she's a beast."

Sasha bit back a groan. Alex's pale skin was a beautiful contrast against the black leather, and his nimble fingers darting over the gear shaft were giving Sasha very inappropriate thoughts.

I could take him out in this car, he thought, *then find a back road somewhere, surrounded by trees. Lay him down in the back seat, all that clear pristine skin on display. Just like in the movies, when the couple finally gets to be together.*

He was tempted to ask Alex out right now, could practically feel the words forming on his tongue.

Thankfully his phone buzzed in his pocket before he could make a fool out of himself. He pulled it out and bit back a curse at the display.

Ed was awake, finally.

"Sorry, I have to go," he said.

Alex slid out of the car with one last caress of the steering wheel. "No problem. Hey, you want to get lunch on Tuesday after practice?"

Sasha grinned. "Yes, for sure. Maybe we'll take my car."

"That's what I was hoping you'd say." Alex grinned, looking very pleased with himself. "Have a good afternoon, Sasha."

"You too."

Sasha watched him head back up the ramp. When he sat down in his car, the seat was warm, and he had to close his eyes and regain his composure before he could start the car and head back home.

Mrs. Merkley… a girl can dream! (@MerkleyFan96)
This schedule is the worst! 11 days on the road, and then only one day off before they have to play again? Poor 'Scades, hope they were able to get enough sleep and recover from the time differences. Nashville is tough!

ALEX WAS in a fantastic mood going into the game on Monday. He wasn't playing, which meant there was no pressure on him beyond showing up and getting his gear on. He'd fed Sunday morning from Heather, and his arm was almost completely healed now. And, to top it all off, he'd had a great conversation the day before with Sasha.

"Dude, I didn't even think about the car thing," Shawn had said when Alex got home from practice. "He loves that damn Camaro like it's a child. I think he did a lot of the work on it by himself. Figures you two would both be gear heads."

"It's a gorgeous car," Alex had said.

Shawn had rolled his eyes. "A gorgeous car, or a gorgeous man?"

Alex had just smirked. "Why can't it be both?"

He'd finished the evening off grilling steaks with Shawn and catching up on some TV, and had gone to bed dreaming of Sasha pressing him down onto the hood of the Camaro and kissing him.

So Alex was almost floating when he got to the arena before the Nashville game, and even a summons to the coach's office wasn't enough to bring his mood down too much.

"Hey, you wanted to see me, Coach?"

Henrique motioned him to take a chair. He didn't seem upset, which was a good sign; in fact, Alex thought he might have seen a hint of a smile on Coach's face when he first tapped on the doorframe to announce his arrival. So he was relaxed as he slid into the office.

"Great game against Buffalo last week, Fanning. Grant says you've been working hard in practices and picking up suggestions easily."

Grant Ogilve was the goalie coach. He'd initially been more focused on Hertzog, spending time helping Matthias get comfortable as the team's unexpected starter; lately, however, he'd been working closer with Alex, and the extra training was paying off.

"Yes, sir," Alex said. "He's great, has some interesting training exercises to help with tracking the puck."

"Excellent." Coach steepled his fingers and studied Alex for a moment. "We're playing Arizona in two days. Grant and I agree that we'd like you to start in that game."

Shock and excitement left Alex temporarily speechless. He hadn't expected to play in another game until the second week of February, when the team had back-to-back games at home.

He finally managed to say, "Thank you, Coach."

But apparently Coach wasn't finished. "Matty was never intended to be a starting goalie for this team, but we've been following your progress with the Loggers since you took over the starting position there. Last season was very impressive. We were hoping that you'd be able to show that ability on the NHL level, and the two games you played so far were fantastic."

Alex managed not to make a face, thinking about the Vancouver game. Coach must have seen something, though, because he definitely smiled this time.

"I know. The loss in your first game stung. But we really liked what we saw." He tapped his desk, clearly thinking. "Grant suggested that you also play one of the two games in Alberta at the end of this week. I'd like to ease you in a bit more, but Grant is convinced that you're capable, and I'll defer to his judgment. So we're going to play you Wednesday for the home game, and then Friday against Edmonton as well, I think."

Alex couldn't help the grin that split his face. "Yes, sir. I know you're putting a lot of trust in me, and I promise I'll do my best not to let you or the team down."

"Good, good. You'd better get moving if you don't want to be late for practice."

With one last thank-you thrown over his shoulder, Alex scrambled from the room.

All goalies, all the time (@GoalieGirl29)

FINALLY! Cascades are giving Fanning the recognition he deserves! They interviewed Rico before the game and he said Fanning is gonna start the two games after this one. He's so good, can't wait to see him play.

Chad (@Despresident)

@GoalieGirl29: he's played 2 games and lost 1 of them... wtf are you talking about? we need despres back before this team misses playoffs.

THE SLIGHT roster changeup didn't really make waves in the locker room, apart from a few guys who fist-bumped Alex, and Matty who grinned and threw and arm over Alex's shoulder, looking proud and not a little relieved.

But to Sasha, the announcement felt like being boarded.

Ed's going to be pissed.

His friend had been gone by the time Sasha got home on Sunday afternoon, and the note had been balled up and thrown into the trash can.

The entire situation had made Sasha furious, until guilt took over and the anger died away. But it was becoming increasingly more difficult for Sasha to find a balance. He wanted to support Ed and see his friend succeed and return to playing, but he couldn't do that if Ed kept drinking and acting the way that he was... and from what Sasha had seen over the last few weeks, he definitely couldn't support Eddie and be friends with Alex at the same time.

I'll call him later this week. Maybe Ed would be sober then, and they could talk things over.

But as much as he hoped for the best, Sasha had a sinking feeling that he was going to have to make a choice soon, and it wasn't going to be an easy one to make.

Chapter Twelve

The NHLPA today filed a motion against Commissioner Heatly's proposal to add genetic testing to mandatory health and fitness screenings for all athletes, calling the move "discriminatory" and "a violation of current CBA regulations." In a written response, Heatly stated that genetic screenings fell under current CBA guidelines regarding testing of players to ensure that "no performance-enhancing drugs or other factors that might unfairly influence a player's ability" be allowed. Heatly has asked that a vote be added to the agenda for the upcoming General Managers meeting, already scheduled for April, following the end of the regular season.
—Ellen DeSmith, ESPN

WATCHING ALEX slide into the passenger seat of his Camaro was one of the sexiest things Sasha had ever seen.

Alex looked good, tight jeans and an even tighter T-shirt clinging to his frame, hair still a little damp from his shower after practice and falling over his forehead. He ducked into the car easily, sliding one hand over the leather seats in obvious pleasure.

"God damn, this is one hell of a car." Even Alex's voice was sexy, low and purring like the Camaro's engine. His eyes were dark when he turned to look at Sasha, crinkling with a smile. "You gonna take us to lunch or just idle here and let me fondle your upholstery?"

Sasha *really* couldn't answer that question the way he wanted to. So he swallowed around the sudden dryness in his throat, shifted gears, and backed out of his spot.

There was no real chance in downtown Seattle to find open roads and show off the Camaro the way she deserved, but he still took the long way around to the restaurant he'd chosen.

Alex sat silently, staring out the window as Sasha drove. At first Sasha thought it was because he was still enjoying the feel of the car and the smooth rumble of the engine, but soon he realized that something was bothering the younger man.

"You okay?"

"Hm?" Alex turned from gazing out the window, smiling a little. "Nothing. Just a tough practice. You know how it goes. Kinda pissed we lost yesterday, but the team was so tired after that road trip."

His tone was upbeat enough, but something about the smile on Alex's face seemed forced.

Sasha pulled into the parking lot of the small restaurant and found a spot in the back, away from any other cars. Alex gave him a knowing look but didn't complain about having to walk a bit farther.

"A sandwich shop? I figured you'd take me something a little nicer on our lunch date."

Alex dropped just enough emphasis on the last word to catch Sasha's attention. *Is he flirting with me?* But no, that wasn't possible. He must have misheard. Still, Sasha had his honor to defend here.

"Trust me. It might not look like much, but I think you'll be pleased by the end." The words slipped out of his mouth before he could think, and Sasha felt a moment of horror. If Alex took it the wrong way....

But Alex laughed. "Oh, I *really* hope so."

The shop was close enough to the arena that the team sometimes stopped here on their way home from practices to pick up food. The staff all knew them, and no one usually bothered them. Sasha ordered, motioned for Alex to do the same, and pulled out his wallet.

"Wait, I'll pay my half," Alex said.

Sasha stopped him with a frown. "You say this is a lunch date. And I brought you here, gave you a ride in the Camaro. So I'm gonna pay, and you can go find a seat."

Alex's eyes went wide, then narrowed teasingly. "Yeah, I guess you did give me a pretty nice ride."

Jesus, what is he doing? But Alex just grinned and left Sasha to pick up their food.

Thankfully, for Sasha's sanity, the flirting died down once there was food between them.

"So hey," Alex said, biting into his sandwich. "Thanks for taking me out to lunch today, seriously."

"Of course." Now that Alex was somber again, focused on his food, Sasha could see the same fake layer of happiness on the surface. Maybe it wouldn't be obvious to anyone else, but Sasha had spent enough time watching Alex over the last few weeks to know that there was something upsetting the other man.

The realization was enough to make Sasha put his own sandwich down and ask, "What's wrong?"

"Huh?" Alex looked up. "Nothing, nothing. Just focused on this sandwich…. You were right. It's fantastic."

But he was tense as he picked up his fork to eat the side salad he'd ordered.

Sasha took another bite and chewed slowly, studying the lean form across the table from him. Alex had his head down and his shoulders hunched, as though trying to make himself unnoticeable. It would have made sense if there were a few fans hovering nearby, but it wasn't a busy period for the shop, and there was nobody around them.

"You nervous about tomorrow's game?"

Alex glanced up, genuine confusion on his face. "Huh? No, it should be fine."

"You break up with your girlfriend, then?" he asked.

Alex dropped his fork. "What? I don't—" He stopped suddenly, then tried again. "No, I didn't break up with anyone."

Hmm. The mystery deepened. Alex definitely looked like something was upsetting him, but it wasn't anything obvious. Still, he'd reacted strangely when Sasha had mentioned Heather, so he pushed forward on that note. "You forget it's Valentine's Day in a week? Worrying about presents?" Sasha had to hold back a laugh when the fork, having just been picked back up, clattered once more onto the table.

Alex's eyes were wide. "No, that's not it. But, uh, that explains why Heather's making me take her out next week. Dammit."

Fond amusement made Sasha shake his head in disappointment at the goalie, even as his own heart ached. Alex didn't seem like the kind of guy who forgot about holidays or important dates. He was usually pretty on top of things, organized and tidy in the locker room.

"Everyone makes mistakes sometimes, yes? Nice to see you are only human after all." Sasha laughed.

For some reason, however, that made Alex's shoulders go up even farther, and frown lines to appear between his eyes.

He's upset because he's not perfect, forgets things sometimes? It didn't make any sense.

But if Alex wasn't going to talk about it, Sasha really wasn't going to force him. They were teammates, and maybe friends, but Alex wasn't Carts or Misha, both of whom Sasha knew well enough to make them spill whatever was bothering them.

They kept eating their sandwiches, Alex plowing through his meal with almost single-minded focus.

And then—*finally*—Alex dusted his hands and squared his shoulders.

"Hey, you see the news about the stuff the GMs are going to be voting on in April?"

Well, that wasn't what Sasha had been expecting. The question threw him for a loop, and he had to think fast to understand what Alex was asking. He could recall having seen mention of it in one of his group chats earlier that day, as the agenda had apparently just been released.

"Yeah. I saw a little." There were at least half a dozen topics that the GMs would be discussing… so which one of them had upset Alex? More arguments about review calls from on-ice refs versus the League officials; another chapter in the eternal debate for-and-against fighting; something about health screenings for Paras; and… *oh*. "You are upset about the goaltender interference discussion?"

Alex blinked, glanced off to the side, and then nodded tightly. "Yeah." His voice was oddly uneven. "That's what I'm upset about."

Sasha leaned back in his seat, proud that he'd figured it out. "I agree, not fair the GMs discuss policy and do not listen to goalies on this."

"Really unfair." Alex hesitated. "You'd think… well, you'd think the NHL would listen to whatever group of people they're trying to make rules about, instead of having a bunch of guys in suits hash it out amongst themselves, right?"

Sasha couldn't disagree. "Sure. If teams are making new rules about fighting, I want them to talk to me so I can say, 'Leave it alone!'" He laughed.

Alex cracked a smile. "You just want to be able to fight more often, you goon. Carts has told me about your tendency to drop gloves given even the slightest provocation."

"Well, Carts is not wrong." Sasha grinned.

Regular Season Fight Card
Name: Alexander Petrov

Height: 6' 6" / Weight: 245lbs
NHL Career Fights: 19

Date: December 5 / Time: 16:30 P2
Game: DAL @ SEA
Opponent: James Benning
Height: 6' 4" / Weight: 220lbs
Voted Winner: Petrov (82.4%) / Rating: 7.3

LUNCH HAD been surprisingly fun. Even with that morning's news hovering in the back of his mind, Alex found himself smiling and laughing as he chatted with Sasha. He'd tried flirting a little, but it had been obvious that Sasha wasn't really sure what to do with Alex's teasing, so he'd eventually dropped it.

In fact, he kept forgetting about the announcement for short periods of time, relaxing completely and trading stories with his teammate.

But try as he might, Alex couldn't escape it entirely.

The vote was more than two months out, but it still loomed over Alex, a potential life sentence waiting to be handed down. If it passed, he'd never play NHL hockey again. Hell, even the AHL wouldn't take him back if the results were released. His pro hockey career would be over because a bunch of rich old dudes were afraid of what they didn't understand.

When it passed, Alex thought fatalistically.

Talk turned from recapping some of Sasha's favorite fights, to talking about their upcoming games.

"You probably heard," Alex said, his joy bubbling up in his words. "They're starting me tomorrow… and again Friday against Edmonton."

Sasha's smile was genuine. "Yes, I heard. Congratulations, is huge accomplishment."

But something in his tone was off. Alex tried not to let it upset him, but it was obvious that Sasha wasn't completely happy about the news. "I'm hoping the increase in starts means they'll give me a chance to make the roster full-time next season," he said carefully, watching Sasha's reaction.

And there it was, a tiny wince. If he hadn't been looking for it, he never would have noticed.

"Very exciting. You're incredible, so much talent." The words sounded genuine, at least, and there was no deception in Sasha's eyes.

And yet. "Now it's my turn to ask: what's wrong?"

Sasha didn't look surprised by the question. If anything, he seemed resigned to it. "It's Ed."

"Eduard Despres, you mean?"

"Yes." Sasha sighed, picking at the remnants of his sandwich. "He's my best friend and having a very rough time right now. The injury, and he has to go to court soon."

Alex had read up on the older goalie once he'd had a chance. "Yeah, for the drunk driving." His second, and Alex knew that meant Despres was in serious trouble in the eyes of the law.

Sasha hissed, looking upset, but he didn't deny it. "He worries that he won't play next season, or even this year in playoffs if we make it."

Privately, Alex thought it was a valid worry for Despres to have. The media made it sound like the charges against the older man were serious, and the injury had been pretty bad; even the best trainers in the NHL couldn't guarantee that Despres would recover full use of his arm again, if the shoulder dislocation had been severe. And he'd seen the words "jail time" mentioned by more than one reporter.

But Sasha was clearly unhappy with the topic, so Alex dropped it.

Eventually lunch had to end. Sasha gathered up both of their trays, and Alex drifted after him toward the exit.

"Hey, Sasha."

Sasha paused, letting Alex catch up so they were walking side by side.

"I was thinking about this earlier. The fight, in the Vancouver game. Why'd you do it?"

He half expected Sasha to get defensive. And Sasha did tense up for a second, but then he relaxed and laughed. "Don't know how they do things in the A, Fanning, but that wasn't a fight. Just little disagreement. But as for why...." Sasha looked contemplative. "Because he insulted you, I guess."

Alex was confused. "He insulted me?"

"He snow-showered you. Rude, had to tell him this isn't allowed, you know? So I shove him, and he shoved me back." Gone was the man who'd stood like a stone statue while Alex berated him in front of their entire team; now Sasha was clearly amused by the entire situation.

"Oh." Alex let Sasha hold the door for him, and followed him outside. "Well, thank you."

Sasha smiled. "You're welcome."

Alex stared up at him, oddly charmed. He smiled at Sasha. "I guess I should apologize."

Now it was Sasha's turn to look surprised. "For what?"

"For getting upset with you. I was too"—*hungry, aching, frustrated*—"emotional, I guess."

Sasha returned the smile, and Alex's heart skipped a beat. It was yet another cloudy day in Seattle, though the sun threatened to poke through that afternoon. But Sasha's eyes were as clear as a summer sky, and the upset from earlier had completely vanished from his face.

He was gorgeous.

They stood on the sidewalk in front of the restaurant, Alex with his hands tucked into his hoodie pockets, staring up at Sasha. *I could kiss him*, Alex thought, not for the first time. But Sasha hadn't responded to his flirting earlier, and he had to remind himself that they were in public.

And a glance at his phone told him it was later than he thought. "Ah, damn. I told Heather I'd meet her this afternoon. Guess we should head back to the arena so I can grab my truck."

Something in Sasha's posture changed subtly. "For sure, let's go."

The car ride back was silence, and there was a strange tension between them now that Alex couldn't figure out the source of. At one point Alex reached out to adjust the air vent, just as Sasha went to change the radio station, and their hands brushed against each other.

"Sasha," Alex said.

But Sasha snatched his hand back with a muttered apology. Instead of turning the air on, Alex rolled down the window and watched the scenery outside.

He turned into the parking garage, then drove up the ramp until they spotted Alex's truck.

"Sasha," Alex tried again. "Thank you for lunch. I had a really nice time."

Sasha's smile was thin but genuine. "Glad we can go, talk. Glad we're friends."

But there was something sad in his tone. As he got out of the car, Alex found himself wondering again if there was something else there as well, the same longing that he'd seen directed at him a few times before.

He closed the door behind him, then turned around to lean over, watching Sasha through the open window. "I'd like to do this again sometime, if you're interested."

Sasha's gaze went carefully neutral, and his smile thinned. "Maybe. Next time we invite Carts and Misha, okay? But I should go now."

Wait, Alex wanted to say, puzzled and not a little disappointed.

"Don't forget about Valentine's Day, hm?" Sasha added, before he could say anything. "Your girlfriend will be very upset if you do!"

He held one hand up in a halfhearted wave, then shifted the car into gear and drove off without even saying goodbye.

What the heck was that? For a second he'd thought Sasha looked… heartbroken, maybe? And the comment about Heather. *Fuck.* It seemed so obvious now. *He's jealous. Because of course he thinks I'm dating Heather, so if he* is *interested, then he would think I'm off-limits. Maybe Shawn was right after all.*

Maybe it was time to put Shawn's theory to the test and see if Sasha really did return his interest.

Emma (@Cascadiac)
GOALIE POINT ALERT! Alex Fanning gets his first NHL assist on a stretch pass up to Engel, who buries it on a breakaway.

I think we can all agree that the performance from Fanning tonight was absolutely exceptional. He was playing like a man on a mission, and even red-hot Arizona couldn't break him. Well deserving of the first star of the game. I wouldn't be surprised if Henrique and the Cascades coaching staff decide to give him even more starts as the season continues.
—Chloe O'Donnell, ESPN Post-Game

SASHA HAD been upset going into that night's game, but after the performance he'd witnessed, he couldn't help but feel much happier. Alex had been sensational, somehow even better than he'd been against Buffalo, and it had been a pure joy to watch him stop Arizona in their tracks at every turn.

It didn't mean the disappointment wasn't still there, however. Lunch yesterday had been fantastic, a chance for him to really connect with Alex one-on-one and get to know the younger man better. But it had hurt, after the meal had ended, to be reminded that there was nothing more that could happen between them; he and Alex could be friends, and that was all.

And I want more.

Looking across the locker room now, seeing Alex looking so happy as he pulled his chest protector off and bent to untie his leg pads, made the longing even worse.

I wish yesterday had been an actual date. I wish the look Alex had given me at the end, before we drove back, was real.

But it wasn't, and it would never be, because Alex had Heather.

Still, Sasha must have been a glutton for punishment, because after he hung his skates up, he found himself walking around the locker room to approach Alex.

"Incredible game," he said, offering a fist to bump.

Alex's returned the fist bump, looking up at Sasha with a smile that was so radiant that it made Sasha struggle for breath. "Thanks. It means a lot, to hear it from you."

The way Alex looked at that moment was too much. His face was lit up, eyes gleaming with joy and adrenaline from the game. He was sweaty, and his hair was getting a little long, falling over his eyes only to be brushed aside unconsciously. His Under Armour clung to his muscular frame.

The realization hit Sasha all at once.

I think I could love this man.

It was a devastating revelation. Sasha forced one last smile and quickly excused himself.

He made his way back to his stall blindly to finish getting undressed, chest aching. *I think I could love him,* he thought, *but he will never love me in return.*

Chapter Thirteen

Edmonton Hockey Updates (@EDM_Ice_Report)
Edmonton falls to Seattle, snapping a four-game win streak, in a disappointing 4-2 loss.

Seattle Cascades (@CascadesNHL)
Another win for your Cascades, and another win for @goaliefanning! Now let's cross our fingers that this snowstorm doesn't stop us from getting to Calgary tomorrow.

"So we're going out, right?" Braiden, one of the team's rookies, asked loudly.

Someone threw a dirty sock at him. Alex couldn't see who, but he heard Merkley call, "You're not even old enough to drink."

Braiden pouted. "We're in Canada, not Seattle. I can drink here!"

Shawn was the one to reply. "Yeah, but none of us want to haul your drunk ass back to the hotel when you can't walk straight after one beer." That got laughter from the rest of the room. Alberta had a drinking age of eighteen, which meant their under-twenty-one teammates were clamoring to hit the bar. The victory over Edmonton had only increased their excitement. "But the kid's not wrong… we should definitely go out tonight, eh?"

"What are you, Canadian?" Merkley balled up his sock tape and tossed it at Shawn's head.

"Minnesota, Canada, basically the same thing, yes?" That was from Rybár, stirring shit up with a grin.

That comment resulted in an eruption of sound, most of the locker room jumping to their feet. The Americans and Canadians were evenly matched in numbers, but the Americans were definitely louder.

Alex watched them with a smile on his face, pushing back into his stall to avoid being dragged into the fray. He'd played again tonight, his second start in as many games, and his second win as well. He was tired but triumphant, and content to bask in the victory on his own.

When the shouting increased, he slipped out of the locker room and into the peace and quiet of the showers.

That was where Shawn found him a few minutes later, pushing the door open and calling out Alex's name.

"Yeah, Carts, in here." Alex flipped the water off and grabbed his towel.

"Hey, you vanished there." Carts was smiling, face flushed from the game and the win. "Living up to your nickname some more?"

Alex returned the grin. "Just didn't want to get dragged into another USA versus Canada debate."

"Dude, I get ya. Like having gravy on fries and Justin Bieber makes them better than us."

His smile widened. "Hey, I saw you singing along to Beebs in the kitchen two days ago."

"And I'll deny it to my dying breath," Shawn said easily. "So after a peace treaty was reached back in the room, everyone agreed to go out for drinks tonight. You in?"

Alex was tired, but the thought of going out with the team was tempting.

Shawn must have caught his hesitation, because he smirked and added, "Sasha's coming."

Dick. Shawn's eyes said he knew exactly what he was doing, and that he knew Alex wasn't going to be able to resist that lure.

"Fine, okay." Alex threw his wet towel into Shawn's smug face and grabbed his clothes. "But *not* because Sasha's going to be there. I'm just going to celebrate with the team, got it?"

"Sure, of course." Shawn's shit-eating grin said he wasn't buying it. "I'll go tell the others."

Akseli Mäkelä (@AkseliMakela38)
Night out with the boys, celebrating a big win over the reigning Cup Champs.

Mrs. Merkley... a girl can dream! (@MerkleyFan96)
so apparently most of the cascades are at some bar in Edmonton tonight even though there's a blizzard. Look what rybar and angel posted on their instas! pic.twitter.com/l5e2Wj....

THE BAR was loud and crowded, but it had a VIP section big enough to contain most of the team, and deep, dark benches that Alex could sink back into and disappear. Alcohol had stopped being fun for him years ago, when he realized that his body didn't process it right; instead of getting drunk, he just got a little tipsy, and then spectacularly hungover the next morning.

But he couldn't explain that to his teammates, who produced a tray of shots and set them in the middle of the table that Alex was currently trying to hide behind.

"Got whiskey, tequila, and something that smells like lighter fluid and probably doesn't taste much better," Otter said with a flourish. "Pick your poison, but don't take the vodka or the Russians will be pissed."

Alex's eyes slid to the next table over, where the aforementioned Russians had a bottle of vodka on the table between them and seemed to be engaged in some kind of drinking contest with Rybár and Sjöberg. Sasha looked really good, his dark button-down open at the collar, hair slicked back. Every so often his eyes caught a bit of strobe lighting from the dance floor a few yards away, lighting up electric blue.

Oettenger was clearly waiting for him to pick up one of the shots, so Alex dragged his gaze away from the other table and back to the tray. With a grimace, he took one that he hoped was whiskey and not lighter fluid, and tossed it back.

A waitress came by with several trays of bar food, which the hockey players descended on like a pack of ravenous wolves. Alex took the opportunity to slide off the bench and away from the table, putting as much distance as he could between himself and the platters of snacks.

A hand caught him on his hip, warmth sinking into the skin only a split second before the intense, brilliant scent filled Alex's nose.

"You'd better get a plate before they eat it all," an accented voice whispered into his ear. Alex shivered at the sensation of warm breath on his neck.

"I think I'm okay to wait a while," he responded, and was proud that his voice was steady.

When he glanced over his shoulder, he saw Sasha hovering beside him, intense gaze watching Alex.

The moment stretched between them, then snapped when Volkov bumped into Sasha, laughing and already a little drunk.

"Food, Sasha," he said.

With a thin smile, Sasha let the rookie push him forward. His fingers brushed once more against Alex's hip before vanishing.

Alex leaned back against a wall, shaking a little. *The way he was looking at me....* It had been the same look Sasha had given him in the hotel lobby in Buffalo almost two weeks before. *He makes me want too much.*

The team dispersed to eat, drink, and dance, and Alex finally reclaimed his spot at one of the tables. He spotted Sasha occasionally, weaving through the tables and accepting drinks when they were offered. Volkov and Rager were definitely past drunk and well on their way to wasted, dancing with a group of equally young women and having a great time.

It wasn't Alex's preferred way to spend an evening. *But this is your team now*, he told himself. *This is what team does.* And watching his teammates enjoying themselves, having a great night, was enough to make the evening out much more tolerable.

So far he'd managed to avoid any further attempts to drink or eat something. Unfortunately, Alex's luck didn't hold.

"Hey! What are you doing, kid?" Merkley swung an arm over Alex's shoulders, smiling loosely. His usual scent was mixed with the sour smell of beer, and his unfocused gaze told Alex he'd had a few shots of something stronger as well. "No drink, no food, no girl to dance with. Not acceptable, Fanning!"

Alex tried to protest, but Merks overrode him. He flagged down a waitress and ordered a couple more beers, then pulled a tray of food over. "C'mon, Fanning, eat something."

Alex glanced at the platter, which was loaded down with appetizers from the bar. There were more mozzarella sticks, chips and salsa, pretzels, french fries, and onion rings—Alex's stomach turned just looking at it.

Alcohol he could manage, even if tomorrow would be hell on his body, but the food on the table in front of him, all of it soaked with grease and not a trace of meat or green vegetable in sight… there was no way his body could handle that.

"Nah, I'm good, Cap," he said.

But Merks was drunk, and he wasn't going to give up that easily. "C'mon, kid. Tell me you're not one of those health nuts like Engel is."

Engel was infamous in the locker room for his love of kale smoothies and his dairy- and gluten-free diet during the season. But a glance across the bar showed that even he had a plate of snacks in one hand and a bottle of beer in another.

Alex tried again. "I'm just not hungry, I guess."

Merks gave him an unsteady look. "You played sixty minutes tonight, Fanning. Sixty amazing minutes, dammit." Merkley paused to grin, still clearly riding high on the victory. "Gotta get some calories in you. C'mon, kid." He grabbed a basket of onion rings and pulled them closer. "Captain's orders, eat something and then have another beer!"

If you refuse, he'll get suspicious, a little voice whispered in the back of Alex's mind. *Humans eat human food.*

With Merkley staring him down, Alex sighed and resigned himself to his fate. The onion rings were delicious, of course, hot and crunchy. It was the kind of food that Alex loved, but which definitely didn't love him in return. *This isn't going to end well.*

He ate a few onion rings under Merkley's watchful gaze, while his captain chattered amicably about the game they'd played and how he was just as excited to beat Calgary in two nights' time.

Thankfully Shawn spotted him and rescued him from Merkley a few minutes later.

"Cap, I need to borrow Phantom here. There are some girls looking for a dance partner, and I can't keep 'em waiting!"

"I have a girlfriend," Alex protested, but it was halfhearted and he let Shawn drag him away from the table without any real resistance.

As soon as they were clear, Shawn pulled him in close. "Bro, I thought you couldn't eat that shit?"

Alex was already feeling queasy. "I can't. The grease… my body can't process it. But Merks was insistent, you know?" And after his anti-Para rant just a week and a half prior, Alex couldn't risk drawing any suspicion, especially not from the captain of the team. "I'm gonna be so sick, though."

Shawn glanced around. "Go on, dude, head back to the hotel now. I'll cover for you if anyone asks. I can say you drank too much or something."

"Thanks, Carts." Alex swallowed around the rising nausea, then ducked around the crowd and started to head for the door.

He didn't make it.

Jonas—in medical school (@futuredocjonas)

Med school is hard enough, but having to learn human *and* para physiology makes it 10 times harder. Why the hell do I need to know about fae metal allergies or vampire food intolerances? I want to treat PEOPLE not PARAS.

Paranormal Rights Activist (@pararights)
@futuredocjonas: Paras are 99% identical to humans when in their human forms. If having to learn about the 1% of anomalies is *so hard* then maybe you should try an easier profession... #ParasArePeople

SASHA WAS looking for Alex.

The goalie had spent most of the evening ensconced in one of the club's large leather benches, watching the team get progressively drunker with a small, amused smile on his face. But now Sasha'd had a few drinks of his own and was feeling good and loose. And what he wanted was to drag Alex from that bench and get him to dance with Sasha.

But Alex wasn't at the table any longer. Sasha looked around. The bar was packed, the Friday night bringing people out to drink and party even with the snowstorm building outside. But he found Alex easily enough, drawn to the familiar dark hair without any problems.

Alex was halfway across the bar, heading toward the front of the building. Sasha watched Alex stumble, knocking into a man who'd been perched on a barstool and laughed when Alex apologized profusely.

He's drunk.

Which, Sasha reasoned, was fair enough. Their goalie had pulled off another spectacular win against Edmonton, putting Hertzog at risk of reclaiming his place on the bench as the team's backup.

His smile faded when he saw Alex stumble again, though, barely catching himself on the edge of an empty table.

Before he could think it through, Sasha had set his own drink down and was pushing his way through the crowd of drunks and dancers, crossing the distance as quickly as possible. He caught up to Alex a few feet from the door and only barely managed to get a hand around Alex's waist before the goalie collapsed to the ground.

"You need an ambulance."

Alex was conscious at least, and not so out of it that he couldn't protest. "I don't. I just need some fresh air."

Fresh air Sasha could do, but it was about negative ten outside right now. He spotted a hallway off to the side and helped Alex walk down there. A door at the end opened into a bathroom that was almost certainly for employees only, but Sasha closed the door behind them anyway.

"Fuck, I'm gonna be sick." Alex's voice was thin, weak, and he was white as a sheet. Sasha helped him over to the toilet and lowered him to the tile.

It wasn't a second too soon, either, because as soon as Alex's knees touched the ground he was hunched forward, gripping the side of the toilet bowl and retching. The acrid scent of vomit filled the tiny bathroom.

Sasha ran a hand through Alex's hair, holding it back from his face, and rubbed his other one in large circles over the smaller man's back. "Shh, солнышко. Deep breaths. You will be okay."

Alex shuddered and heaved again, then sat panting for a second. His entire body was shaking beneath Sasha's hands, and pained whimpers escaped him with each exhalation.

He settled a hand between Alex's shoulder blades, thumb rubbing the soft skin above the goalie's T-shirt. He expected Alex to be warm, sweating from the exertion, but instead he was surprised to find the skin ice cold beneath his fingers.

When it became clear that Alex was done, Sasha helped him sit backward, propping him against a wall. He flushed the vomit, then grabbed a handful of paper towels and ran them under the faucet.

"You drink too much?" he asked, helping to clean up Alex's face. This wasn't the first time that he'd helped a teammate who'd had one too many.

Alex shivered in his grasp. His entire body was like an icicle. "Just one shot."

Sasha frowned. "Sick, then? Flu?"

There was no answer. He turned his head to find Alex's eyes were closed. His lashes were dark against his pale cheeks, and there were bruise-like circles beneath the younger man's eyes.

"Oh, солнышко," he murmured. His phone was in his back pocket, and he had to perform some acrobatics to get it out without moving Alex too much. "I'm going to text Carts, okay? And we'll get you back to the hotel."

"What's that mean? Sol—solshenko?"

Sasha paused in typing one-handed, pulling Alex closer while he thought. "Solnishko. It means sunshine," he said eventually. "Like little sunshine. Is… like nickname? But for friends."

Alex huffed out a weak laugh. "Funny," he murmured. "Don't like the sun."

"Yes, I can tell. You are pale like Siberian tundra. Good thing you play hockey, not beach volleyball, hm?"

"Good thing," Alex whispered.

There was a light knock on the door. It cracked open a second later, and Shawn's head poked in.

"God damn," he said. "Is he okay?"

Sasha glanced up. "I think so now. Ate something bad, perhaps, or maybe the flu. But he has no fever."

Shawn slipped in all the way and squatted down in front of Alex. "Hey, Phantom, bud. You still awake?"

Alex's nose wrinkled. "Yeah."

"Good. Me and Sasha are gonna help you up. There's a back door out of the bar, and I'll get a cab to come around and meet us. Then we'll go back to the hotel, okay."

"'Kay." Alex shifted. "Carts. I need Heather. Can you get Heather?"

Sasha stiffened.

"We're in Edmonton, Phantom, not Seattle. Heather isn't here."

"Need—"

Shawn nodded even though Alex's eyes were still closed. "I know, man. I've got you. Don't worry. C'mon, up we go now, okay?"

Together, he and Sasha managed to get Alex on his feet. Shawn went on ahead to get a taxi, leaving Sasha to carefully lead him toward the back exit, away from the crowds of people and their still-celebrating teammates.

Chapter Fourteen

Ellen DeSmith (@EllenDeSmithESPN)
Hearing word that Cascades G Alexander Fanning may be out for tomorrow's game against Calgary due to stomach flu. He's the fourth NHL player to go down with the flu this season. If he's not recovered, an emergency backup will be called in.

THE DAY after the Edmonton game was a blur of pain, nausea, and stomach cramps for Alex. He spent most of it lying down on whatever flat surface he could find: his hotel room bed, a row of seats as the team flew up to Calgary, a massage table in one of the trainer's rooms at the arena, and yet another hotel bed.

The first moment of clarity he had that day was somehow making it downstairs for breakfast, only to have Coach Rico send him right back up to bed again. A trainer had stopped by soon after, smelling medicinal and pressing a warm hand to Alex's forehead.

"No fever," the trainer said, "but this definitely looks like the stomach flu that's been going around. I'll send Cartier in to keep an eye on you until the flight, and I want you to stay hydrated as much as possible. If you can't keep liquids down, tell Shawn to come get me, okay?"

"Okay," Alex rasped.

The trainer passed him a Gatorade. "If you're not feeling better tomorrow, we'll call up one of Calgary's emergency backups to sit on the bench."

Alex hummed and closed his eyes as another wave of pain wracked his body. His insides felt like they wanted to claw their way out.

"You know," Shawn said, some indeterminable amount of time later. "If you needed to, you could feed from me. If it would make you feel better."

"No." Alex shook his head, then stopped abruptly when the motion made him feel even sicker. "You have to play tomorrow. Don't want to risk taking too much and making you sick too."

And Shawn was at his side when they had to leave for the airport just before lunchtime, helping him onto the plane and covering him with a blanket for the short flight.

But it was Sasha who filled most of Alex's moments of awareness throughout the day.

Sasha, whose scent was the only thing that seemed to help the nausea and whose strong arms wrapped around Alex's waist as they stepped off the plane.

And Sasha, who found him after practice, when Alex was curled up in a back room trying to nap while a trainer came in occasionally to check on him.

"Hey, солнышко." Sasha's warm callused fingers caressed down Alex's jaw and neck.

Alex opened his eyes slowly, inhaling deeply and feeling some of the stomach cramps fade away. "Hey," he whispered.

"Feeling any better?"

"Yeah." Alex tilted his head up, finding Sasha's bright eyes in the dim light of the room. "Time 's it?"

Sasha glanced at something on the wall. "Just after two." His voice was soft, soothing, and the hand on Alex's neck had moved up to card through the short hairs at the top of his spine. "Came to help you get to the bus so we can go to the hotel. Coach said you gotta sleep more, and maybe tomorrow you'll be feeling better."

"Mmh." Alex closed his eyes again, sinking into the rich scent and the comforting feeling of Sasha's hand against his skin.

Until another cramp struck, and he groaned, curling up on his side and clenching his eyes shut.

"Oh, Alex." Sasha rubbed his hair tenderly, then wrapped an arm around his shoulders. "Come on, we need to get up now."

Alex lost some time between leaving the arena and getting to the hotel. Even with Sasha at his side, the pain was intense, and he had to breathe carefully to avoid losing whatever liquids he'd managed to keep down so far that morning.

He was distantly aware of another voice talking to Sasha—Shawn, he realized, recognizing the fresh scent of him. Normally Shawn's scent was comforting, but today Alex just wanted to bury his nose in Sasha's neck and ignore everything else.

But Shawn helped Sasha get him upstairs and into a room with a soft, warm bed and heavy blankets.

Then Sasha was pulling away, and Alex couldn't help the moan that escaped him.

"Wait," he whispered.

Sasha returned to his side, bringing his scent with him.

Alex swallowed. "Can you stay? Just for a while."

Shawn said something from behind him, but Alex couldn't focus enough to hear it. He did see Sasha nod, though, and say, "I've got it. I'll call you if anything changes."

And then Shawn's bright scent was gone, and it was only Sasha left in the room.

Alex relaxed, and closed his eyes. "Don't go yet," he murmured.

"I'm not going anywhere," Sasha said.

Alex fell asleep that way, Sasha warm at his side and his scent filling the room.

Emma (@Cascadiac)

anyone else watching this #SEAvsCGY game right now? Every time the camera pans over the bench, it looks like Fanning is about to pass out. Hope Hertzog doesn't get injured, because I doubt Fanning is well enough to play.

Seattle Cascades (@CascadesNHL)

Cascades manage to hang on for a win, 4-3 over Calgary!

SASHA KNOCKED on the door to Ed's sprawling Medina mansion, feeling the guilt return as he stood in the chilly afternoon air.

He felt even worse when the door swung open to reveal Ed, the hand of his uninjured arm propped on his hip, staring at him with a frown. "Well, then," Ed declared, "look who finally remembered his best friend."

Sasha shifted his weight on his feet and looked away. The last week had been busy; they'd had two games at home to deal with, and two games in Alberta, with practices every day in between.

It's no excuse, he berated himself. *Eddie's your friend, and you keep letting hockey distract you from spending time with him while he's hurt.*

Of course, it wasn't just hockey that was distracting Sasha. Brown eyes and pale skin flashed through his mind, and the guilt in Sasha's chest grew heavier.

"Sorry, Eddie."

He must have sounded apologetic enough, because Ed finally scoffed and stood aside to let Sasha in. The weather had rebounded back to the more expected Pacific Northwest temperatures, but it was still windy and damp outside and Sasha was happy to get indoors.

"I figured you'd come see me after the Nashville game or even before you flew up to Canada, but all I got was silence. No calls, no texts, and now you show up on my doorstep like everything's fine?" Ed clicked his tongue, closing the door behind them. "I thought we were friends, Sasha."

"We are!" Sasha straightened. "I said I'm sorry. It was just a hectic few days, you know? We got back from Calgary last night, and I came here as soon as I had time."

It wasn't a lie exactly. *But you had time to get lunch with Alex the day after the Nashville game, instead of coming to see Ed. You had time to go out with your teammates when you could have texted Ed to see how he was doing.*

He'd actually planned to call Ed the day after the Edmonton game. Their schedule that day had been light; a short flight in the morning, a lunchtime practice, and then the entire afternoon to themselves. But Alex had been so sick, and Sasha....

He hadn't been able to stay away. Alex had skipped practice, resting in one of the trainer's rooms instead as he tried to shake off the stomach flu he'd caught. Sasha had found him after practice ended, asleep on a massage table and curled up beneath a thin blanket, sound asleep.

Alex had blinked his eyes open when Sasha had nudged him, and for a split second, he'd just stared up at Sasha, barely awake and so full of tenderness that the breath had caught in Sasha's throat. Then stomach cramps had wracked his body, and he'd groaned, curling up on his side as his eyes fluttered shut.

So instead of calling his friend, Sasha had offered to help Alex back to the hotel, getting him to his room and pulling the heavy comforter over his body. He'd curled up in a chair in the corner and listened to Alex breathe, and he hadn't even thought about Eddie once.

After the game against Calgary—after Alex had somehow managed to sit on the bench for three full periods, looking miserable and pale—they'd flown home. Sasha had sat beside him, letting Alex sleep on his shoulder until the plane had touched down in Seattle.

And then, for the second time in as many weeks, he'd watched as Alex got off the plane and went straight to the gorgeous blonde woman who had been waiting for him, looking at her like she was made of pure gold.

It had hurt. It still hurt.

But Sasha couldn't say that aloud.

So instead he gave Ed his most weary stare and said, "You know how it is, man. You'll be back soon enough anyway, so you can join us on these hellish road trips."

"Damn right I will," Ed replied. "Docs said the break and the shoulder should both be about twelve weeks, and it's been four already. I talked to the trainers, and they said I could come in starting the second half of February to do physical therapy and train."

That was unexpected. "They're letting you come back?"

"I'm still on the team." Ed's voice rose as he talked, going from even-keeled to upset in the blink of an eye. "They can't just kick me off."

Sasha took a step back. "No, I meant, I thought with the trial and all...."

"Well, obviously the team isn't worried about that." Ed waved a hand dismissively. "They know I won't be convicted, so why not let me train until then?"

The raw confidence in Ed's voice made Sasha uncomfortable. "You have a trial date scheduled?"

Ed nodded. "First week of April. It was the soonest my lawyer could get me in, even pulling whatever strings he could. But it means I'll be ready for playoffs for sure, especially if I can start back with the trainers in a couple of weeks."

"That's great, Eddie."

It *was* great, Sasha told himself. He wanted Ed back, playing in the net behind him and making sarcastic comments during breakages in play. He wanted the familiar face on the other side of the locker room and the easy familiarity of having his best friend around to talk to.

But if Ed comes back, Alex leaves.

And that... was not great.

Ed walked farther into the house, and Sasha trailed behind him, biting his lip in thought.

"Anyway," Ed continued, "I'll send you the info for the trial. Date, time, location, all that. You have two days off between games that week, and I made sure the trial is on one of them so you can stop by and testify on my behalf."

And that was another problem altogether. Sasha followed him into the kitchen and leaned against the fridge, watching Ed move around confidently to pull a couple of glasses from a cabinet.

"Ed, I want you back on the team so badly," he began.

Then Ed reached up and pulled a bottle of whiskey off the shelf, unscrewing the top and pouring them both a generous amount.

It's only two o'clock in the afternoon.

Ed took the sudden silence as an affirmative, turning to pass one of the glasses to Sasha. "Glad you're on my side, brother." With his now-free hand, he dug a bottle out of his pocket and popped the lid one-handed, shaking a small white pill out on the counter before returning the bottle to its place.

I want you back on the team, Sasha mentally finished, *but something is seriously wrong here, and I'm not sure that me lying to a judge is going to make anything better.* He was a hockey player and spent most of his free time surrounded by hockey players. He knew how to drink—hell, his team could put an entire frat house to shame, given a really good night. But everyone on the team knew where the limits were, knew to only drink with their teammates and not get too carried away. This? Drinking straight Jack in the middle of the afternoon, popping pain pills and washing them down with booze? This was so far past those limits that Ed couldn't even see them anymore.

Sasha cupped his hands around his own glass and didn't take a sip, physically queasy from what he was witnessing. "Yeah, Eddie, I only want what's best for you." *Even if that means getting treatment... because I'm starting to think you need it.*

"Cheers, my friend," Ed said, and poured himself another drink.

Chapter Fifteen

Seattle Cascades (@CascadesNHL)
We're home for three games in a row, and a day off on the 14th in between! Haven't gotten your special someone a #ValentinesDay card yet? No worries, we have you covered with these #CascadesValentines! https://t.co/hHgW3igrM0

Mrs. Merkley… a girl can dream! (@MerkleyFan96)
Okay, these @CascadesNHL Valentines win the internet today. "I love my significant Otter!" "I would Rybar be with you than anywhere else!" "I love you more than I can Bayer!" I CANNOT STOP LAUGHING!

"You're distracted," Heather said, taking a sip of her wine. "Is the steak not good?"

The steak was excellent, as was the wine and the rest of the lavish meal spread out between them. Alex glanced down at his half-eaten plate and sighed. "It's fine."

"It's one of the most expensive steaks in Seattle, cooked to medium-rare perfection, so tender that it melts in your mouth, but it's *fine*?" Heather laughed.

Alex stared down at the plate, moving a pile of mashed potatoes from one side to the other methodically.

It wasn't that anything was wrong, exactly, but every time he looked across the table, with its vase of roses and expensive wine, he couldn't help but wish there was someone else sitting across the table from him.

"Oh, Alex," Heather murmured. "You have it bad, don't you?"

Alex nudged his steak around and didn't look up.

She laughed again and tapped the table with her perfectly manicured nails. "If I was any other woman, I'd probably be a little insulted. Most people don't want their Valentine's Day dinner partner to be longing for someone else and moping throughout the entire meal."

"I have no idea what you're talking about."

Heather leaned in closer. They were at an intimate two-person table, tucked away in a private corner of one of Seattle's finest dining establishments. There were bouquets of red roses everywhere Alex looked, more than enough to block them from casual view of their fellow diners. It was as isolated and secure a location as they'd find in public, but Alex was still thankful when Heather lowered her voice to a whisper before saying, "You know that I can sense when you're thinking about him, right?"

He knew, but that didn't mean he was going to admit to anything. "There's nothing to sense."

She licked her lips pointedly and curled her mouth in a teasing smile. "No? We're out on Valentine's Day. Everyone around us is overflowing with so much love and sexual desire that I could stay here all night feeding and none of them would notice a thing. But you, Alex, are a black hole. A pit of misery and longing that is adding a very sour taste to a *very* lovely meal."

Alex set his fork and knife down and fumbled for his water glass. "Heather, you know that I—"

She rolled her eyes. "I know, I know. You're gay, you're a professional athlete, you don't want to draw any attention to yourself, and the man you're desperately pining after probably doesn't return your affections anyways. Did I get it all?"

Alex stared moodily down at his plate. "The problem is, I think he might actually return them."

Heather set her wineglass down, and her eyes went wide. "What?"

"I said, I think he might—"

"No, I heard you." Heather kicked him under the table. "When were you going to tell me about this? How long have you known?"

"Ow, geez." If Shawn was like a brother to him, Heather was fast becoming like a sister—complete with every annoying stereotype he'd ever heard of. Alex pulled his leg back out of her reach. "I don't actually know for sure, okay. Just... we've been getting closer, and he keeps giving me these looks, like he's interested."

Heather picked her glass back up, eyes gleaming with delight. "But he hasn't made a move yet?"

Alex shook his head. "We had lunch last week. There was a second where I thought... well." He blushed and lowered his voice even more.

"Anyways, I realized that even if he's interested, he's not going to do anything about it."

"Because of your teammates?"

"No, because of you," Alex said.

That took Heather aback. She blinked, then exhaled as understanding washed over her. "Of course."

Alex finally took a bite of his food, chewing slowly while he thought. "I want to tell him the truth. Not," he rushed to add, "about us being... you know. But that we're not really dating."

"You should. If you want to break this off entirely, you know—"

"No." Alex cut her off. "Just Sasha."

The smile that passed over Heather's lips was a little sad but full of understanding. "You're still worried about your teammates knowing?"

It wasn't that Alex was worried. Shawn had joked about the bet they had going, but he'd also made it clear that the locker room would be welcoming enough if he came out. But he still didn't have a fixed place on the team, and anything that could rock the boat could jeopardize his chance to get a shot at the roster for real.

"It would be easier," he finally said. "Simpler."

Heather nodded.

But the more Alex thought about it, the more he wanted to let Sasha know that he was gay. *But I can't just tell him.* Sasha had been looking at him lately with such blatant longing and had taken such tender care of him when he'd been sick in Calgary, but that didn't mean he'd leap at the chance to be with Alex.

Heather reached across the table and squeezed his hand, then leaned back in her seat. "You should say something to your Sasha."

"He's not my Sasha." *Not yet, but maybe someday.* "And I will. I just need to figure out the right way to do it."

"And you'll tell me all about it once you manage to get your man into bed?"

Alex laughed, head falling back. *Succubi*, he thought, amused. "You only want us to have sex so you can feed off the residual emotion."

She winked. "Well, I wouldn't complain if you wanted to tell me all about it. Every time you think about him, it's like biting into a truffle—rich, earthy, decadent."

The words were eerily familiar. *That's how Sasha smells to me.* Even though the defenseman was miles away right now, Alex could still conjure that mouth-watering scent.

"Yes," Heather said, licking her lips. "That's it exactly."

Alex swallowed hard. "I can't—I won't get my hopes up yet. I like him a lot, and we've finally started to become real friends. And I know he cares about me, and I care about him, but I can't risk messing that up until I'm sure."

"Subtlety, then."

"Yeah. For now." Alex laughed again, shaking his head. "And if he doesn't take the hints, I'll probably just have to corner him and kiss him senseless."

Heather finished her wine and dabbed her mouth with a napkin, careful not to smear her lipstick. "That sounds like a plan. Now, I think we should skip dessert. You still need to feed before tomorrow's game, and I definitely wouldn't mind seconds of the lovely meal you just shared with me."

Her amused gaze said she wasn't talking about the steak.

"I hope you all had a nice, sweet day yesterday, because tonight is going to be a bitter one as the Cascades take on Pittsburgh here in Seattle. There's a rivalry between them going back to the Stanley Cup Finals from seven years ago, when Seattle lost to Pittsburgh in overtime of Game 6 after an illegal check behind the play didn't get called by the refs. So even though these two teams meet up only twice a season, it's always a vicious matchup when they do."

KTCP Radio 102.7, Cascades Pre-Game Show

SASHA WAS sweaty and sore by the start of the first intermission. He hadn't been on the team when the rivalry against Pittsburgh had been established, but he'd heard about it from Klausman, one of the only guys on the team who'd been playing back then. But just because he hadn't been involved in the rivalry personally didn't mean Pittsburgh was going to pull their hits on him. He could feel bruises coming up, and his muscles were screaming for relief.

So he was in a mood when he walked into the locker room for intermission, trying to radiate *leave me alone* as loud as possible. Most of his teammates picked up on the silent signals easily enough… except, of course, for Alex.

"Good period," he said cheerfully.

"Ugh." Sasha found his stall and slumped onto the bench, breathing hard. "Not gonna survive forty more minutes of this."

"I believe in you." Alex passed over a bottle of cool water, which Sasha took gratefully. "You want me to grab you a protein bar or something?"

"No." Sasha glanced up, draining half the bottle of water in one long pull before catching his breath again. "Sit down. Stop hovering."

Alex was the only guy in the room who wasn't dripping with sweat, since he was on the bench again tonight. He pulled up a folding chair, facing Sasha's stall, and at least had the good sense to look a little guilty. "I wish there was something I could do to help. This is one hell of a game."

"Just—" Sasha motioned with the bottle in his hand. "—talk about something. Distract me from painful bruises for a few minutes."

From what Sasha had seen, Alex wasn't much of a talker with other people. When he was hanging out with Shawn, or even Sasha himself, he tended to open up more. But otherwise he was more likely to watch in silence and live up to his nickname.

"Oh, okay." Alex seemed thrown. "Well, how was your Valentine's Day? Did you do anything last night?"

Sasha grunted again.

Alex laughed. "Sorry, when you said talk to you, I guess you meant a one-sided thing. Well, I guess I can tell you what we did."

If Sasha was being honest, that was the last thing he wanted to hear about. He'd rather face another twenty minutes of Pittsburgh jamming him into the boards than hear about Alex's perfect evening with his perfect girlfriend. But he was too exhausted to protest… and too pathetic to want to miss anything that made Alex smile the way he was right now.

"We went to La Fleur downtown," Alex said. "Disgustingly fancy and overpriced, but probably the best steak I've ever had in my life. Heather got us a table… guess being friends with a celebrity pays off sometimes."

Sasha finished off his bottle of water, listening to Alex describe the meal he'd eaten, and the celebrity diners he'd spotted. He couldn't blame the goalie for taking a date to La Fleur; it was supposed to be the best French restaurant in the city, and even Sasha had been eager to give it a try.

It took him a second to realize that the food was the only thing Alex was talking about, though.

"What about girlfriend? You have a nice time together?"

Alex stumbled midsentence, describing the wine he'd had. "Oh, Heather? Sure, we had a great time. She's hilarious, you know, like the sister I never had. Told me I have an 'unrefined palate,' whatever that means, just because I didn't like the soup. It was weird, Sasha, I'm telling you."

He thinks of his girlfriend like a sister? Sasha blinked in confusion, watching the goalie continue to chatter.

"Anyways, we skipped dessert. I needed to—" Alex paused for a split second. "—to get ready for the game today, and she had an early on-set call this morning."

Alex was watching him with a strange expression in his eyes as he talked, and Sasha blinked away some of the lingering pain and exhaustion from the first period, trying to interpret it. *Is he upset that he didn't get to spend the night with his girlfriend for Valentine's Day?* But that wasn't upset in Alex's gaze.

Sasha shook his head, too tired to figure it out now. "Glad you had a good night," he said simply.

A flash of disappointment flittered across Alex's face, there and gone in an instant, and was followed by something that looked like resignation. "Yeah. It was a nice meal. I'll let you finish resting. Good luck in the second, okay?"

He patted Sasha on the shoulder as he went.

I feel like we were having two very different conversations there. But then Coach came in to prep them for the second, and he had to push Alex's strangeness out of his mind and focus on the game once again.

Chapter Sixteen

The problem, Alex thought, *is that Sasha is completely oblivious.*

No, not oblivious. He'd fixed it in his mind that Alex was in a loving, committed relationship with Heather, and nothing that Alex hinted at could shake him from that resolute belief.

Even blatantly flirting with him wasn't helping.

He ran into Sasha and Mikhail in the parking garage as they arrived for the game against Atlanta on Friday night. Alex was getting another start, his third of the month so far, but any attempt to focus on the game and get himself prepared mentally went right out the window when Sasha pulled up in the Camaro and stepped out, dressed in his game-day suit—which clung to his body like it was perfectly tailored, hugging his broad shoulders and making Alex stop dead in his tracks.

"That suit looks great on you," he said, when Sasha got close enough for him to speak.

Mikhail rolled his eyes and muttered something in Russian, then gave them both a pat on the shoulder and took off ahead of them into the arena.

Sasha's cheeks were a little flushed, but that was the only sign that Alex's words had affected him. "You too," he said. "Very nice."

Alex's suit was off the rack, something he'd picked up back in Portland. He knew it looked good enough on him; he was lucky that even when he was bulking at the end of summer he was still relatively thin and lanky, and didn't need special tailoring to fit into a suit—*Unlike Sasha*, he added, *with those arms and that ass. God damn.*

But his game-day suit was nothing compared to what Sasha was wearing. The dark gray suit made Sasha's blue eyes pop even in the dim light of the parking garage. Add in the classic sports car, and Alex wasn't sure how anyone could possibly expect him to focus on the game ahead.

"I'm serious." Alex caught and held Sasha's gaze, then stepped forward to brush an imaginary piece of lint off Sasha's arm. This close, he could smell Sasha's cologne, a hint of something woodsy and expensive mixing perfectly with his natural rich earthy scent. "You look really good today, Sasha."

Sasha shrugged off the compliment, but the flush on his cheeks remained. "I'll give you the name of my tailor. You can impress your girlfriend. She coming to the game tonight?"

Ugh, it was like Sasha refused to see what was right in front of him. And every time Alex's attempts fell flat, the doubt flared back up. *Maybe he's really not interested.*

He allowed the subject change, though, turning to walk beside Sasha into the arena. "Nah, Heather's not a hockey fan."

Sasha stumbled a little. "You date a woman who doesn't like hockey?" He sounded incredulous. "Why?"

Alex held the door open and followed Sasha inside. Finally, the perfect opening for him to tell Sasha the truth. *If he's not going to accept subtlety, I'll just have to hit him with the truth head-on.* "Well, I don't."

"Hm?"

Before Alex could explain, though, Akseli came up behind them. "Gentlemen. Ready to destroy Atlanta this evening?"

Dammit. Alex glanced over at Sasha, frustrated by the interruption, and let himself get drawn into a conversation with the Finnish forward.

I'll have to catch him at practice tomorrow or on the road trip next week. I can't keep playing this game... I need to know one way or another.

Seattle Sports News (@SeattleSportsNews)
Spotted injured goalie Eduard Despres on the ice today, skating with no equipment. Trainers say he's still recovering, but they're working with Despres to maintain muscle mass and ensure injuries heal properly.

sports fan in the emerald city (@SEAyaLater)
Wasn't this guy ARRESTED for DRUNK DRIVING like 6 weeks ago?? Cascades should suspend him, not let him come skate with the team.

Chad (@Despresident)
@SEAyaLater: dude hasn't been convicted yet. Innocent until proven guilty, ring any bells?! Despres is the best goalie on this team, glad to see him back to skating so we can get back to winning!

sports fan in the emerald city (@SEAyaLater)

@Despresident: this team is 13-7-2 since Despres was injured, and Fanning is 4-1. Looks like he and Hertzog are doing just fine. We'll see about the trial, but I doubt cops accuse Despres unless they have proof!

SASHA WAS in a great mood when he came into the practice facility on Saturday morning. They'd defeated Atlanta the night before, he'd played well and gotten a point, and Alex had given another stellar performance in net. Today's practice was optional, which meant the locker room had a more laid-back air to it as guys pulled their gear on, while those who had taken the option not to skate sat around and chatted before hitting the gym or meeting with trainers.

Alex looked to be in an equally good mood when he arrived. He set his bag down but didn't bother to change before heading straight over to Sasha's stall.

It was honestly infuriating. Alex was spending so much time around him that Sasha was going crazy trying to constantly restrain himself. *He's off limits*, he reminded himself, but as usual his resolve started to crumble when Alex flashed that bright smile at him.

"Hey, Sasha." The locker room was empty enough that Alex could slide onto the bench beside him, a long line of muscle and heat seeping into Sasha's skin through his base layers from shoulder to knee. "You got a second?"

God, Sasha would always be weak for this man. "Sure. For you, always."

Alex smiled shyly, eyes going soft as he glanced up at Sasha through his lashes. He looked nervous, but also sweet, smile a little tentative around the edges.

"I really wanted to talk to you about something. And I know this isn't really the best place, but it's important and I didn't want to wait."

Sasha turned to face Alex, curious. "Of course, anything."

Alex hesitated. "This might sound a little weird, and maybe it doesn't matter to you after all, but—"

He didn't get a chance to finish his sentence, because Bayer suddenly stood up and shouted across the room, "Hey hey! Look who finally decided to show his face!"

Sasha caught a glimpse of frustrated disappointment on Alex's face before he tore his eyes away to see what the commotion was about. His easy smile drained away as he spotted the body filling the locker room doors.

"Eddie, my man!" That was Merkley, stepping forward to give a one-armed hug as Ed moved farther into the room.

Beside him, Alex tilted his head. "Oh. That's Despres?"

"Yes."

"Huh. I've seen him play, of course, but didn't expect him to look like that."

"Like that" was what had reduced Sasha to single-word responses. He'd seen Ed less than a week prior, but he was shocked by how much had changed since then. Or maybe it was the setting, seeing Ed surrounded by large, bulky, healthy-looking hockey players. Of course his friend looked thinner, less muscular; he'd been in the hospital, and then restricted in working out by the injuries he'd sustained. But now he looked small, almost, and tired like he hadn't slept for a couple of days.

Sasha hung back at his locker, watching as his teammates took turns greeting Ed, giving him hugs and handshakes. But that vantage point also meant he could see who chose not to approach the goalie, who looked away awkwardly or whose hugs didn't linger.

They're uncomfortable with him. Even Merks seemed a bit anxious, like he wasn't pleased with Ed's presence in the room. It could have just been the captain's displeasure with having the practice schedule pushed back unexpectedly, but Sasha doubted it. Somehow, in the last six and a half weeks, Ed had stopped being the Cascades' beloved number one goalie.

"Sasha!" Ed finally spotted him, and his call jerked Sasha from his contemplations. "Look, I'm back!"

Sasha smiled and hoped it looked more genuine than it felt. "Looks like you are. How's the arm?"

"Eh, it's healing. Trainers are optimistic." Ed turned his head, and his eyes widened in recognition as he spotted Alex sitting beside Sasha, before narrowing in obvious dislike.

Sasha spared a glance at Alex and was surprised to see him wrinkle his nose, as though he'd smelled something awful. Sasha inhaled subtly. *Ed doesn't smell like alcohol.* But Alex was backing up too, pushing into the stall he was sitting in as inconspicuously as he could, like he wanted to put distance between himself and Ed.

"You must be Alexander Fanning." Ed's voice was flat, but anyone who knew would know what that tone meant.

Alex smiled, a fleeting there-and-gone moment of politeness. "Call me Alex. It's really great to meet you, Mr. Despres." He didn't stand up or offer his hand to shake.

"And you." Ed looked between Alex and Sasha, and his frown deepened. "I should get going, so you can get to practice. Sasha, let's have dinner next weekend when you're back from your trip, eh?"

Sasha managed another smile. "Of course, Eddie. I'll text you later."

Ed raised his good arm, waving at Sasha. He spared Alex one last look, and Sasha glimpsed anger in his gaze before he turned away to talk to a few other players.

He didn't realize how much Alex had tensed up until he felt the smaller man relax at his side.

"So, that's Despres," Alex said again. "Can't say I'm a fan. He looked at me like I was something he wanted to scrape off the bottom of his shoe."

Sasha sighed. "He's just upset about not being able to play."

"Sure, I guess." But Alex didn't sound convinced. "Hey, I should go get dressed. I don't want to be late on the ice; Rico will bag skate me for sure, goalie gear or not."

"Okay. See you soon."

He watched Alex go, and it was only when the goalie was back across the room that he remembered Alex had wanted to talk to him about something before Ed had shown up.

He kept thinking about that through practice. Whatever Alex had wanted to tell him had seemed important, and Alex had looked nervous.

Sasha tried to track him down after practice ended, only to find him and Shawn tucked in the player's lounge, talking without realizing he was nearby.

"He smells horrible," Alex hissed. "And I get the feeling that he'd do something pretty drastic if he thought I was going to steal his place on the roster."

Shawn frowned but didn't seem too concerned. "You might be overreacting, Phantom."

But Alex shook his head, adamant. "Something's wrong with him, I'm telling you. It's not the alcohol, either, though I could definitely smell it. It was the way he looked at me; Sasha didn't seem to notice, but I could see it."

They moved on before Sasha could hear anything else, and neither of them seemed to be aware that he'd overheard.

Sasha exhaled and found a couch to flop down onto.

He'd known for a while that he was going to have to make a decision between his best friend and the man he was becoming more and more attracted to with every passing day. But Sasha had figured the issue was one-sided, that he just needed to placate Ed in order to find a balance between two of the most important people in his life. Now, though, it seemed like Alex had caught on to the problem too.

Everything was getting more complicated, and Sasha wasn't sure how he was going to get through this with both Eddie and Alex in his life.

Seattle Cascades (@CascadesNHL)
A short practice this morning, and then we're off to Minnesota! Hope everyone packed their jackets… it's going to be a bitter cold Midwest roadie. https://t.co/t9Ci5CUNe7

DESPRES WAS back at the arena the next day, much to Alex's frustration.

The older goalie had been one of his idols for years. When he'd been drafted by the Cascades at age eighteen, he'd immediately started following Despres's career, modeling his own play after the veteran goaltender and dreaming about a day when he'd get to play side by side with him. But now that he'd met Despres, he was quickly beginning to revise those dreams.

It wasn't that Despres was an alcoholic, though that was obviously a very large problem. Alex understood that it was a disease and that even someone as talented and set in life as Eduard Despres could fall victim to it.

No, it was what came along with the alcoholism—or, maybe, what was already there before and was now amplified with it.

He *hated* Alex.

It was obvious, and Alex wasn't the only one to have noticed it, though no one else seemed willing to discuss it. But every time Despres caught sight of Alex, his eyes narrowed and he looked furious. At one point Otter came up to talk to him about the Chicago game, where Alex would be getting yet another start; the smell of something foul had caught Alex's attention, and when he looked over, he'd seen Despres practically seething a few yards away, clearly listening in.

"Why is he even here?" he asked Shawn, once he'd escaped to the ice.

Shawn grimaced, eyes darting over to where Despres was on skates but dressed casually, working one-on-one with a trainer. "I heard from Wilson, who heard from Klausman, that the team is waiting until the results of the court case before they pass any judgment on Ed. Like, they won't suspend him until they know for sure. So until then, they're letting him work with the coaches and trainers here so he can maintain muscle mass as he heals."

It would have been fine, if Despres didn't stink up the entire arena with his hate.

And if he seemed interested in actually healing. Because as he watched, Despres skated to the bench to pick up his own water bottle… only the liquid inside wasn't water. Alex could smell the clear scent of alcohol all the way across the ice, though he doubted anyone else would have been able to smell it.

But the question of *why* Despres hated him so much wasn't answered until they were getting ready to board the bus to head to the airport for their afternoon flight.

Sasha was talking to Despres in the back hallway, apparently saying goodbye, and Alex caught a hint of the conversation as he passed by them.

"You'll be back soon," Sasha was saying. "No one's trying to steal your spot. I promise."

Alex nodded politely as he walked around them, smiling blandly like he hadn't heard. But inside he was raging.

He thinks I'm going to take over for him as starting *goaltender? That's why he hates me so much?* He boarded the bus and threw himself into a seat. *Fine. If he wants to be an asshole about it, then he'd better watch out. Because I want to stay on this team. I'll gladly share the position with him, but if he forces me, I'll prove to Rico and GM Dubois that I'm better than he could ever be.*

Chapter Seventeen

Emma (@Cascadiac)
Ouch. Just… ouch.

Seattle Cascades (@CascadesNHL)
A bitter loss to Minnesota, as the Cascades fall 7-1 here in Minneapolis. An overnight here in MN thanks to the snow and then we're off to Illinois tomorrow to take on Chicago.

Sasha didn't smash his stick, but it was a close call. He did throw his gloves when he stepped into the visitor's locker room, chucking first one and then the other into his stall as hard as he could manage.

He was supposed to have postgame media, but Alyssa took one look at him and kicked him out. "Go. Take a shower or something, I don't care, just go."

So Sasha went. He stood under the shower spray for far longer than he needed to, letting the scalding water burn a layer of skin off and hopefully wash away the rest of the evening with it.

You messed up tonight, дурак.

He'd played like shit, end of story. Coach had pulled him off the top pairing with Shawn before the end of the first, though things hadn't improved after. Nothing had worked, nothing had clicked, and every time Sasha had tried to make a play he'd found himself three steps behind.

He toweled off roughly and dressed quickly, keeping his head down and pulling a baseball cap on to hide his face. The seat next to him on the bus ride back to the hotel remained empty, and no one talked to him or tried to approach him.

No one, that was, except Alex, who cornered him in the hotel elevator.

"Not tonight," Sasha growled.

Alex raised an eyebrow. "I'm heading up to my room. Which happens to be down the hall from yours."

The seemingly innocuous words made Sasha's mood blacken even more. He slumped against the elevator wall, staring intently at the display.

"Oh, for fuck's sake." Alex's words were exasperated and amused. "Put that damn pout away. So you had a bad game. It happens. The loss wasn't your fault, you know."

"Yes, it was."

Alex scoffed. "You're giving yourself way too much credit. Matty had a bad night. Merkley's line got shut down every time they even looked at the puck, and Minnesota knew exactly how to stop us in our tracks. It happens."

"Shouldn't happen."

The door finally opened, and Sasha stormed out.

"Sasha, wait." Alex jogged a few steps to catch up. "Hey, come on."

Sasha slowed, ostensibly to locate his key card, but he was secretly pleased when Alex stopped beside him and bumped their shoulders together. "Just angry. Need food, sleep, tomorrow will be better."

"Well, food I can do. Come by my room? We can order room service, maybe put a movie on." Alex reached out, resting his fingers on Sasha's arm. "You shouldn't be alone right now; you'll just stew in your thoughts all night."

If he concentrated, Sasha could feel the heat from Alex's touch through his shirt. He shuddered, then ducked his head. "Yeah, okay."

Alex's room was as neat as Sasha would have expected. Housekeeping had made up the bed, but there were clear signs of habitation: a book and phone charger on the nightstand, a six-pack of sports drinks on the desk. Alex's suitcase was laid out on the unused bed, his belongings arranged tidily across the comforter. Sasha's own room looked like a tornado had blown through it, even after only twenty-four hours.

"Grab a seat. I'll call down for dinner. Let me know what you want?"

Sasha passed along his order, then sat uneasily on the desk chair to watch as Alex hung up the phone and tugged at his tie. "Food's gonna be about half an hour. You want some sweats to change into?"

"I'm fine."

"Suit yourself." Alex yanked his tie loose, folded it neatly, and set it on his suitcase. His jacket went directly on a hanger, and then he unbuttoned his dress shirt and shook it out before hanging it up as well.

And then—

"What are you doing?"

That damn eyebrow went up again. "Changing out of my gameday clothes. If we're going to hang out, I'd like to be comfortable." His dexterous fingers undid his belt and rolled it up, before returning to unbutton his slacks.

Sasha tore his gaze away, face heating up. The team undressed in front of one another in the locker room all the time, easily walked around nude—or nearly so. You couldn't really have body shame as a hockey player, but what happened in the locker room was different. This—glimpsing Alex slide his pants off out of the corner of his eye, seeing him in only tight boxer briefs and miles of smooth, pale skin, just the two of them in a hotel room—this felt different. Intimate.

Alex sounded amused when he spoke again. "You can look now."

He was wearing sweats and a tank top, showing off his arms and muscled shoulders. His hair was ruffled, probably from pulling the shirt on, and his eyes looked darker than usual as they met Sasha's.

"I'll put the TV on. Maybe there's a game to watch." Alex sat on the bed—the one he'd slept in last night, Sasha noted, hoping his face wasn't as red as it felt—and grabbed the remote. "Dude, you can't see the TV from over there. C'mere." He patted the bed beside him.

Sasha didn't move.

"Sasha." Alex's eyes darkened even further. "You coming?"

The question was innocent enough, but it made Sasha's mouth go dry. He nodded once, stood slowly.

"You can take off your shoes and jacket, you know. Relax."

Sasha did as he was told, toeing off his shoes and hanging his jacket on the back of the chair. He unbuttoned the cuffs of his shirt, rolled them up to his forearms, then froze and eyed the bed.

Alex waited patiently, watching Sasha with an unreadable look.

Swallowing around the dryness in his throat, Sasha took a step forward and climbed onto the bed.

"Cool." Alex sounded happy. "Let's see what's on."

He flipped channels, pausing sometimes to watch for a minute or check a sports score before moving on. Sasha sat beside him, stiff and unmoving. He could feel Alex only inches away, arms sometimes brushing together as Alex shifted or laughed at something on the TV.

The sound of a hockey game caught Sasha's attention, and he looked up in time to see a flash of teal-and-white jerseys.

"Wait."

Alex froze in the process of changing the channel. "Sasha, I don't think—"

Sasha shook his head. "Just wait."

The sports channel currently on TV was recapping that night's game, the two announcers going over the highlights. "Petrov was out of position here, moving up from the blue line to play the puck, which resulted in the odd-man rush that made the score 4-0 Minnesota."

It was only one of many mistakes he'd made that night.

The TV clicked off, silence falling on the room.

"Sasha," Alex said softly.

Sasha stared at the black television screen, unblinking.

Alex repeated his name. "Hey, it was a good play on your part. You were trying to help Leduc out. It's not your fault that Minnesota's D got there first."

Sasha closed his eyes, miserable. Alex could be as nice as he wanted, but that didn't change the result of the game.

"You know," Alex said softly, "you're only one person on this team. One piece in the puzzle. Even if you have a bad night, there are five other defensemen and twelve forwards on the ice as well. One guy has a bad night, it's up to the rest of the team to help fill in for him. The entire team has a bad night? Well… you get a game like this one. This was a team loss, Sasha."

"Still feels like shit," Sasha mumbled.

Alex moved closer, eliminating the remaining distance between them so Sasha could feel the heat from his body all down his side. "Yeah, and it's gonna sting for a while. But tomorrow we play Chicago. You just have to let it go and move on."

A gentle hand cupped Sasha's cheek. He opened his eyes as Alex turned his head so he could meet those beautiful brown eyes straight-on.

"Tomorrow's a new day," Alex said quietly. "Fresh scoreboard, fresh ice."

In the low light of the hotel room, Alex looked like something straight out of a dream. His hair was soft, falling down in front of his eyes, which were bright and full of tenderness. He looked younger in the lamplight, flawless in a way that Sasha couldn't tear his eyes away from.

There was something else in his gaze too, that Sasha was terrified to put a name to. But it drew him in, making Sasha's heart beat in his chest like it was trying to escape.

"Sasha." Alex's voice was barely a whisper, and his palm was warm against Sasha's jaw, his skin smooth and white except where it was flushing a pale pink along the top of his cheeks.

God, he's beautiful. Sasha had battled temptation and want constantly for the last few weeks. He'd looked, sure, but he hadn't given in to the desire that coursed through him every time he was near Alex.

But now Sasha found the last of his resolve crumbling. Alex was so close that he could see every eyelash, could track the way Alex's tongue darted out to wet his lips. Sasha could hear the hitch in his breath and feel the heat from Alex's body.

So he did the only thing he could do. He leaned forward and kissed Alex.

Alex responded immediately, eyes fluttering shut, a tiny *oh* escaping his lips before Sasha covered them with his own once again.

Sasha had weeks of longing built up, and he poured every ounce of it into the kiss. He pushed forward, and Alex fell backward easily, dragging Sasha with him until they were more horizontal, Alex stretched across the bed with Sasha hovering over him, pressing their lips together over and over until they were tingling.

Alex was moaning, little sounds of want that lit a fire beneath the surface of Sasha's skin.

And Alex's body beneath his was everything he could ever have imagined. He fit against Sasha perfectly, cradled between Sasha's arms, a line of warmth pressed against Sasha's chest. At some point Alex's hand had migrated from Sasha's cheek to his hair, and now his fingers were tangled up in the short strands, pulling Sasha closer, refusing to allow any space between them as he returned Sasha's kisses with an equal amount of desperation and desire.

Yes.

Sasha kissed him until his lungs were burning and his lips were numb, and even then he couldn't find the strength to pull away.

And then a knock on the door echoed through the room.

It yanked Sasha back to reality with all the force of an atomic bomb. He pulled away quickly, chest heaving and horror rising where lust and want had previously been.

His skin felt hot, prickly. In front of him, Alex was flushed like he'd just been exercising, eyes so dark they were almost black. He licked his lips, the movement apparently unconscious, and Sasha tracked the flash of pale tongue hungrily.

The knock on the door came again.

"Fuck. Oh fuck." Sasha yanked himself away as he realized what he'd done. Shame crashed over him, and humiliation as well, because even though Alex had responded, had kissed him back, Sasha knew that what he'd done was wrong.

Alex didn't move, still sprawled out across the bed.

God, I let him comfort me, and then I took advantage of him being a good friend. Sasha felt sick to his stomach. "I should—I need to go. Now."

That spurred Alex into action. "Wait, please." He hurried to sit up as Sasha threw himself from the bed. "Sasha, don't leave yet. We need to talk."

Sasha shook his head. He could imagine what Alex needed to say, and that was painful enough. Hearing him say the words—*You're my friend, but that's all we can be*—would slice him to shreds.

Sasha shoved his feet into his shoes and grabbing his jacket. "Nothing to say. I'm sorry. I'm—" He paused, hand on the door handle. "I should not have done that. Alex, you—you have a girlfriend, and I took advantage. I'm sorry."

Alex opened his mouth to respond, but Sasha didn't want to hear it. He yanked the door open, brushed past the startled and confused room service delivery person and the cart of food, and fled down the hall.

eenie-minni-hockey-mo:
my friend is a huge cascades fan (why becka?? you live in st. paul, not seattle!) so we decided to head down to the hotel the players were staying at after the game, even though it's cold as balls out here, because she wanted to try and meet some players. obvi all the guys were really bummed but like sjoberg and engel stopped to sign her jersey and makela took a selfie with both of us! nice guys, even if I'm glad my boys beat them tonight. (sorry scades fans.)

anyways, we're about to call it a night and go somewhere warm, when suddenly petrov comes tearing out of the hotel. no jacket, still in his gameday suit, lookin like he'd just gotten some really bad news. might just be the bad loss, but hoping everything's okay with him?

#hockey #cascades #minneapolis #alexander petrov #still can't feel my toes #the things I do for my friends
198 notes

ALEX TOOK a deep breath, let it out. He texted Shawn and told him to come by.

And then he fell back against his pillows, closed his eyes, and evaluated the last few minutes.

Sasha had kissed him. *Sasha* had kissed *him*. After weeks of watching and waiting, Alex had started to wonder if Sasha was ever going to say or do anything about the palpable tension that built up whenever they were in the same room.

But he had. Sure, Alex had been flirting with him. He could have moved his suitcase off the other double bed and given Sasha his own space, but he'd seen the dark red flush on Sasha's cheeks and neck when he'd gone to change out of his suit, and he'd been... curious.

That curiosity had paid off so beautifully too. The heat in Sasha's eyes and the way he'd kissed Alex like a starving man discovering a buffet, had been everything Alex had dreamed about.

Of course, then Sasha had remembered his chivalry or whatever, and fled.

I kissed him back. Did he even notice? I was 1000 percent on board with everything he was doing, and he still thought he was taking advantage. Alex cursed under his breath, tempted to throw the remote across the room. *I should have just told him about Heather weeks ago.*

This time the knock at the door was a welcome one. Alex rolled off the bed and opened it, moving aside to let Shawn in.

Shawn immediately spotted the tray of food, which Alex had already managed to forget about. "You ordered me dinner? Nice, thanks, bro."

"Not... quite." Alex winced. "It's Sasha's. Or, I guess, it was his. You can have it, though."

Shawn's eyebrows disappeared behind his bangs. "Um."

"Sit down," Alex said. "It's a long story."

They were both athletes, which meant they could eat a full meal even in the middle of an emotional crisis. Shawn steadily devoured the salmon he'd claimed, eyes glued to Alex as he explained what had happened from the moment they got to the hotel until Sasha had stormed out of the room and vanished.

"Dude."

"Yeah, I know."

Shawn chewed thoughtfully. "You just need to find him and tell him Heather isn't your girlfriend."

"I tried calling him. He sent me to voicemail. And it's not exactly something to explain over text, you know?"

"I guess." Shawn shook his head. "The two of you are an equal emotional mess. Maybe you deserve each other after all."

He knew Shawn was joking, but the words sat heavily in Alex's chest. *Maybe we're made for each other.* The way he felt about Sasha, how quickly he'd started to fall for the other man—*And he feels the same way. Now I know he does.*

"I just hope I can get him to listen," Alex said.

Chapter Eighteen

The Seattle Cascades may have one of the most difficult schedules going into March, but that's not going to stop them from dominating on the ice. The loss of goaltender Eduard Despres made playoffs look unlikely as the Cascades started their late push toward the end of the season, but the team has held on against all odds. After a devastating loss to Minnesota on Monday, they went on to win handily over Chicago the next day with rookie Alex Fanning in net, and managed to keep the game tied against St. Louis through 65 minutes of play on Thursday before falling in the shoot-out. Now they're home briefly before heading to Colorado, Arizona, and California for yet another road trip, where we expect them to continue to rack up points on their way to the playoffs.
—Mark Lund, contributing writer, NHL.com

ALEX HAD planned to talk to Sasha the next day before their game against Chicago, but that plan fell through in about five minutes flat the next morning, when he walked into the dining room at the hotel to find Sasha already seated at a full table, refusing to look at him.

In fact, Sasha did everything in his power to put distance—or, failing that, other teammates—between himself and Alex at every opportunity over the rest of the road trip. He sat next to Misha on the flight to St. Louis, shared a row with Mo on the bus, and spent every free second of practice working with the defense coaches or in the gym with his headphones on.

Try as Alex might, there was no chance to catch him alone. Road trips were great for team bonding, but they also meant there was very little privacy or opportunities for a one-on-one. Even if Sasha hadn't been pretending like he didn't exist, there wouldn't have been much chance for Alex to corner him and beg for a chance to explain.

"What if I walk across the locker room after the game, push him against the wall, and kiss him senseless until he finally lets me talk?"

Shawn, who was sprawled across Alex's spare bed while playing a game on his phone, just laughed. "I think you'd give the guys a nice show. But there's got to be a better way to make Sasha listen to you."

"He's being stubborn."

His friend started laughing so hard that he had to pause the game. "Wait, *he's* being stubborn? God, Phantom, it's like the vampire myth is real after all and you can't see yourself in a mirror."

Alex scowled. "I'm not stubborn."

"Sure," Shawn said.

Okay, Alex realized as they were flying back to Seattle. Maybe he was a little stubborn. But Sasha was way worse.

The locker room kissing thing is starting to sound better and better.

Seattle Cascades (@CascadesNHL)
Have you bought your tickets for #ScadesAndSkates yet? Our annual charity night will be held on March 11! Get dressed up and come on down to meet your favorite players for a night you won't forget. Benefiting the Seattle Children's Hospital. https://t.co/tpoM6TRNsu

MEETINGS BEFORE practice were fairly common. Meetings involving Alyssa from PR before practice, however, were not.

Sasha sat in his stall and tried to duck out of her line of sight while she did her best to get the attention of twenty-something rowdy men.

"Hey, shut up," Merks yelled, "or I'll have you all skating lines for the first part of practice."

That made everyone quiet down, at least. Alyssa folded her arms and gazed evenly around the room until everyone was settled.

"All right. As you would know if you read your emails, 'Scades and Skates is coming up in two weeks. You are all required to be there. You are all required to be in formal dress. That does *not*," Alyssa emphasized, giving Mo a dirty look, "mean nice jeans and a button-down shirt."

Morgan looked away guiltily, and the rest of the team snickered. No one could forget the look on Alyssa's face after last year when Mo had shown up late and dressed comfortably casual.

Alyssa cleared her throat and continued. "You all get a plus-one. Bring a date. If you don't have a date, let me know and I'll note you down for the Bachelor's Auction."

Sasha glanced around the room and was amused to note how many guys suddenly looked very, very nervous. The auction was harmless; local socialites bid their money for the Cascades' charity, and winners got to spend the rest of the evening with a player on their arm. Usually it was the younger guys who got suckered into it, the ones who didn't have significant others and who didn't mind having a couple of drinks with an attractive—and wealthy—woman.

"I'll keep reminding you over the next two weeks," Alyssa finished. "If you forget, I'm putting you on bench interviews with that one guy from the NHL Network for the rest of the season. Got it?"

With that final threat, Alyssa smiled and left the room.

Conversation sprung up in her wake. "Damn, she's terrifying," Rager proclaimed.

Sasha winced. Braiden usually didn't realize how loud he was and how well sound carried. There was little chance that Alyssa hadn't heard that one.

"She has to be terrifying," Oettenger joked. "She's got two dozen idiots to wrangle. I wouldn't do her job for all the money in the world."

Carts laughed. "You wear an A, Otter..., pretty sure that makes you a professional Idiot Wrangler by definition."

The rest of the guys started pulling on gear, getting ready for practice. Sasha grabbed his chest and shoulder pads, half listening to the chatter around him. He had a friend who he called on for events like this, the sister of one of his teammates from back in Russia who was studying medicine in Seattle, who would come with him to team-mandated events like 'Scades & Skates. It got her out of studying for a night and got him out of being on the auction block.

"You gonna bring Heather, then?" he heard Carts ask.

Sasha tugged a jersey over his head, then peered over to see Shawn and Alex talking a few feet away.

"I guess." Alex glanced to the side, then found Sasha's eyes and didn't look away. "I mean, it's not like I have anyone else to take, right?"

He held Sasha's gaze for another few seconds, brown eyes intense, before turning back to Shawn.

"What about you? Didn't you break up with that girl you were seeing months ago?"

The two of them moved off, heading to the ice to start practice, but Sasha was frozen in place.

What the hell was that?

IF SASHA had made it difficult for Alex to approach him over the last few days, he made it practically impossible over the next week and a half.

The team had a hectic schedule, with a brief few days at home to play Winnipeg before heading back out on the road again, heading south to Colorado and Arizona before looping back up to hit Anaheim and Vegas. It was a warm-weather, sun-drenched trip that Alex wasn't especially excited about. His bad mood about four away games—and no chances to start—was only augmented by the way Sasha cleverly avoided any contact him with over that time period.

"I know it's technically illegal to knock him out, tie him to a chair, and force him to talk to me," Alex said while they were in Vegas. The team was banned from going out to the Strip, which meant he and Shawn were holed up in a hotel room, playing video games on the system Shawn had brought in his suitcase. "But I feel like a judge wouldn't actually blame me if I explained why I had to."

Shawn snorted, jamming a few buttons on his controller. "You gotta tell him before 'Scades and Skates. He's gonna see you there with Heather if you don't."

Bringing Heather to the charity event had seemed like a no-brainer when Alex had first proposed it. It was great publicity for her, a chance to meet and mingle with some of the city's elite, while also showing off Alex's "girlfriend" to all of his teammates and the Cascades media.

Except now Heather's planned appearance was causing more and more strain between him and Sasha.

"I would tell him if he'd just acknowledge my existence for ten seconds." Alex cursed as his character on the screen took fire and he had to quickly maneuver to safety. "I tried knocking on his hotel room door last night, and he wouldn't even answer. I know he was in there, though—I could smell him."

"It's kinda creepy that you can do that," Shawn admitted, though he didn't actually sound disturbed.

Alex whacked him with an elbow. "Trust me, it's way creepier for me. Especially when I have to walk by your bedroom."

Shawn squawked in outrage, then muscled Alex out of the way so Shawn could attack his player on the screen. "Uncool, bro. Anyways, there's gotta be some way to make him hear you out."

"If there is, I haven't thought of it yet."

"Well, if worse comes to worse, you can trade me tables at 'Scades and Skates and talk to him there."

Alex threw his controller across the bed in disgust as his character died. "It's assigned seating. Alyssa said so, and I'm not gonna risk her wrath by sneaking over to your table halfway through dinner."

The game switched back to the menu screen, and Shawn set his controller down to grab a bottle of water and stretch out his back. "So let's just tell Alyssa we want to switch. I sit with Sasha at every one of these events. I bet she won't mind switching things up."

It was a tempting idea. If Sasha wouldn't give Alex a chance to talk to him, or even be near him, then 'Scades & Skates was a guaranteed opportunity to be feet apart for a full hour. Maybe Alex wouldn't have a chance to actually talk to his idiot crush at the dinner, but he could corner him after for sure.

"All right, Carts," he said. "Let's go with your plan. But you've gotta ask Alyssa… I don't want her to get mad at me when I've only been here for two months."

Chapter Nineteen

Seattle Cascades (@CascadesNHL)
#ScadesAndSkates is here! Our annual charity event gives you a chance to enjoy dinner, drinks, and some casino-style card games with all of your favorite players. And for the third year in a row, 'Scades & Skates is SOLD OUT!

Emma (@Cascadiac)
damn, wish I had $300 to spare. all the guys are postin pics of themselves in their suits, looking super hot!

"Hey, smile."

Valentina subtly elbowed him, and Sasha pasted on a thin smile as a photographer came up to take their picture. He recognized the guy as being from one of the local newspapers and quickly ducked away with Valentina on his arm before any questions could be thrown his way.

"You know, you could at least pretend to be enjoying yourself," Valentina said in Russian as she snagged two glasses of champagne from a passing server. "When you asked me to come along with you to this event, I assumed it was an invitation to a party, not a funeral."

Sasha accepted the flute that she passed him and took a long sip. "I just don't enjoy these kinds of events."

'Scades & Skates happened every year in March, and every year he dreaded it. It wasn't the dressing up that bothered him or even the fans—most of whom were polite, clearly thrilled to be there, and respectful of obvious boundaries. No, it was the fact that every year his teammates came with their wives and girlfriends, and he had no one.

Well, he had Valentina, but she was a friend and nothing more. Sasha's teammates knew she was a medical student and a family friend, but they'd long ago moved on from teasing him about his gorgeous, supermodel-like doctor "friend" when he'd failed to rise to their baiting.

"Come on, let's go find our table." Valentina took his arm and guided him through clumps of people toward the cloth-draped tables in the back of the room. The food was one of the bright spots of the night, at least—an elegant three-course meal. Each table would host two players, their dates, and a handful of fans. Sasha was always paired with either Ed or Carts at these types of events, but with Ed still on Injured Reserve it looked like it was going to be the two D-men tonight.

"Hey, Sasha!" And speak of the devil.... Carts threw an arm over his shoulder, grinning as a blinding flashbulb went off from a few feet away.

Sasha forced another smile and turned to his friend. "Shawn. You've met Valentina, of course."

Valentina smiled politely and brushed a kiss on his cheek in greeting. "It's good to see you again," she said in English. "And where's your date?"

Shawn shrugged. "I'm a single man tonight. On the auction block. You guys want to donate a couple grand to the Cascades Foundation and bid on me?"

"Not a chance." Finally Sasha's smile felt genuine. "But I am going to record the entire thing for Instagram."

"Rude!" But Shawn laughed. "I'm starving. Let's find our seats."

Valentina spotted their table first, pointing it out to Sasha who followed her. He glanced over, expecting to see Shawn beside him, but missed a step when he realized that Shawn was across the room, sitting down at a table with Mäkelä and his wife.

What the— Sasha glanced around, confused. *Who am I seated with, then?*

The answer came a second later when they finally reached their table.

"Hey, Sasha."

No.

But there were the nameplates, *Alexander Petrov* and *Valentina Maximova* spelled out in delicate script. And there, in the seats across from theirs, was a gorgeous, smiling blonde, and....

"Alex." Sasha swallowed hard. "You're at our table tonight?"

"Looks like." Alex stood, offering his hand to Valentina. "Alexander Fanning. It's lovely to meet you. You must be Sasha's friend who we've heard so much about."

Valentina was polite, all smiles and poise, but she picked up on the tension immediately.

"And this," Alex continued, "is Heather Bell, my date for the evening."

Sasha couldn't even pretend to smile. He shook Heather's hand briefly, pulling his hand away as soon as he could do so without it being rude. She didn't seem offended, though; in fact, she seemed to be trying not to laugh at him.

They took their seats, waiting for the rest of their table to arrive. With nothing else to do, Sasha had a chance to study the couple before him.

Alex's girlfriend was beautiful, Sasha had to admit. She was even more stunning in real life than she was in the magazines or television shows that he'd seen her in. They looked good together, both of them young and attractive, her light hair contrasting with his dark as she leaned over to whisper something in his ear, which he laughed at.

Valentina elbowed him again, this time far less subtly. "Что с тобой не так?"

"Ow, careful." Sasha scowled. "Nothing's wrong."

She leveled him a look that said she didn't believe him.

CascadesTV: What's your favorite part of the evening been so far?

Emily Cole, Cascades Fan: I came here hoping to meet Merkley, because he's my favorite player on the team. But the seat selections were random, and I ended up sitting next to Alex [Fanning], the new goalie? And he was honestly so nice, attentive and funny and polite. His girlfriend is really lovely too. Sasha [Petrov] was across the table from us so I didn't get to talk to him as much, but Alex was just really charming. (Laughs) I think I might have a new favorite player now!

ALEX DRAINED his third glass of champagne and set the empty flute aside. He loved the taste of a good champagne, but any more would leave him feeling miserable the next morning.

Dinner had been fantastic. Shawn had told him a little about the event over the last week, so Alex had known what to expect. Several fans had joined them at their table, and Alex had alternated between eating his steak and answering whatever questions they had for him.

At least Shawn had agreed to trade tables with him, so Alex could sneak glances at Sasha throughout the meal. Sasha, to no one's surprise, had managed to avoid looking at Alex as much as possible. Heather had been shaking with laughter by the end of the third course, clearly picking up on some very loud emotions from them both.

But now dinner was over, and Heather had escaped to talk with some people who she recognized. Alex scanned the room idly. Most of the fans had gravitated to the more popular players: Merkley was dealing cards at a full table across the room, with a dozen observers circling around as well. Oettenger and Mäkelä were in the middle of an interview with Cascades TV, and Alyssa was hovering nearby. Even Shawn was occupied, talking to a mixed group of fans, everyone laughing easily.

But there was one man in particular he was keeping an eye out for. He spotted Valentina, towering over everyone around her in her sky-high heels. If Shawn hadn't explained about the arrangement they had, and assured Alex that she was only a good friend, he might have felt a twinge of jealousy.

Instead, her appearance only made him more eager to talk to Sasha as soon as possible.

Only... the man in question was nowhere to be found.

"Hey." Alex caught Sjöberg's arm as he passed by. "You seen Petrov anywhere?"

The Swedish defenseman shrugged. "Last I saw he was heading toward the back to get some air."

"Awesome, thanks."

It was as good a place to start as any, Alex reasoned. He circled around the outside of the room, ducking his head to avoid being spotted—by fans or Alyssa, either of whom would be more than happy to prevent his escape—until he found a hallway leading toward the back of the venue.

As soon as he stepped down the corridor, he knew he was going the right way. Sasha's scent, always on the edge of Alex's awareness these days, was much more noticeable here. Alex followed it, smiling politely at a few surprised caterers, until the rich, earthy scent was as strong as if Sasha was standing right beside him.

There was no Sasha, but there *was* a door. Alex tried it, found it unlocked, and slipped inside. A familiar form sat hunched over on a chair, facing away from him.

"You know, Alyssa will skin you alive if she finds you skipping out on media obligations back here."

Sasha went from relaxed to tense so quickly that Alex worried he might pull something.

"I'm just taking a break." Sasha's words were barely audible, and he didn't turn around. "Tell her I'll be back out in a minute."

"Or," Alex said, locking the door behind him and stepping farther into the room, "we can take that minute to talk."

Sasha, somehow, went even tenser.

The room was full of extra tables and chairs, some stacked against the walls and others sitting out and ready for use if needed. Alex wove around the furniture, each step taking him closer to the room's other occupant.

"Okay, then, you don't have to say anything. I'll talk, and you can listen, okay?"

He slid around one last table, then came to a stop directly in front of Sasha. With only a few feet between them, the scent was almost overpowering. Alex took a deep breath, held it, then exhaled.

"First of all, your kissing technique could use some work."

Sasha's eyes jerked to Alex's face, surprised. Clearly, that wasn't what he'd expected to hear.

"The thing is," Alex continued, "it was really great right up until you stopped and ran away. So, you know, A-plus for the initial execution, but a solid F for the conclusion."

Sasha's mouth opened, then closed.

"I debated for a long time about saying anything to you. I was pretty sure you had feelings—that you returned *my* feelings—but I wasn't positive. Until I knew for sure, I couldn't risk being wrong."

There was a hint of something in Sasha's stunning blue eyes. It looked like hope, but there was still a healthy amount of fear and confusion too. Alex wanted nothing more than to see the latter disappear.

"When you kissed me, I had all the confirmation I needed. And *damn*, Sasha, that kiss. You have no idea how long I've been thinking about that."

Sasha cleared his throat. "But…."

Alex smiled. "Heather. Yeah, I'm getting there. Shawn told me right from the start that the Cascades locker room is a good one. That people are pretty tolerant and understanding. But this is the NHL, and it's hard enough being a rookie goalie. Being a *gay* rookie goalie? It was terrifying to even contemplate."

Being a gay Para *rookie goalie,* he mentally corrected. But that was another matter entirely.

"You're—" Sasha was leaning forward now, eyes wide.

"Gay, yeah." Alex shrugged. "Heather is just a good friend."

"Oh."

Alex rocked back on his feet, tucking his hands into his pockets and waiting. Sasha appeared to be processing what Alex had told him, and he looked like he was going to need a minute.

"So," Sasha began, then stopped.

Alex laughed. "So, what I'm saying is, if you want to try that kissing thing again…."

Now it was his turn not to finish a sentence, because Sasha was on his feet and closing the space between them in the blink of an eye. One second he was sitting; the next he was inches from Alex, pressing against his front and walking him backward until Alex hit the wall.

Yes, Alex thought as Sasha eliminated any remaining distance between them and kissed him.

Sasha kissed like he played—skilled, confident, and a little vicious. He covered Alex's body until his front was nothing but heat and his back was flat against the cool wall, nipped at Alex's bottom lip hard enough to sting before running his tongue over the spot in apology.

"You know," Alex said, panting around the words as Sasha's mouth moved down to his jaw, his neck, "I've been kinda crazy about you since the moment we met. Even when I thought you hated me."

Sasha pulled away. His pupils were blown, the blue only a thin circle around the outside. "What? You hated me from the start, were so cold to me before we were even introduced."

"Huh?" Alex blinked.

"Never mind." Sasha shook his head. "More important things now. Stop talking."

"Sasha," Alex said, but was cut off by Sasha's mouth covering his own again.

Then Sasha's lips were gone, and the rest of Sasha, because he was—

"Oh fuck."

Sasha looked up at him from where he'd dropped to his knees, a wicked grin crossing his face. "Been thinking about this for a long time."

Alex was glad there was a wall behind him, because he wasn't sure his legs could completely support him anymore. Sasha's fingers brushed down his stomach, hovered over his waistband for a second before easily undoing Alex's belt.

"You teased me that night in the hotel room." Apparently Sasha was a talker.

Alex groaned, let his head fall back to thump against the wall as the lightly accented words washed over him.

"When you got undressed in front of me. Я так хочу тебя, tried not to look."

"I wanted you to look," Alex gasped.

Sasha flicked open the button of his pants, tugged the zipper down so slowly that Alex could feel every click of the teeth.

"Looking now," Sasha said.

Alex forced his eyes open and gazed down. Sasha stared back up at him with an intensity that rocked him to his core.

"Please, Sasha." He was hard, aching, and Sasha hadn't even touched him yet, cock straining against his briefs as Sasha inched his slacks down.

Sasha leaned forward, still not breaking eye contact, and pressed his lips to the fabric-covered bulge.

"You locked the door?" Sasha spoke the words against Alex's cock, breath hot even through the cotton.

"Yes," Alex sobbed.

"Good."

Then Sasha's fingers slipped beneath the waistband of Alex's briefs and slid them down, torturously slow, until Alex's cock was exposed to the air and he was trembling with need.

The first brush of Sasha's lips to his cock was almost too much. Alex inhaled sharply, clawing his fingers into the wall to try to find something to hold on to.

Sasha huffed out a laugh, hot and wet against Alex's cock. "Here." His voice was already rough with want, and he took Alex's hand and moved it to his own hair, eyes fluttering shut when Alex dug his fingers into the short strands. "Yeah, like that."

And then he closed the distance between them, wrapping his lips around Alex's dick and sucking hard.

"Holy fuck, Sasha." Alex's hips moved forward on their own, and only Sasha's quick reaction stopped him from choking as he slid one arm across

Alex's hips and pinned him to the wall. The other hand wrapped around the base of Alex's dick, his mouth sliding down to meet the fingers.

Alex spared a moment to wish that he'd sat down in one of the chairs, because his knees were going weak and the wall wasn't going to be enough to keep him upright for much longer.

Not that he was going to last much longer, he thought, and then his mind went blissfully blank, pleasure flooding through him as Sasha bobbed his head and sucked harder. He was aware that he was tugging Sasha's hair and tried to loosen his fingers.

"Sasha, Sasha, please, more." His own voice sounded alien to his ears, high and desperate, the words interspersed with moans.

Sasha gave him more. He swallowed Alex down until his nose pressed against Alex's pubic hair, holding himself there while Alex choked out a garbled curse, before moving back to catch his breath. At some point Alex had closed his eyes, and he forced them open again to see Sasha pulling back to suck on the head of his dick, watching Alex through his lashes.

The sight before him stole his breath away: Sasha, on his knees, lips swollen and red, skin flushed all the way down his neck to disappear into his shirt. Alex's hand moved without conscious thought, brushing down from Sasha's hair to his jaw, thumb tracing along Sasha's lips where they were gently sucking Alex's length. A hint of tongue darted out to meet him, and Alex groaned.

Then Sasha's mouth was gone, and his hand was back, jacking Alex slowly while he licked his lips for real. Alex made a noise that he'd deny later, a high-pitched whine.

"I'm a hockey player," Sasha said. "You can pull my hair harder, you know. I don't mind a little pain."

Oh fuck.

"Also," Sasha said, and his voice was hoarse—*because he was just swallowing my dick, oh my god*—"you can come in my mouth."

Alex almost came right then and there from the words alone. "Sasha, god, you're going to be the death of me."

Sasha's grin was filthy.

And then both of Sasha's hands were pinning Alex's hips to the wall, and his mouth was on Alex's cock again. He went down, down until Alex's cock bumped the back of his throat, swallowing around the length.

Alex stared down at him, arrested by the sight. Sasha's lips were stretched wide around him, and his blue eyes were almost completely hidden by his pupils as he stared up at Alex. It was filthy and gorgeous, and Alex couldn't do anything but moan and chant his name, twisting his fingers in Sasha's hair and pulling hard.

Sasha groaned, eyes falling closed with his own obvious pleasure.

Heat started to build, flames licking up Alex's spine. "Sasha, Sasha, please," he managed. Everything was wet heat and perfect pressure, and the scent of sex and *Sasha* rising between them, filling the air until Alex felt it coating his lungs and his tongue.

And then the fire overtook him, magnesium-white passion racing through his body. Alex's back arched off the wall, eyes falling shut, and he was distantly aware that he was moaning—*too loud, too loud, someone's going to hear*—but he couldn't help himself.

Sasha moved his head back, just enough to catch Alex's release as he came, swallowing it down neatly.

Alex slumped back against the wall, sated and worn-out, and was embarrassed to feel his fangs starting to descend. He pressed his lips closed as he sank to the floor, letting Sasha catch him, and tried to wrangle control back over his own body.

Emma (@Cascadiac)

Following the #ScadesAndSkates tag obsessively. Wilson, Thompson, and Cartier just got auctioned off… for charity! Haven't seen any pics of Fanning lately, but his girlfriend is in a few and she's so gorgeous.

Mrs. Merkley… a girl can dream! (@MerkleyFan96)

@Cascadiac: I'm here! I don't see Fanning anywhere right now, but if I find him, I'll try to get a pic.

Emma (@Cascadiac)

@MerkleyFan96: bless you. Also I'm so jealous that you got to go!

SASHA WRAPPED an arm around Alex's waist, catching him as he fell back against the wall and eased him down to the floor.

It was pretty obvious that they wouldn't be going back to the event anytime soon. Alex looked completely fucked out, hair a mess and eyes heavy with contentment. Sasha leaned forward to kiss him, but Alex kept his mouth closed as he returned it gently.

Some men didn't like the taste of cum when they kissed. Sasha moved to press his lips to Alex's neck and collarbone instead, and Alex tilted his head back lazily to allow him.

"You okay, солнышко?"

Alex hummed, smiling sleepily.

Sasha was still hard, but it felt almost insignificant. Right now he was cradling Alex to his chest, feeling his heart beat beneath his lips, and that seemed far more important.

"Gimme a minute," Alex whispered, "and I'll return the favor."

This time when Sasha leaned up to kiss him, Alex returned it eagerly.

"It's fine. We should head back soon."

"Then after the party ends." Alex was apparently finding his second wave of energy, gradually perking back up. "Come home with me tonight."

Sasha kissed him again, then pulled away reluctantly. "You have a roommate."

"So do you," Alex pointed out. "But seeing as how mine has been betting on us to fuck since January, I think he can find somewhere else to sleep tonight."

Sasha felt a moment of panic at that revelation, but Alex seemed so calm about it. Plus, he trusted Carts and knew his D partner wouldn't do anything to hurt either of them. "He was betting?"

"Apparently."

Sasha laughed softly. "In that case…."

Alex grinned. "Exactly." The grin faded, and he leaned forward for one last kiss. "But you're right. We should get back before anyone notices we're gone."

Between the two of them, they managed to get Alex from "clearly well fucked" to "only a little rumpled" in a few minutes.

Sasha stopped him at the door, before Alex could leave the room. Alex stared up at him, eyes heated.

"Thank you." Sasha bent down to kiss Alex quickly.

Alex had no interest in *quickly*, though. He went up on his toes, deepening the kiss, one arm wrapped around Sasha's neck. "Pretty sure

I should be the one thanking you," he said, pulling back only an inch to speak the words against Sasha's lips.

Sasha smiled. "Maybe I'm thanking you for later tonight."

"Oh, in that case…," Alex said and kissed him again. "I'll get out of here as soon as I can. See you soon?"

"Not soon enough."

With one last check to make sure they both looked okay, they left the room. Sasha gave him a once-over before they got back to the party, heavy with promise, and Alex returned it with a grin before vanishing to find Shawn.

Soon, Sasha told himself. He'd have Alex back in his arms soon.

Chapter Twenty

Alex got his first hint that something was wrong two days later.

Heather had given Alex a mock-scandalous look when he'd emerged from the back hallways with Sasha in tow, then winked and made excuses to leave soon after. But that meant they hadn't had a chance to talk, and he had no doubt that she was going to be eager to hear all about it. *That's what I get for making friends with a succubus.*

So Alex drove out to Heather's condo on Monday evening, parking in the guest spot as he usually did and waving to her doorman as he headed up the elevator.

Heather opened the door before he could even knock.

"God, I could taste you as soon as you got off the elevator." She yanked him inside, looking delighted. "Finally. The unrequited pining was getting a little stale."

Alex laughed. "I guess I don't have to give my we-need-to-end-our-fake-relationship talk, then."

"Mmh, no." She licked her lips. "Shame, I was enjoying our little dinner dates. But I suppose the gossip rags will enjoy talking about our angst-ridden breakup instead."

"I'll be sure to look properly depressed in my next few postgame interviews," Alex confirmed. "But in all seriousness, I'd like to keep the feeding arrangement going. Sasha knows we're friends, and the media will have a field day trying to figure out what's going on."

Heather hesitated. "Are you not—you're not going to feed off your Sasha?"

Alex blushed. "He's not *my* Sasha. We've spent one night together. And he doesn't know about the, y'know." He gestured to his mouth, where his fangs were already peeking out in anticipation of a meal.

"Oh." Heather seemed flustered, but she shook it off quickly. "Of course, then. I'd be happy to." Now the amused grin returned. "Like I said, the pining was getting old, and this happy, sated version is much more appetizing."

After two months, feeding from Heather was an easy routine. She pulled her hair up in a messy bun, flipped the TV off, and pulled her legs up to sit comfortably on the couch. Alex joined her, taking off his jacket and shoes so he'd be comfortable.

And then he leaned in, inhaling Heather's familiar scent of spices.

That was when he first realized something wasn't right; Heather smelled the same, sweet and dark and a little floral, but the smell made Alex want to recoil in distaste.

Strange, her scent has never bothered me before. He exhaled, forcing himself to focus on the vein right beneath the surface of her skin.

Biting into Heather was just like biting into any other meal. When Alex was younger, he'd struggled with the concept of feeding on blood, wishing desperately to be more human, more "normal." But now in his twenties, he'd come to accept that blood was sustenance exactly like any other nutrition his body needed. It helped that Heather tasted delicious, her Para ancestry giving her blood an extra boldness.

But once again, something wasn't right. Alex swallowed, but the blood didn't taste the way it normally did.

No, he realized. *It tastes fine… it's just not filling me up.*

He tried to drink more, but soon Heather was gripping his shoulder and saying his name. "That's enough, Alex."

Alex pulled back, sealing the bite marks as he usually did. He'd drunk his fill—more than, if he was being honest. But he didn't feel satisfied like he normally did. And Heather might be Para, but even she had her limits.

"Sorry," he said.

"It's fine." Heather was watching him, a little concerned. "You okay?"

"Yeah, fine." Alex shrugged.

"If you need more," Heather started to say.

Alex shook his head. "No, I'm fine. I have to get going soon, anyways. We play tomorrow, first in a back-to-back. I was probably busy thinking about that and lost track of how much I was taking."

Heather laughed. "Sure, because the game is what you're thinking about right now."

Alex hadn't been thinking about Sasha, but Heather's grin brought his mind right back to the defenseman and the night they'd shared after 'Scades & Skates.

He could still feel Sasha, if he focused: his mouth around Alex's cock in the back room of the party, and later that night Sasha spread out on Alex's bed, and Alex returning the favor. He hadn't been able to go down as far as Sasha had, but the other man hadn't seemed to mind, if his energetic shouts and moans were anything to go on. It had been a very, very good thing that he'd made Shawn crash elsewhere that night.

"Oh," Heather said, her eyes darkening. "My turn to feed, then."

Alex laughed and let the strangeness from his own feeding slip away. Heather was fine, and so was he. Better than fine, to be honest, because now he had Sasha. Finally.

And tomorrow night he'd get Sasha again, in the privacy of a hotel room.

He couldn't wait.

Seattle Cascades (@CascadesNHL)
You want a rivalry rematch? We'll give you a rivalry rematch. Your Cascades are taking on Vancouver in a home-and-home series. Two games, two teams, two cities, two days. Are you ready? #TealAndWhite https://t.co/xBeehEGuIf

Emma (@Cascadiac)
LET'S GO CASCADES! I have a car, a passport, and tickets for both games. Ready to see my boys destroy Vancouver!

Akseli Mäkelä (@AkseliMakela38)
Hyvää huomenta! Good morning! We are all excited to play Vancouver again, and this time we will emerge victorious! #GoCascades

THE HOME-AND-HOME was going to be one of the biggest matchups of the season, and the Cascades locker room was fired up when Alex walked in on Tuesday afternoon. He returned a few high-fives and fist bumps, rolled his eyes with Shawn over Akseli's god-awful Finnish music, and took his time getting into his base layers.

"Hey."

Alex glanced up from where he was stretching on the floor, to see a pair of smiling blue eyes staring down at him.

"Hey, yourself."

Sasha lowered himself to the ground, stretching his legs out in front of himself. "You're starting tonight?"

Alex shook his head. "Tomorrow. Matty and I did rock-paper-scissors for who would get the home game. He won." Well, Coach Rico had asked them if either had a preference, and Alex had noticed the exhaustion in Hertzog's frame when he'd shaken his head. At thirty-four years old, Matthias wasn't prepared to play as many games as he had this season, and it was showing in his performance. Coach had noticed as well; Alex was getting more and more starts as the end of the season loomed. So he'd offered the home game to his fellow goalie, knowing the screaming crowd would help energize him.

"Tomorrow, then. We'll make up for your first game, get you a shut—"

"Shh!" Alex lunged forward, frantically slapping a hand over Sasha's mouth. "Don't *say* it. You'll jinx us."

Sasha laughed behind his hand, grabbing Alex's wrist to press a quick kiss to his palm before Alex could pull away. A glance around the locker room showed no one was watching. "Weird goalie superstitions?"

Alex scooted back to his spot and resumed stretching. "Um, pretty sure that's an everyone-involved-in-hockey superstition, not just mine. You don't walk over the logo on the locker room floor, you don't mess with someone's stick once it's been taped up, and you *never* say the S-word."

"Superstitious." Sasha sounded fond as he rolled to his feet easily, then bent down to run a hand through Alex's hair. "We drive up to Vancouver tonight after the game, stay in hotel up there. You have superstitions about having someone come by your room the night before a game?"

"I guess you'll have to find out." Alex winked up at Sasha, then held eye contact while he spread his legs and twisted his body into the splits.

Sasha groaned. "Tease."

"Only a tease if I don't follow through," Alex pointed out. "Go get ready. I'll see you on the ice."

Steven in BC (@VanYouBelieveIt)
WHAT THE HELL REFS! ARE YOU BLIND?! That was totally a goal, Bilovsky got screwed on that call.

Seattle Cascades (@CascadesNHL)
A tough 60 minutes, a lot of back and forth scoring, and one very controversial no-goal later…. Cascades win! 5-4 in the first half of our home-and-home with Vancouver.

SASHA COULD get used to this.

He woke up in a hotel in Vancouver with a smaller body pressed against his own, soft, steady breaths on his shoulder, and messy brown hair tickling his chin. In sleep, Alex looked impossibly young. Sasha rolled on his side, throwing a leg over Alex and pulling him closer. The alarm said they still had another half hour before they had to be up.

Besides, Alex's body was cool and he was shivering ever so slightly, and Sasha knew of a very good way to warm him up.

Alex came to slowly, arching like a cat under Sasha's hands. Sasha smiled, caressing Alex's spine and enjoying the feel of smooth, bare skin beneath his fingers, before finding the waistband of his briefs and running one finger along the edge.

"Who's the tease now?" Alex was barely awake, his words mumbled.

They hadn't had time or energy for much the night before, getting into Vancouver after midnight. Both of them had been worn-out from the game, and it had been all they could do to strip off their travel clothes and climb into bed. Sasha had wrapped himself around Alex, tucking the smaller man to his chest, and that was the last thing he remembered.

But now they were both awake, rested, and they had nowhere to be until breakfast.

Alex kissed him first. His breath was sour, but Sasha knew his was as well, and it didn't matter after a second when Alex deepened the kiss and made pretty, breathy sounds against Sasha's lips.

"Good morning," Alex whispered.

This close, Sasha could see the flecks of gold in his eyes, illuminated by the dim light that filtered through the heavy hotel curtains. It made Sasha want to throw the curtains open and watch Alex's skin light up and glow in the sunrise. But that would mean having to leave the bed and leave Alex, and that was an unbearable thought even for a few seconds.

Instead, he pulled Alex closer, kissing him again, his hand on Alex's spine trailing lower to rest at the top of his ass, fingers just dipping inside the waistband of his briefs. When Alex's hips made an abortive thrust forward, Sasha exhaled and kissed him again.

It still wasn't enough, though. He wanted Alex closer.

Sasha pulled Alex on top of him, groaning when Alex slung a leg over his waist to straddle him. His briefs were tented, and he took a second to grind his hips down against Sasha's before ducking to moan into Sasha's mouth.

Sasha licked up into him, framing Alex's thighs with his own hands, enjoying the way they trembled beneath his touch. If he spread his fingers, he could brush the side of Alex's dick with his thumb. He trailed the digit along the hard line of Alex's shaft, teasing through the fabric until he found the head of Alex's dick and could rub the ball of his thumb against the growing wetness there.

"You should get rid of these," he murmured against Alex's lips.

Alex pulled back enough to smile. "Oh, should I?"

But he scrambled to get off of Sasha and rush out of his briefs. Sasha took a moment to appreciate him, strong limbs and the long, pale line of his body. Then Alex was back over him, hands eager to get Sasha's boxers off as well.

When they were both naked, Sasha dragged Alex to him, kissing him hard, biting his bottom lip only to lave his tongue over the swollen flesh in apology after.

Alex's hands were roaming aimlessly, desperation clear as he mapped out the smooth planes of Sasha's skin. Sasha snagged one, and then the other in his larger grasp, fingers wrapped around Alex's wrists. Then he hitched one leg up on Alex's hip and twisted, rolling them until Alex's back was on the bed and his hands were pinned above him.

The sound that came out of Alex should have been illegal—a low, needy moan as Alex arched up off the bed, his entire body taut.

"Sasha," he gasped. "Oh, god, Sasha, please."

"I've got you, Милый." Using his free hand, Sasha caressed Alex's body. He started at Alex's neck, teasing with his blunt nails over the younger man's shoulders and clavicle, stopping to rub a nipple between two fingers. Alex's eyelashes fluttered at that, and he made a high, breathy sound in response. Pressing more firmly earned him a groan, and Alex's eyes fell shut.

Alex's cock pressed against his leg, hot and hard, the tip leaking wetness against Sasha's skin.

Trailing his hand down over Alex's abs, muscles sharply defined as Alex stretched out his entire body beneath the caress and strained for more contact.

Then his fingers were wrapping around Alex's cock, skin like silk hot in his palm. Alex moaned, chanting Sasha's name, hips jerking up into the touch.

Sasha jacked him once, twice, collecting the precum at the tip to help his hand glide more smoothly.

"More, more," Alex pleaded. His biceps were bulging as he tried to pull free from Sasha's grasp. "Let me touch you, Sasha, please."

And there was no way Sasha could resist a request like that one. He loosened his grasp, and Alex's wrist slipped free, immediately falling to Sasha's shoulders, down his chest, and to his own cock.

They groaned in tandem, grips tightening around the other.

"I want you to come," Alex said. "All over me. I want to make you, want you to mark me up."

"Yes," Sasha managed, letting his head fall forward and working his hand over Alex's dick frantically.

Alex's grip vanished for a second, and Sasha followed his hand intently as Alex brought it up to his own mouth... and licked a broad stripe down the center, tongue peeking through between his fingers.

When he grasped Sasha's cock again, his hand slid easily.

"God, you're so big," Alex groaned. "Wish you could fuck me like this, right now. I want you in me."

It was a game day, and Sasha knew there was no way they could risk it, knew it was impossible. But he still closed his eyes briefly, imagining the hot, tight slide into Alex's body, the way the goaltender would stretch around him.

"Fuck, Alex." He was distantly aware that he'd lapsed into Russian, but right now Sasha could barely think, could only feel and react. "I want that. As soon as we get home, I want to feel you, to be inside you."

There was no way Alex could understand him, but he gasped nonetheless. "Yeah, babe. I want to come, want to make you come. Please, Sasha."

Liquid fire raced down Sasha's spine, lighting him up from the inside. He jerked his hand over Alex's shaft, thumbed the head, and twisted his wrist. At the same moment, Alex's own grip tightened around his dick, and his free hand curled over Sasha's hip, cupping his ass and teasing Sasha's hole with one dry fingertip, just enough to light up the nerve endings there.

And then they were both coming, heat spilling between them, over Alex's stomach and Sasha's hand.

Sasha managed to bite back his own shout, bury it against Alex's shoulder as he slumped forward. But Alex was louder, less restrained, and he tilted his head back and moaned Sasha's name as Sasha milked him until he was empty and shaking.

"Holy fuck." Sasha barely kept himself from collapsing onto Alex, only sliding to the side at the last second and falling onto the mattress. "Alex."

"Yeah." Alex turned, languid and sated, and kissed Sasha lazily.

Silence fell between them as they both panted for breath, sweaty and sticky but equally unwilling to untangle from each other. They traded soft, sleepy kisses until Alex yawned and tucked his head against Sasha's chest, breathing in deeply and humming happily under his breath.

"Best wakeup ever," he murmured.

Sasha used his clean hand to run his fingers through Alex's hair. Alex smiled, eyes closing in obvious pleasure.

"Я обожаю твою улыбку," Sasha whispered. He pressed a kiss to the corner of Alex's mouth, right where his lips curved up.

"What's that mean?"

Sasha kissed him again, this time on the other side of his mouth. "Means I love when you smile like this. When you look so happy."

Brown eyes flickered open, and the smile deepened.

Sasha allowed his eyes to close as well. Like this, entwined with Alex as he was, he could almost feel the other man's contentment and sleepy, happy pleasure.

I could get used to this, he thought, and let himself doze until the alarm went off.

Chapter Twenty-One

west-coast-best-coast-hockey:
bilovsky looked pissed after his goal got overturned in review last night. bets on if he starts some shit tonight?
#hockey #cascades #there's gonna be a fight #i'd put money on it
24 notes

A<small>LEX SPRAYED</small> water into his mouth, then flipped his helmet back down and shrugged some of the tension out of his shoulders.

"You good?" Sasha skated up to him, tapping his stick on Alex's shins. There had been a volley of shots on goal, and Alex was still panting from the exertion of blocking them before he'd finally been able to glove the puck and force a stoppage of play.

"Yeah, all good."

Sasha grinned, tapped him again, and skated off to take his place for the face-off.

The game so far had been a blast, the kind of intense rivalry match that reminded Alex of why he loved to play hockey. Vancouver was playing great, but Seattle was playing even better, all of the lines gelling together.

It was 5-2, and Alex just needed to hold his end down for the next nine minutes to help bring his team another win.

The refs signaled for the face-off, and Alex hunched down, ready. He noticed Sasha out of the corner of his eye, moving out of position, but the whistle blew before he could spare a second to glance over.

Vancouver won the face-off, passed the puck back to one of the defensemen, and then—

The whistle blew again.

What?

The crowd in Vancouver was on their feet, screaming and banging on the glass. Alex turned and immediately spotted the problem: a Cascades player tangled up with one of the Vancouver wingers, gloves off and punches flying.

Not just any Cascades player. That was Sasha, throwing fists with everything he had. And the Vancouver winger? *Bilovsky. Go figure.*

Alex sighed and relaxed, watching the fight and the surrounding chaos as his teammates approached the two fighters.

Rybár had been one of the Cascades players on the ice next to Sasha during the face-off. Alex waved him over. "What happened?"

He got a shrug in response. "Bilovsky said something to him. Couldn't hear what, but then they're fighting, so must have been bad."

The fight intensified as Sasha managed to get Bilovsky's feet out from under them, sending them both plummeting to the ice.

"Ah, shit." Rybár took off, and so did the refs and linesmen, who'd previously been hesitant to jump in and break the fight up at the risk of getting injured themselves.

Alex hovered in his crease, not sure what to do, while the rest of his team circled Sasha and Bilovsky. He lifted his mask, turning away from the fight for a second to grab his bottle of water.

And then—

The scent that hit Alex was like being smashed with a wrecking ball. He staggered forward, grabbing on to his goal post in order to remain standing. That scent was—

That's Sasha. The rich earthiness that clung to Sasha's body was now filling the entire arena, only it was a thousand times stronger. Alex tried to take a breath and almost choked on it, the richness turning cloying and sticking to his nose and throat.

His fangs came out, completely uncontrolled, dropped along his gums as saliva flooded his mouth. Alex pressed his lips closed, ducking his head and fumbling to pull his mask back down, hoping no one could see him. The entire arena seemed focused on the commotion, though, and no one appeared to be looking at him as the refs finally managed to separate Sasha and Bilovsky and haul them to their feet.

It was obvious, once they were both standing, that Sasha was bleeding. Bilovsky was too, blood dripping from a nose that looked too bruised and swollen to be anything but broken. But Sasha had blood around his mouth, down his white jersey, the red almost obscene in the bright arena lights. A split lip, but it was more than enough to cut away any restraint that Alex had over his vampire half.

He tried to skate it off, doing short laps with his head down and mask once again firmly in place while the refs sent both fighters off the ice and gathered to assess penalties.

As Sasha vanished down the hall to the locker room, the overpowering scent of blood and earth vanished with him. Alex took a tentative breath, then another. He was distantly aware of the crowd's split cheering and booing when the penalties were called, and then when the linesmen went to work on cleaning up the remaining spilled blood.

The entire situation from start to finish had only been a minute or two, but it had felt like an eternity. And finally—*finally*—Alex's fangs retreated.

He took one last shaky breath, then skated back to his crease.

Seattle Cascades (@CascadesNHL)
Alexander Petrov and Joel Bilovsky both get 5-minute fighting majors and 10-minute game misconducts for their late 3rd period fight.

SASHA STORMED down the hallway, ignoring the trainers who tried to stop him. He stripped off his gear as soon as he hit the locker room doors, flinging his jersey in the direction of the laundry bin and his pads in the general vicinity of his locker. Someone would bring his gloves and stick eventually, he assumed, but for now he had more important things to think about.

Like that fucker Bilovsky.

I should have hit him harder. The rage from the fight hadn't faded at all, though his adrenaline was starting to crash, bringing with it the incessant throbbing of his lip, his hands, his... entire body.

"Fuck." Sasha slumped onto the bench in front of a locker that might or might not have been his, legs spread, and let his head fall forward.

Bilovsky was a goon. Everyone knew it, but Sasha had been adamant that he wasn't going to take the other man's bait, wasn't going to let Bilovsky get under his skin.

Until Bilovsky had opened his big fucking mouth. "You know, when we played in January, I almost didn't stop? Thought about it, about just skating up to that kid you got in your net, running him right over. You think a guy that small would be able to take a hit? Maybe I should give it a try now, hm? Knock him down, *boom*. I can do it midplay; refs might give me two in the bin, but it'd be worth it."

The mental image of Bilovsky, who was as big as Sasha and ten times meaner, purposefully angling to hurt Alex, had been enough to send him over the edge.

Should've hit him harder, Sasha repeated. *Shown him what it's like to get knocked down by someone bigger than him.*

A trainer found him like that a minute later. "Petrov. Up, c'mon. I need to get that lip stitched and check your knuckles for fractures. There's a TV in the trainer's room if you want to watch the end of the game."

Sasha trailed behind obediently, let the trainer get his skates off, pull his padding away so he could check for bruises. The TV was, indeed, on and showing the game. Sasha glanced up at it, then looked back down as the trainer examined each one of his knuckles, probing the bruising painfully.

Then awareness of what he'd actually seen filtered through, and Sasha's head shot back up.

"What happened?"

The score had been 5-2 Cascades when the fight had started. Now it was 5-4, and the goalie in net for Seattle was too tall to be Alex.

The trainer glanced over his shoulder at the TV. "Fanning got pulled. Two goals in about two minutes."

Holy shit. Sasha didn't even feel the trainer prodding at his lip or the needle that poked into it to numb the wound. His eyes were fixed on the TV, which was finally showing a brief replay of what had happened.

There was Alex, looking a little shaken but otherwise okay in net. The face-off in the Cascades' defensive zone had been repeated, since the fight had interrupted the initial attempt.

Vancouver won the face-off again, passed the puck to the winger, who lifted his stick, brought it down—

And the puck was in the net. Just like that, a one-timer that Alex didn't even appear to have seen.

Then, a minute and forty seconds later, Vancouver was back in Seattle's end, and it was like Alex hadn't even been trying. The puck had slid in behind him neatly, effortlessly, Alex's leg a full second too slow to kick out and stop it.

At that point Coach Rico must have seen something, because he called Alex to the bench, sent Matty in, and now it was Hertzog holding down the fort for the remaining five minutes of the game.

"Fanning's okay, though? Not injured?"

The trainer hissed. "Don't move, and don't talk." He held a needle up threateningly. "But to answer your question: if he is, no one's notified us. Fanning's still on the bench. Spooked by the fight, maybe."

Maybe the first goal had caught him off guard and shaken his resolve. If it was any other goalie, Sasha might have simply assumed as much and moved on. But he knew Alex; he might have a bit of a temper lurking beneath the surface, but he was as calm and collected as anyone Sasha knew. Even Ed couldn't maintain that level of cool in the net.

The trainer kept him until the final buzzer sounded, doing an X-ray on his hand to check for any fractures. He caught the end of the game—a win, but only barely. By the time Sasha escaped back to the locker room, Alex was nowhere to be seen.

Shawn was just coming out of the shower, though, so Sasha cornered him.

"Damn, you look awful. Your lip is already swelling. I'd feel bad for you, but you deserve it after that stupid fight."

Sasha ignored him. "Do you know where he went?"

Shawn gave him a long look, then shook his head. "Leave him alone right now, okay? I know you want to see him, make sure he's okay, but … give him some space."

That was the last thing Sasha wanted to do. But when they boarded the plane to head back to Seattle an hour later, he forced himself to pass over the sweats-clad form already curled up over two of the seats, hoodie pulled lower over his face.

He ran a hand over Alex's knee as he passed, then took a seat in the row behind him. Alex didn't budge for the entire short flight home.

"I'm not going to answer that question. If there are any injuries to be reported, Coach Henrique will address them. But I will say that Fanning has been an absolute wall in the net for us since he came up. Everyone has a bad game sometimes. For Fanning, he just had a bad couple of minutes. No one here blames him for that, and we're all excited to have him back between the pipes next week against Atlanta."

—Derick Merkley, postgame interview

Chapter Twenty-Two

THE PROBLEM was this:

Alex wanted to be near Sasha. He wanted to bury himself in Sasha's strong arms, curl up against that hard chest, listen to Sasha's heartbeat, and fall asleep warm and comforted. He just also wanted to be as far away from Sasha as humanly possible.

Alex escaped off the plane the second it came to a stop. He'd driven himself to the airport before the game the day before, and now he was grateful that he hadn't caught a ride with Shawn like his roommate had suggested. It meant he could flee as soon as his feet touched the tarmac. He sent a quick text, asking Shawn to grab his overnight bag for him before peeling out of the parking lot.

Heather didn't seem surprised when he knocked on her door, even though it was almost one in the morning.

"Half a dozen people texted me about what happened," she said, stepping aside to let him in. "The perks of *dating* a hockey player, I suppose."

Alex fidgeted inside the doorway, hands clenching and unclenching over his thighs. "Something is wrong."

She sighed. "Come on. We should get comfortable for this one."

The couch was comfortable in its familiarity. Alex curled up on one side, knees tucked under his chin, and arms wrapped around his legs. "I've played hockey for my entire life, and I've never lost control over my vampire side because of blood on the ice. Until tonight."

Heather made a low sound. "Alex."

He shook his head sharply. "I don't—I don't want to talk about it. Just, I know we weren't going to feed again until tomorrow, but can we do it now instead? Maybe it'll help with what happened tonight."

"Alex." Heather looked like she wanted to say something else, but instead she sighed and nodded. "Yeah, that's fine. You can feed."

Relief flooded through Alex. *This is such a mess. But if I can feed now, whatever* this *is will go away.*

Maybe something had been wrong with the feeding from two days prior. He'd noticed then that Heather hadn't smelled right, that he'd felt strange after, as though he hadn't gotten enough blood. And Alex half expected something similar to happen again today, but when he bent his head in and inhaled Heather's scent, he was relieved to find that it was the same as always, saffron and spice.

When he bit into her, the first rush of blood in his mouth was another relief. Heather tasted as usual, the same as she had for the last two months of their arrangement. *Maybe it was a one-time fluke.* He'd never encountered anything like it in his life, but he'd heard of stranger things. *She tastes fine. Not as good as Sasha would, of course, but—no, that's not an option.*

Still, just thinking about Sasha made Alex's eyes fall shut. He could picture the blood—everywhere, on the ice, on Sasha's jersey, his face, painting his mouth a lurid shade of red. The smell had been at once the best and worst thing he'd ever experienced, but all Alex wanted to do now was kiss Sasha and run his tongue over the cut, lap at the hint of blood there and see if it tasted as good as he imagined it would.

Heather groaned, but it wasn't a pleasurable noise. "Alex," she hissed. "Enough."

Shit, shit, shit. Alex pulled back as quickly as he could, pressing his lips to the incision until the blood stopped. Then he backed away quickly, dread making his breathing shallow. "I'm so sorry. Are you okay?"

"I'm fine." She didn't look fine, though. Heather was pale beneath her tanned skin, and she looked worn-out. "I figured you needed it, so I let you take more than usual."

Alex curled back up into a ball, gripping his shins as tight as he could. "You shouldn't have. I could have really hurt you." *Again*, a tiny voice told him. This was the second time in two days that he'd lost control while feeding and taken too much.

Heather's smile was tired, but there was a hint of sharpness to it. "I'm not entirely defenseless. If you hadn't stopped immediately, there were methods I could have used to make you."

The words and her tone sent a shiver down Alex's spine, and he knew she wasn't wrong. Still….

"I don't know what's wrong with me. Maybe it was the fight, or I'm coming down with something?"

The look in Heather's eye said she had a theory, but if she did, then she kept it to herself. "Maybe you should tell your Sasha about this," she suggested carefully.

"You know I can't do that."

"I know you *think* you can't do that."

But Alex shook his head. She hadn't been there in the locker room on that first day, to see the way Sasha had laughed at the slur. Even if Sasha was okay with it, could he really take that risk? The thing between them was so new, so fragile; telling Sasha the full truth could mean losing him completely… or worse: having him tell others that Alex was Para, costing him his job.

I really like Sasha. And maybe someday in the distant future I'll feel confident enough to tell him. But until I know if he's truly anti-Para—until I know if I can trust him to keep my secret, I just can't risk it right now.

Mrs. Merkley… a girl can dream! (@MerkleyFan96)

Finally, a Saturday night home game! It's so hard to get to a game on a weeknight, so I splurged and got tickets down near the bench for tomorrow vs. Columbus. #GoScades

Emma (@Cascadiac)

@MerkleyFan96: Oh, I'll be at that one too! But I'm in the upper bowl. Want to meet up during intermission?

ED FOUND Sasha at practice a few days later.

They were just wrapping up. Coach had left the ice, as had most of the trainers and almost all of Sasha's teammates. Sasha was working his way methodically through a bucket of pucks, practicing his slap shots while also burning through two days of worry.

Alex had barely talked to him since the game in Vancouver. He hadn't talked to anyone really, as far as Sasha could tell, though Shawn spent a lot of time hanging out by his side, chatting without getting any real response.

"He's just doing his Phantom thing," Carts said. "Don't worry. Give him space, like I said."

But giving him space was getting more difficult with every passing day.

He had his head down, passing a puck back and forth between his stick, when Ed skated up. His friend was only dressed in sweats, but the sling was finally gone.

"Penny for your thoughts?"

Sasha snorted. "You're a millionaire. I'll need more than a penny."

Ed laughed, grabbing a puck with his skate blade and nudging it across to Sasha, who shot it toward the net. It pinged off the post, and they both watched it roll away.

"Seriously, Sasha, you look miserable. Did the trainers not clear you to play tomorrow?"

Tomorrow would be a home game against Columbus, but Sasha didn't have the energy to even think about that right now. "No, I'm fine. No injuries except my lip." He sighed, eyeing the rest of the bucket of pucks, spilled across the ice nearby. "I'm worried about Alex."

Ed didn't respond. When Sasha glanced up, Ed had a cold look on his face.

"I know, you do not like him much," Sasha said quickly. "But I'm getting to know him while he's up, yes? And he's good. Good man, good player. Not a threat to you."

"Sasha." Ed glanced around, then looked satisfied when he noticed that they were alone on the ice. "I need to tell you something. About Fanning."

Sasha grimaced. "He's not stealing your starting position, Eddie. I promise."

"No, he's not," Eddie said, "because he's not going to be on the team anymore."

What?

"What?"

Ed exhaled. When he looked up at Sasha, there was triumph in his eyes, and something else—something a little cruel. "I was at the game a few days ago. In the press box at first, but one of the reporters kept giving me looks like he wanted to grab me for an interview, so I left at the start of the third and headed down to some empty seats at the glass. Figured I'd watch from among the fans, and no one even noticed me with a baseball hat on."

No one had noticed him, Sasha thought, because Ed looked different. Ten weeks had made a huge difference; gone was the handsome, charming man who effortlessly attracted women in bars. He looked older, thinner. There were bags under Ed's eyes now, and his skin looked clammy. Maybe it was just the injury, the lack of exercise, but Sasha couldn't help but wonder.

"So I was down behind the Cascades net when the fight broke out," Ed continued.

"And?"

Ed lowered his voice, even though there was no one in sight. "And I saw Fanning. I saw what he is."

Sasha blinked. "Yes, of course you saw Fanning. He was in net when the fight broke out."

"Dammit, Sasha." Ed kicked at the pile of pucks, sending them scattering. "He's a goddamn Para. That's what I saw. He tried to hide it, but I was looking right at him. Clear as day, the son of a bitch grew fangs right there on the ice."

Sasha's jaw dropped. "What? Ed, what are you talking about?"

He'd spent hours, days with Alex. Sasha had kissed him, had run his tongue over Alex's teeth, had made out until their lips were numb. Alex didn't have fangs.

"Ed, have you been drinking?"

Ed's eyes were hard, lips pursed. "I'm serious, Sasha. I know what I saw. He's a fucking dirty Para freak. And when I tell Coach and Dubois, they'll kick him off in a heartbeat. They're voting in a few weeks, you know. They're going to test everyone, kick all of the Paras right out of the NHL."

Sasha's mind was whirling. *Maybe he is drunk.* But this wasn't the ramblings of a man who'd had a couple of drinks. Ed seemed possessed, vengeful and victorious. He seemed… dangerous. The look on his face made Sasha want to skate away from whoever this man was, because this was not his best friend, his brother.

"Eddie." Sasha took a deep breath, thinking fast. "Okay. Wait, think about this. Maybe it's true what you say, yes? If Al—if Fanning is Para, this is big. But remember what you told me when I first came to Seattle?"

Ed frowned.

Sasha plunged forward. "You tell me *team comes first*. Remember?"

"I remember."

"So maybe right now, team needs to come first for this. You still can't play. Sling is gone, and that's good, but still not skating in practices, not cleared to wear full gear. If you report Fanning, we lose a goalie, no chance of making playoffs." Sasha swallowed, his mouth dry, and kept talking. "Gonna be close, the conference is very tight. Maybe we make wildcard spot, if we can keep winning. But Matty? He won't be winning enough games."

Finally, Ed's face relaxed as he processed Sasha's words.

"You think two, maybe three weeks tops before you play? So we need Fanning in net. And then when you're cleared, you tell Coach. Okay?"

Sasha was out of breath by the time he finished, but Ed no longer looked like he was about to storm off for the coach's office to play his trump card. Instead, he was nodding slowly. He looked calmer, thoughtful.

"I see what you're saying." Ed frowned. "I don't like it. Don't like that you all have to play on a team with a dirty Para bloodsucker. But team comes first."

"Yes." Sasha nodded as well. "So we keep secret for now. I will watch Fanning at game tomorrow and—and next week! Road trip, I will watch carefully. We will make sure he is Para, and then only three full weeks from now until season ends and you can be back."

Ed was smiling now. "Good thinking." He patted Sasha on the shoulder with his good arm. "All right, we'll do it your way, then."

Sasha mentally sighed in relief.

He'd just bought three weeks to figure out what the hell Ed was talking about... and to figure out what the hell to do about it if Ed was right.

Chapter Twenty-Three

Seattle Cascades (@CascadesNHL)
You win some, you lose some. Cascades fall 4-2 to Columbus. But cheer up, we're off to sunny Georgia and Florida tomorrow for a week in the sun (and on the ice)!

Seattle Sports News (@SeattleSportsNews)
Cascades GM Martin Dubois discusses upcoming General Managers meeting, to be held April 7 in Toronto. "I think it's going to be very productive. There are several important votes on the agenda."

Para Rights—Seattle Chapter (@ParaRightsWatch_SEA)
We're calling on Cascades GM Dubois and all other NHL managers to abstain from voting next month to force genetic testing of players. Sign our petition here: bit.ly/p4Ra….

"Got you a present."

Alex look up curiously up at Shawn as his best friend appeared on the other side of the kitchen island. His glance turned to a glare when Shawn's "present" was revealed: a bottle of SPF 100 sunscreen.

"You dick." Alex took a pointed bite of his sandwich, then used it to gesture at his laughing friend. "You know I'm freaking out about this road trip."

Shawn nodded, wiping away tears from his eye. "I know, I know, but the look on your face was worth it. Besides, I told you, man. I got this. The only team bonding event is the volleyball thing on the day off between the Tampa and Florida games. You scheduled that interview with ESPN for that time, right?"

Alex nodded.

"So you're fine. Nobody's gonna say a word. Trust me. Besides, it's not like Rybár or Wilson are going out in the sun either." Rybár was almost as pale as Alex was, and had already vocally proclaimed his disinterest in beach volleyball ("Sand, everywhere!"), swimming in the ocean

("Sharks!"), and sunbathing ("Sun *burning*, you mean."). Wilson had just lifted one eyebrow when the outing was proposed, then pointed up at his bright orange hair; no one had even tried to involve him after that.

But while Shawn's reassurances went a long way, Alex couldn't help but feel nervous. It was one thing for him to walk outside in the sunshine to get from the bus to an arena, or a hotel to a restaurant over lunch. But going to the balmy, sunny Southeast was considered a highlight for everyone on the team… except Alex.

"Could you imagine," Shawn said, reaching over and grabbing the other half of Alex's sandwich. "What if you'd been drafted by Atlanta or Dallas even?"

Alex grimaced. "I've thought about it. I might not have signed or I might have tried to request a trade. I always knew I was going to the AHL for a couple of years, so I figured not having the spotlight on me would give me time to figure things out. If worse came to worse, I would have gone to play for a college team up north for a bit."

Shawn finished the sandwich half in about two bites. "Never really thought about how hard it is for Paras to play in this league."

"Could be worse," Alex said. "I've heard shifters have to navigate pack dynamics wherever they end up, and fae need a nature source nearby… which sucks if they end up in a big city like New York. It's what we do to play the sport we love, though."

"And if that vote goes badly in a few weeks?"

Alex eyed the rest of his sandwich, suddenly not hungry anymore for human food. He handed it over to Shawn. "Then I guess all that work was for nothing."

Akseli Mäkelä (@AkseliMakela38)
I love Seattle but miss lots of sunshine. Thanks NHL for the weeklong trip to Florida! Ahhh, beach + ocean + drinks with little umbrellas, here I come! (Maybe we play some hockey in there too?)

THEIR PRIVATE lounge at the airport was bustling with excited noise when Sasha arrived. He handed his suitcase over, then found an empty seat so he could charge his phone. The flight to Atlanta for the first of three road games was going to be a long one.

Alex joined him a few minutes later, sliding into the chair beside Sasha so quietly that the defenseman almost hadn't noticed him. *Phantom.* Sasha smiled at the younger man.

"Excited for five days of sun and heat?"

"Ugh." Alex made a face. "I guess. Forecast says it's going to be humid; I might just stick to indoors and air-conditioning as much as possible."

Eddie's words teased through Sasha's mind. *Dirty Para bloodsucker.* Sasha had gone home after that practice, had pulled up a search window and dug into research. The Russian sites talked about how dangerous vampires were, how they seduced and murdered innocents, talked about how they were Паразло. Simply seeing the slur on the page had made Sasha sick, even though he'd heard it dozens of times; it was a common insult in Russia, hurled across locker rooms and among friends and enemies alike.

But Alex wasn't Паразло.

The English sites had given more information: how they fed, their increased sense of smell and sight, and their allergy to sunlight.

Alex went out into the sun all the time. Not that it was often sunny in Seattle, but he'd definitely seen Alex step out into sunlight without immediately beginning to burn.

Then why is he the only person on the team who does not want to go to Georgia and Florida?

Alex laughed suddenly, pulling Sasha out of his contemplations. "Did your rookie have too much sugar before you drove here?"

Sasha followed his gaze to where Volkov was practically bouncing off the walls. "Nah, he's been like this for days. Has good friend playing for Atlanta, excited to see him."

"Oh yeah, the kid he was drafted after? I remember reading about them: they met at the draft and became best friends overnight even though everyone expected them to be bitter rivals."

"Yes, that's him."

Alex nodded and fell silent again, fiddling with untangling his headphones. Sasha watched him for a moment. It was tempting to file away Ed's accusations, his own research, and ignore it all. His friend was jealous, angry, and he was definitely drinking more than he should be. It felt safe to say that Ed was wrong—or at least he hadn't seen whatever he thought he'd seen.

Or, another part of Sasha's mind added, *you could just ask Alex if it's true.*

Alex finished sorting out his headphones, then turned to look at Sasha. When he noticed the other man watching him, his entire face lit up in happiness.

Yes, I could ask him. Clear this up now, so I don't worry about it for the rest of the trip.

"Alex," Sasha began.

The intercom dinged, and a voice announced that it was time for their flight to board. Alex was on his feet in a second, tucking his phone away and offering a hand to help Sasha up.

"I promised to sit with Shawn on the flight. We're going to watch a movie on his tablet. But"—he lowered his voice, grinning wickedly—"maybe you can come by my room later?"

Or maybe I could ignore it. Just for now.

He returned the grin and pressed his fingers to Alex's hip out of sight where none of their teammates could see. He slid the hem of Alex's shirt up until he found warm skin. "Yes, I'll see you tonight."

Atlanta Forecast—March 19
High: 77°F (25°C)
Low: 57°F (14°C)
Sunny
0% Chance of Rain

BEING IN Atlanta sucked.

It wasn't too hot, thankfully, but it was *sunny*. Their plane landed midafternoon, and Alex could feel the strength of the sun beating down on him every time he had to walk outside. He kept his hoodie on and his hat pulled over the top of his ears and low over his forehead.

Thankfully, there were good things about Atlanta too. Like Sasha, who tapped on Alex's door the second the team got back from dinner that night.

"You know," Alex said, leaning a shoulder against the doorway and peering down the hall to make sure they were alone, "the last time we had sex before a game, you ended up getting into a fight." *And I got pulled from the game because your blood was all over the ice and I couldn't focus.* "Maybe we shouldn't risk it."

Sasha frowned, but there was a glimmer of amusement in his eyes. "One bad game for us both. Not proof that sex before games is cursed. We should try again, yes? To be certain."

Alex feigned a thoughtful look. "Well, I guess we could test it out one more time. For science."

With a growl, Sasha pushed into the room. Alex laughed as he was scooped up and then promptly deposited on the bed as the door fell shut behind Sasha. He bounced back against the mattress, propping himself up to watch as Sasha stripped off his shirt, tugging it up over his head to show off the long, muscled line of his torso.

"You just going to look?" Sasha's hand hovered over the button on his jeans as he watched Alex with one eyebrow raised.

Alex crossed his legs before him, falling back against the pillows. "I wouldn't want to get distracted from the show."

A slow, wicked grin curled across Sasha's lips. "You want a show?" He flicked the button of his jeans open, then dusted his hands down his hips, taking a step closer to the bed. "Or you want to get off?"

Alex licked his lips, gaze flicking down to the bulge that was tenting Sasha's pants. "Who says I can't have both?"

Sasha was elegance and brutal strength on the ice, and that carried over to the bedroom. It wasn't a striptease, but there was clear intent in each of Sasha's motions. He took his time unzipping his pants, hooking his thumbs in the waistband to lower them down over his hips, slowly revealing his ass and powerful thighs.

Hockey asses were a definite thing, and Alex had seen some pretty incredible ones over the years, but the thick, corded muscle that ran up Sasha's quads and glutes were in a category all by themselves.

As was his cock, heavy and already damp at the tip, soaking through Sasha's boxers.

Now Sasha definitely was teasing, because instead of stripping off the final piece of clothing, he brought one hand up to cup his balls and run a fist over his cloth-enclosed cock, letting his head fall back as a soft groan escaped him. It was more than Alex could handle; he wanted Sasha and skin and his hands running over Sasha's body.

With a curse, he pushed up from the pillows, shed his own T-shirt, and flung it across the room before scrambling down the bed.

"Impatient." Sasha laughed, but his voice was strained with want and he opened his arms to wrap them around Alex as soon as he was standing.

And finally—*finally* they were kissing, tongues tangling together, Sasha pulling Alex close and licking into his mouth. Alex relaxed into Sasha's strong arms, tilting his head back and welcoming the onslaught.

He was distantly aware of hands skirting down the sensitive skin over his ribs and sides, and then fingers were tugging at the drawstring of his sweats, Sasha nipping at his lip in frustration while he tried to get the offending clothing undone.

He groaned in triumph when the sweatpants finally came loose and puddled to the floor at Alex's feet—

And cursed, eyes going dark as he realized that Alex wasn't wearing any underwear.

Alex smirked, moving back just enough that Sasha could look his fill.

"Fuck," Sasha said reverently.

"Not tonight unfortunately," Alex replied, "but if you wanna get naked, I'm sure there are plenty of other things we can do."

He'd planned for this, so while Sasha was still dumbstruck and staring at Alex's body, Alex turned around and bent over to grab something from his suitcase.

Sasha cursed again, this time accompanied by the rustle of clothing being discarded. Alex grabbed the items he was looking for, then paused to close this eyes and inhale as Sasha's scent grew thicker. It was only a split second later that the man himself appeared, running his large hands over Alex's back, tucking his hard, thick cock against the crack of Alex's ass.

"Could take you like this." Sasha's voice had dropped, and it rumbled through Alex as he spoke.

It was tempting. Alex was flexible enough to do it, to brace himself with one hand on the top of his suitcase, another braced against the wall, and let Sasha fuck him like this, nearly bent in half. And Sasha would be strong enough to hold him up, one arm wrapped around Alex's waist as he fucked into him, hard enough that Alex would be feeling it the next day.

But that was the exact reason it had to remain a temptation and nothing more. "Game tomorrow." Alex straightened, shivering as Sasha used that same strength to lift him up and tug him backward until Alex's back rested against Sasha's broad chest, and Sasha's chin was hooked over his shoulder so he could press heated kisses to Alex's jaw.

"Fuck hockey," Sasha growled. "Would rather fuck you." But he sighed and stepped away, moving toward the bed and pulling Alex with him.

"I've got something almost as good," Alex promised.

He let Sasha tug him onto the mattress, position him so Alex was lying on top of the big defenseman, their cocks bumping together and leaving sticky traces of precum on the other's hip and stomach.

"This is good," Sasha groaned.

Alex held up the item in his hand. "Yeah, but this will be better. I promise."

Sasha's eyes were already so dark that the icy blue irises were barely visible. Now his lips parted, and his skin flushed with arousal as he took the bottle of lube from Alex's hand and turned it over. "But the game tomorrow?"

"There are other ways to fuck." Alex took the lube back, flipped the cap with one hand, and poured a generous dollop over his fingers.

He lowered his hand, watching Sasha track the motion with the same intensity he used to track the puck on the ice, only to have those brilliant blue eyes flutter shut when Alex wrapped his hand around Sasha's cock, lube making the glide perfectly smooth. He didn't tighten his grip, only coated Sasha's shaft, making sure he was slick.

"Alex, милый, please."

Alex leaned forward to kiss him, smirking against Sasha's lips when he pulled his hand away and got a desperate moan in return. "Trust me, babe." He whispered the words against Sasha's mouth. "I've got you tonight."

There were tiny beads of sweat forming along Sasha's hairline, and his eyes were damp with need when he flicked them back open.

"Gonna follow my play, Petrov?"

Groaning, Sasha licked his lips. "Yes, tonight you're Captain. Just do something, please."

Alex kissed him once more, hard and fast, then grabbed the lube and poured more onto his already-wet hand.

Sasha didn't complain when he pulled away this time, but he made a little sound, like he was trying not to whine at the loss. Alex took a second to run his gaze over Sasha's body from head to toe, appreciating the way his muscles quivered and the flush that ran down his neck and chest, the way his skin looked tan and smooth against the plain white sheets of the bed.

Then he turned around, repeating the position he'd been in before when they'd been standing over his suitcase. He rolled on his side, tucking his back up against Sasha's chest, and grinned when Sasha's arm immediately wrapped around his stomach.

"Like this," Alex said.

He reached between his legs, coating his thighs with lube, then reached behind him to find Sasha's hard, hot dick and guide it between his legs.

A rush of breath escaped Sasha as he realized what was going on, the hot air hitting the back of Alex's neck and sending a shiver down his spine.

"Yes, like this," Sasha agreed. Then he moaned, hitched Alex up against him, and thrust his hips forward.

Yes. This was perfect. At this angle, Sasha's hard shaft rubbed over Alex's perineum and teased at his hole with every thrust, and the head of his cock nudged over Alex's balls. Alex squeezed his thighs together tighter and felt more than heard Sasha's breath hitch in response.

Everything was hot and slick and wet, and the friction was absolutely delicious. Alex let his head fall back against Sasha's shoulder, sinking into the embrace and the overwhelming sensations.

His own arousal was pressed up against his stomach. Sasha grunted, shifting his arm and pulling Alex closer, then worked one hand around Alex's neglected cock, stroking it in time to his own thrusts.

"Sasha." Alex was getting close and knew this wasn't going to take much longer. He could feel the way Sasha's breathing had picked up behind him, how his body was straining, and knew Sasha wouldn't last much longer either.

He clenched his thighs tighter, reveling in the drag of Sasha's cock against his ass. Sasha's dick hit Alex's balls with every jerk forward, and his hand sped up on Alex's cock.

Alex's orgasm was almost a surprise, sweeping over him in a tidal wave of pleasure. Behind him, Sasha dug his teeth into the meat of Alex's shoulder, muffling his own groans into the skin there as he thrust forward once, twice, the sensation almost too much against Alex's sensitive body before he was coming as well, spilling hot cum between Alex's thighs.

Sasha wrapped around him like a heavy blanket, nuzzling his face into Alex's neck and pressing tiny, sleepy kisses into the skin as he wrapped Alex tight.

Alex let his body sink into the heat and muscles, breathing in Sasha's rich scent with every inhalation. He tilted his head to the side to give Sasha better access, enjoying the feel of silky lips over his pulse.

After a minute, Sasha grunted and rolled over. Alex made a sad noise as the heat along his back vanished, turning his head as Sasha stretched and walked into the bathroom. He could see Sasha through the open door, like a Greek statue backlit by the bathroom light as he grabbed a washcloth off the counter and turned the water on to get it warm.

When he returned to the bed, it was to clean himself and Alex up. He wiped the lube and cum from between Alex's legs gently, though Alex couldn't help but shudder at the feel of the coarse fabric against his oversensitive skin.

Then Sasha threw the cloth across the room, climbed back on the bed to cover Alex up once more, and spooned around him. The room was cool from the air conditioner blowing across the bed, but Alex felt warm and sated in Sasha's arms. He started to doze off like that, safe in Sasha's arms and content as the lingering pleasure of his orgasm seeped through his body.

Sasha took a deep breath, held it, and let it out slowly. Alex could feel the warm breath on his neck, and the expansion-contraction of his chest against his back.

"Whatcha thinking about?" he asked drowsily.

Gentle fingers teased up and down Alex's side, tracing a path from his ribs to his hip and back up again.

"If I ask you a question, will you answer it honestly?"

Alex stirred, rolling over just enough to peer over his shoulder. Sasha looked awake and troubled. "Yeah, babe. Of course."

Another slow, deliberate inhale, then the caress stopped, replaced by a firm hand against Alex's hip. "Alex," Sasha asked, "are you a vampire?"

ALEX FROZE in his arms.

It wasn't just that he held his breath and went still; his skin went ice cold beneath Sasha's hand, and a full-body shudder ran through him.

"Alex." Sasha whispered the name.

"How did you find out?"

Alex's words were barely audible, even though only inches separated them. He sounded afraid. *No, not merely afraid. He is terrified.*

It was all the confirmation Sasha needed. All of the air in his lungs fled in a *whoosh*, and he rolled onto his back, stunned.

"So it's true, then." Sasha stared up at the ceiling. "Okay."

A flurry of movement from beside him alerted Sasha that something was wrong. Alex scrambled from the bed, limbs flailing as he untangled himself from the sheets and got to his feet.

"Alex, calm down."

The words had no effect. Alex moved away from the bed as quickly as he could, putting distance between himself and Sasha.

"I—you—" Panic was obvious on the goalie's face, in every movement he made. He tripped over something on the ground, and then he was pulling on his pants with shaking fingers. In the dim light of the room, he looked impossibly frail… inhuman, almost. Pale skin stretched for miles, and brown eyes caught the light of the lamp and flashed every time he glanced at Sasha.

"It's okay, солнышко. Let me talk."

Alex shook his head once, hard. "How did you figure it out?" Every word was brittle. "Are you going to tell anyone?"

Sasha sat up. "No. Of course not."

"You can't—the GMs, if they find out…." His voice broke, and Alex hunched in on himself. "I just want to play hockey. You can't tell anybody. Please."

"Alex, listen. We won't—"

Alex cut him off, any last trace of color vanishing from his face. "We? Someone else knows?"

Sasha felt like he was trying to grasp at water that kept slipping from his fingers. "No!" He swallowed, then backtracked. "I mean, just Eddie. That's it."

"Eduard Despres. The alcoholic goalie who wants me gone." If he'd been terrified before, now Sasha was seeing what Alex looked like when he was petrified. "You told Eduard Despres that I'm a—a—*a vampire?*"

Alex didn't give him a chance to answer the question before he was pulling his sweatshirt on in a flurry of movement and rushing toward the door.

"Wait," Sasha tried. "I can explain."

"Don't—" He cut himself off, wide eyes looking everywhere except at the bed where Sasha still sat. "I knew this would happen. I—I thought I was being paranoid, but I knew—" He froze, a deer in headlights, looking so frail that Sasha thought he might shatter into a million pieces if he even tried to draw a breath.

"This is why I couldn't tell you," Alex said. Fear vanished behind a wall of ice as Sasha watched, Alex catching his breath and visibly building a barrier between them. "I was so afraid that if I told you, you wouldn't be able to keep it a secret. And—I guess I was right." He laughed, but there was nothing funny in the sound.

"Alex," Sasha begged. "Солнышко, wait."

Alex paused, hand on the door handle. "Don't call me that. I have to go. I—I can't be here."

Then he was gone, fleeing down the hall and leaving Sasha alone in the hotel room, shell-shocked and speechless.

Sasha buried his face in his hands. *I only wanted to know the truth. How did this go wrong so quickly?*

Chapter Twenty-Four

Alex fled down the hallway blindly, bare feet rough against the hotel carpet. Shawn's room was at the end of the corridor, and at that moment it was the only safe place he could think to go. Sasha was still in his room. Sasha, who—

A well of fear threatened to bubble up from inside his chest. Alex stopped at the last door on the left and knocked as quickly as he could, praying that he had the right room.

When Shawn's familiar face appeared seconds later, Alex didn't hesitate. He pushed through the barely open door and straight into his friend's arms.

"Alex?" Shawn's voice sounded far away, but Alex couldn't focus on it. He couldn't focus on anything except the scared, angry tears that burned his eyes and the feel of strong arms around him. "Phantom, bro, talk to me. Are you okay? Do I need to call someone?"

Alex shook his head. He was distantly aware of Shawn moving them both farther into the room, of being lowered to sit on the bed. Shawn must have turned the show he was watching off, because the room went silent all of a sudden, and then Shawn was wrapping an arm around his shoulder and running tender fingers through Alex's hair.

"What happened?"

Somehow, Alex found the words. "Sasha knows."

Shawn didn't have to ask for clarification. He cursed and pulled Alex closer. "I'll kill him if he hurt you."

"He told Despres. They both know."

The cursing this time was more creative.

Alex wasn't sure how long they sat there, side by side on the end of Shawn's bed, before he was able to catch his breath and begin to speak haltingly. "The first time I met him, he was laughing at an anti-Para slur that Volkov had called him."

"Mikhail is a dumb kid," Shawn said. "Not excusing him, but the shit those kids hear and say before they come to the NHL doesn't mean anything."

"But Sasha *laughed*. Like calling someone that word was funny."

Shawn didn't have a response to that.

"Despres doesn't like me. Sasha told me that they're best friends and they've been close since he joined the team years ago." Alex's hands were shaking, and he clenched them into fists to try to make them stop. "When Despres was in the locker room, he kept glaring at me, and I overheard him tell Sasha that he thinks I'm trying to steal his spot on the team."

"Alex." Shawn hugged him close but didn't say anything else.

The fragile calm that Alex had managed to hold on to started to crack, and panic slipped through, making it difficult to breathe. Alex closed his eyes, struggling to inhale around the sensation. "If he tells Coach, they won't let me play anymore."

Alex didn't clarify which *he* he was talking about, because either possibility was equally horrifying. Sasha had revealed his biggest secret to a man who wanted him off the team and could use that information to make it happen. Even if it wasn't Sasha himself who knocked on Coach Henrique's door to spill the beans, the betrayal was just as immediate and heartbreaking.

"Hey, no." Shawn gripped his shoulder, turning Alex to face him. He used his free hand to lift Alex's chin, and Alex blinked his eyes open to see Shawn staring at him dead-on, serious in a way that his best friend rarely was. "That's not going to happen, man."

The laugh that escaped Alex was hollow, not remotely humorous. "Yeah, Carts. That's exactly what's going to happen. I'll never play pro hockey again."

"Then fuck 'em." Shawn's eyes were blazing. "If they want to get rid of you because 50 percent of your blood isn't human, then that's their loss, because they'll have to find a new first-pair defenseman too. I'll go play in the Swedish leagues before I let them kick you off this team because you're Para."

"No! Carts, that's not—you can't do that."

Shawn grinned crookedly. "Pretty sure I can, dude. Anyways, I hear the men *and* women in Sweden are way hotter, and they have really amazing Para equality laws."

Something loosened in Alex's chest. The panic was still there, but he could manage a few shaky breaths around the weight on his ribs. "I was so careful," he said quietly, glancing away. "I can't figure out how he guessed."

"Who cares?" Shawn got up off the bed, digging a bottle of water out of the hotel fridge and passing it to Alex, who took it gratefully. "If he tells, he's an asshole. Don't let yourself worry about the *how* right now… we have a game tomorrow. You should go out there and show him that you don't give a fuck what he says or does, or who he tells. Play your heart out; show them that getting rid of you is the biggest mistake they'll ever make."

Oh god. He was starting against Atlanta in less than twenty-four hours. This time the panic was something he could grasp on to, at least.

"Stop, Phantom." Shawn hauled Alex to his feet, meeting his gaze once again. "What do you *want*?"

"I want to play hockey," Alex whispered.

"Then do it. You can freak out and spend all night going over the what-ifs, or you can drink that water, climb into the spare bed to crash for the night, and wake up tomorrow ready to play hockey. What's it gonna be?"

The answer was obvious. Alex took a deep breath, and then another.

If Sasha or Despres wanted him off this team, he was going to show them exactly what they'd be losing.

"If his performance tonight is anything to go on, I think Alex Fanning is going to drag this team to the playoffs kicking and screaming. Especially when you look at how poorly the defense played tonight… if it wasn't for Fanning being a force of nature between the pipes, this team would be looking at a loss to Atlanta instead of a win."

"Absolutely agree, Bob. But I also want to highlight how Mikhail Volkov played tonight. He absolutely made the most of every shift, and his two goals and one assist were the driving force behind the Cascades' offense. If both of these rookies keep playing like they are, the Cascades will have to postpone their summer vacation plans for sure."

—Bob Rousseau and Emily Burnwood, Seattle Cascades Post-Game Report

ALEX HADN'T looked in his direction even once since the night before the Atlanta game.

Sasha knew this, because he'd spent every waking moment watching Alex instead, feeling like there was an entire canyon of misunderstanding and heartbreak between them.

Even Shawn wasn't speaking to him, unless it was a call to pass the puck, or something else related to hockey.

"Hey, you and Fanning fighting again?" Merkley asked, finding him before they headed out for warmups before the game against Tampa.

Sasha resisted the urge to look over toward Alex, dressed in his full goalie gear and talking animatedly with Bayer and Mo about something. "No," he said shortly.

"So, yes, then." Merks nodded. "I don't need to tell you to sort it out, man. I don't know why the two of you were at each other's throats back in January, and I don't care why you're back to this frozen silence now. But get it together before it starts affecting this locker room, okay? We have a real chance to make playoffs this year. But if you two fuck with the team chemistry, summer vacation is going to come too early. Got me?"

"Yeah, Cap. I got you." Sasha watched his captain head across the room and sighed.

Merkley is anti-Para. The thought came out of nowhere. He didn't make any secret of it in the locker room, though Merks had gotten better about using certain phrases and being too vocal since he'd gotten the captaincy. *If he knew why Alex was so upset with me, he* would *care. He'd insist that Alex be kicked off the team.*

And that, Sasha resolved, was *not* going to happen. Alex could hate him until they were both retired or traded to teams across the continent, but Sasha wasn't going to let anyone kick him off this team because he was Para.

Of course, knowing he was Para meant so many little oddities finally made sense. It was honestly a miracle that no one else had noticed—though, Sasha reasoned, hockey superstitions and weird goalie quirks definitely helped to mask any Para behavior.

But some things, put into context, now finally made sense. Like the burn on Alex's arm, which had looked vicious and painful when Sasha had seen it. But now, thinking about it, the burn had been completely gone a few days later when they'd all been fucking around in the player's lounge before video review one day. And the girlfriend, Heather—

Does he feed from her? Alex had seen her every few days before he and Sasha had gotten together, based on gossip from their teammates and cell phone pics posted online. And Alex had been upfront about the fact that they were friends, that he still "hung out" with her sometimes.

The thought of feeding, of Alex drinking someone's blood, was where Sasha got stuck, however.

He's Para. Vampires drink blood.

Sasha was gay. In Russia, that was spit upon at best, criminal at worst. But while being gay was bad enough in his culture, being Para was… unthinkable. And Alex *drank people's blood*, which was somehow even more terrifying than simply being Para.

There were too many questions, too many things Sasha didn't understand.

He found Shawn during warmups. "I need to talk to Alex."

"Fuck off," Shawn replied. "If you're going to threaten him by going to Coach or the NHL officials, you can just tell it to me. He doesn't need to hear any of that shit."

Sasha glanced at the net, where Alex was focused on his own warmup routine. "I'm not going to threaten him. I only want to talk. I need answers."

Shawn spat on the ice. "Alex doesn't owe you anything, especially answers to whatever questions you might have. If you want to see how badly you're about to fuck up his life, go google 'Para pro athletes.' But leave him alone."

With that, his partner skated off. Sasha watched him go, deep in thought. He couldn't imagine the horror stories that would come up if he searched for stories about Para athletes, couldn't even fathom how difficult things were for people like Alex.

But… he *could* do some research. And maybe, if he figured out what he was dealing with, he could figure out a way to stop Ed from telling anyone. Maybe he could fix this, so Alex didn't need to be afraid anymore.

The majority of Paranormal beings have two "forms": their natural state, in which their Paranormal status is obvious; and a human state. While few tests have been done on the difference in abilities between these two forms, what little research we've seen proves that Paras who are in their human form are, for all intents and purposes, human. So far, no testing has revealed any performance-enhancing benefits for Paras in human form, apart from minor sensory increases (i.e., hearing, scent). Even allergies, which may be deadly to a Para in his natural form, are significantly less impactful in the human form.

Patel, A. N. (2017). An analysis of Paranormal abilities. *The American Journal for Paranormal Studies, 3*(3):44-49.

Let me break this down for you: Patel collected dozens of research papers and test results, and showed that Para athletes get ZERO benefit from being Para when they're playing. Like sure, a wolf can run really fast, but a werewolf sprinter can't go any faster than his human-form body allows him to. The science proves it! Unless your Olympic swimmer suddenly grows a tail in the middle of a heat, the only way they're going to win is if they work hard and train diligently—same as any other human competitor.

—Cole Whitesmith, for Deadspin.com

THERE WERE only so many things that Alex could focus on at one time, and he was fast reaching his limit between hockey, Sasha, and the gnawing hunger that he couldn't seem to shake no matter what he did.

At first he'd thought it was just a physical manifestation of the heartbreak that sat heavy in his chest every time he spotted Sasha on the ice or at a team dinner. He'd fallen hard for Sasha, and quickly. The revelation that Sasha—and, through him, Despres—could ruin the one thing Alex loved more than anything… well, he hadn't been surprised when he'd started to feel lethargic, aching, and unsettled.

He'd pushed the discomfort aside to play his second game of the road trip against Tampa. Hockey came first, always, which meant he couldn't waste time worrying or hurting over something beyond his control.

But then they'd lost the game against Tampa, and Alex had been forced to reevaluate.

It hadn't been a bad game. The Cascades were hungry for every point they could get, vying desperately for one of the wildcard spots in the Western Conference, and they'd played like a team hungry to win. Tampa hadn't been able to hold together against them.

Unfortunately, neither had Alex.

Something's wrong. It wasn't the first time he'd thought that in the last few weeks, but now it was becoming frighteningly obvious.

"I was too slow," he told Shawn later that night. He had his own hotel room again in Tampa; it was pristine, bland, and empty of both Sasha's scent and Sasha himself, unlike the room in Atlanta. But Shawn's room smelled bright and fresh just like his best friend did, and Shawn didn't seem to mind Alex crashing on his spare bed. It was comfortable, and Alex was craving comfort these days.

Shawn made a back-and-forth gesture with his hand. "You looked a little off at times, but you were playing fine."

"I wasn't, trust me." Alex stretched out on the bed, and every muscle in his body protested at once. "I couldn't move fast enough tonight. Like my body wouldn't respond the way I needed it to."

Silence made him turn his head, only to spot Shawn looking troubled. "When's the last time you fed, bro?"

Alex shrugged, then regretted it when the ache radiated down his back. "Sunday morning, before we left for the airport. I ran by Heather's early, since she had a midmorning set call and we had our flight."

"And you're okay? On blood, I mean."

Shawn held his wrist out hesitantly, as though to say *I can help if I need to*.

"I fed four days ago," Alex stressed. "It can't be that."

But even as he said the words, he knew they were a lie. He was *hungry*, bone-deep. Feeding from Heather hadn't worked for some reason. Maybe it hadn't been working in a while, but now he was really noticing the effects.

"I'm fine," he said. "Maybe I just need more sleep."

Chapter Twenty-Five

Seattle Cascades (@CascadesNHL)
A loss to Tampa last night isn't going to stop these guys from enjoying a day on the beach! Tomorrow we take on Florida… today, we play an epic game of beach volleyball! https://t.co/Ergk5bTG0D

Mrs. Merkley… a girl can dream! (@MerkleyFan96)
Finally, my favorite day of the year: when the entire Cascades team runs around in the sun wearing just a pair of shorts. #hot #somuchmuscle

The beach was paradise. The sun was hot, the sand was white and beautiful, the ocean was blue, and they had a cooler with water and sports drinks set up beneath an umbrella.

Sasha lounged in the shade, sunglasses firmly in place, and tried to enjoy it.

The rest of the team was engaged in what had begun as a civil game of volleyball, before devolving into chaos. Sasha had escaped as soon as the match had turned into a winner-take-all elimination contest, grabbing a cold drink and finding somewhere to sit in the shade.

He was having fun, but he couldn't help but notice the holes in the team where people were missing. Rybár and Wilson had ridden down to the beach with them on the bus, only to vanish into a nearby restaurant for some Cuban food. "And air-conditioning!" Wilson had added, grinning.

The only other person missing, though, was the one person Sasha wanted to see more than anything. Alex had apologized profusely, explaining that he had a phone interview that he'd scheduled weeks ago, before the team bonding day was announced, and he couldn't get out of it. So their goalie was back at the hotel, and Sasha was miserable in paradise without him nearby.

"How on earth can you look so sad right now?" Misha threw himself onto the sand beside Sasha, chatting happily in Russian as he sprayed his face down with a bottle of water. Alyssa came by, dressed down in shorts and a tank top, and snapped a photo of the two of them for the Cascades' social media account before moving on.

Sasha took another sip from his own drink and stared moodily out at the volleyball game. "Not sad," he responded eventually. "Just thinking."

"Thinking deep thoughts about Fanning?"

The Gatorade he'd just taken a sip of caught in his throat, and Sasha coughed and almost spit it right back out. "What?" he gasped.

Misha, the little shit, laughed at him. "We might be hockey players, Sasha, but none of us are dumb. When you and Alex go from being best friends who sit on the bus together, to not even looking at each other, people are going to notice." He stretched his legs out in front of him and tilted his head back. "Also, I live with you, dumbass. You come home late all the time, and the next day Fanning looks like he's the happiest boy in Seattle."

The casual reveal hit Sasha like a freight train—or like being boarded by Bilovsky, that asshole. He shook his head to clear it, and then studied his rookie carefully. Misha had left Russia only a year prior, had spent his entire life before that entrenched in Russian culture and politics as one of Russian hockey's rising stars. Sasha had been spending most of his year in America for half a decade, but he still fought against the deeply engrained stereotypes and stigmas of his childhood.

So for Misha to be so relaxed about this…. Sasha couldn't fathom it. Either he was being deceptive, or Sasha had vastly underestimated his rookie.

"What if—" He cleared his throat, took another sip of his drink. A glance around showed they were completely alone, even though they were speaking in Russian. "What if Alex and I were dating?"

Misha shrugged. "Good for you, I'd say. You're too uptight, old man. Maybe a good fuck every once in a while will help you relax a little."

At least this time Sasha only had air to choke on, instead of his sports drink. "Jesus, Misha. If I told your mother about some of the things you said…."

Misha laughed. "My mother played hockey as a young woman, and she married a hockey player as well. I don't think anything I could say would surprise her."

It was true. The Volkovs were Russian hockey royalty, and Maria Volkova could curse just as fluently as her male family members, given the right incentive.

They drank in silence for another minute. The yells and chirps of their teammates carried over the sand to them, and the ocean was a soft roar beneath that.

"You know, Sasha, it's okay here to love another man. This is America; here you can love whoever you want… man, woman, even both—I hear that's a thing. You can even love a P—"

He cut off suddenly, face going red.

Sasha turned, eyebrows going up. Misha was focused again on the game in progress, eyes fixed on the ball as it went back and forth over the net. *He almost said more than he wanted to.* He replayed Misha's words. *You can even love a Para. That's what he was about to say, I'm certain.*

He'd welcomed the rookie into his home when Misha had signed with the team, but he'd never seen any sign of his housemate dating anyone. Was he gay? Or was it something else?

Is he *dating a Para?*

Misha looked uncomfortable, shoulders up like he clearly didn't want Sasha to talk about it any further. But Sasha needed to. The only person who knew about Alex—other than Shawn, who was angry at Sasha on behalf of his friend—was Eddie, and Sasha couldn't trust him. But Misha—Misha, who might be in love with a Para himself, might be the only person in Sasha's life who could understand.

"What if—" His voice was hoarse, and he whispered even though there was no way for anyone to hear or understand him. "What if I did love someone who was a man? And—and a Para?"

Misha jerked, like a lightning bolt had struck him head-on. His water slipped from his fingers, the half-empty bottle rolling a few inches before spilling out into the sand. Misha didn't seem to notice.

"What are you saying, Sasha?" he asked. Every word was careful, precise.

"This is not my secret to tell," Sasha said, "but I'm thinking maybe you're the only person who can help me."

"Sasha."

"I think I'm in love with Alex," Sasha said slowly. "And I think he's a Para. No, I know he is. I confronted him about it, and now we're no longer speaking."

Misha turned his entire body, any pretense of watching the volleyball game abandoned. His eyes were wide, darting from side to side, and his entire body twitched slightly. "I think I'm going to need a little more than that."

What was the English saying? *In for a penny, in for a pound.* It was a dumb saying, but at this point Sasha wasn't sure he had any path except to push on forward. Eddie already knew, was already threatening to tear Alex's entire world apart; surely telling Misha, who might actually be sympathetic, couldn't be any worse?

So Sasha told him everything. He laid out the weird things he'd noticed about Alex, the burns and the mood swings, the way he dated Heather but still flirted with Sasha once they got to know each other. And he told Misha about the fight on the ice, and how Ed had discovered Alex's secret, had revealed it to Sasha, hoping for support and encouragement in going to Coach Henrique until Sasha had convinced him to wait.

Through it all, Misha sat silently, shaking a little but otherwise watching Sasha, unmoving.

"I didn't get a chance to explain to him what had happened," Sasha concluded. "So he thinks I went to Ed, and that I'm going to be instrumental in him getting kicked off the team."

When it was clear he was done, Misha deflated like a balloon, slumping forward. "Oh, Sasha. This is a fine mess you've gotten us into."

Huh?

"Us?"

Misha looked up, and there was a strange glint of determination in his eye. "Yeah," he said. "Us. The Paras of the NHL. If the team kicks Alex off before the season even ends, it's going to give more strength to Commissioner Heatly's resolution to do genetic testing."

What. The. Hell?

"I—you—that is—"

Misha tilted his head to the side. A hint of his usual humor had appeared now, lips turning up at the corners. "What, you didn't think your boyfriend was the only Para to play pro hockey?"

"You're a—a—"

"A Para. Yes." The grin appeared in full, but Sasha could still see the nervousness that lurked beneath it. "A werewolf, in fact."

That was impossible. Волколак were violent, diseased, vicious beasts with no reason who would come for you and your children in the night. Misha was funny, immature, but ultimately a good man. He couldn't be a werewolf.

Except вампиры are supposed to be evil, manipulative bloodsuckers who will hypnotize you and drain you dead, and Alex is nothing like that.

"A werewolf." Sasha shook his head in disbelief. "You lived with me all season, but I never had any idea."

Misha looked uncomfortable again. "Well, that's the point, isn't it? You couldn't have any idea, because if you did, then anyone could find out. Right now, Para groups are fighting to get the vote canceled, but until that happens we're all at risk of discovery."

"How many?"

"Hm?"

Sasha blinked. "How many Para are in the NHL?"

"Oh." Misha shrugged. "Lots. I don't know. Werewolves like me, we all know each other, right? You can smell it, and it's important to know where pack boundaries begin and end. And I've heard about others. But I won't tell you any names," he added defiantly.

"No, of course not." A thought came to Sasha suddenly, and he laughed. "Oh, goodness. Your last name. Of course, it's so obvious now."

Волков and волколак. Put side by side and it was so obvious. The last name was rather common in Russia, but Sasha had never assumed that a man with the last name Wolf would be an actual werewolf.

"Hiding in plain sight, my papa likes to say." Misha smiled. "So now you know."

"Now I know." Sasha dug his fingers into the sand, feeling the heat against his palm. "So…."

Misha reached out and put a hand on his knee. "So let's figure out how to help you win back your love, and then we can figure out what to do about Ed and this entire anti-Para agenda, hm?"

Seattle Cascades (@CascadesNHL)

Finishing off our trip to sunny Florida with a win! The guys will bring home four out of six possible points from this trip, plus a few sunburns.

Mrs. Merkley… a girl can dream! (@MerkleyFan96)
can we please take a moment to discuss the many MANY photos of half-naked hockey players covered in sand that resulted from this trip? seriously @nhl thank you.

BY THE time the road trip finally came to an end, Alex felt like he was about to lose his mind.

The hunger was a living, visceral thing now, clawing at him every time he wasn't in skates between the pipes. Even playing hockey was barely enough to keep it at bay, and the second he was back in the locker room, it was the only thing he could focus on once again.

"Phantom, dude, you really don't look good."

Shawn's concern wasn't helping. He hovered constantly, worry twisting up his scent and making it come off as faded and a little sour. He'd offered to let Alex feed again, after the game against Florida, but Alex had just shaken his head.

The other thing that wasn't helping was Sasha, who had somehow managed to increase the intensity of his staring. Every time Alex happened to look his way, Sasha would be focused on him. He didn't seem eager, or even anxious; instead, he was patient, calm, like he was waiting for the right moment to approach—or, Alex thought bitterly, waiting until he noticed a moment of weakness so he could strike.

But Sasha hadn't gone to Coach Rico yet, so Alex tried to push him to the side. There were more important things to focus on.

"You need a ride home?" Shawn asked, once the plane finally touched down in Seattle. Six days in the sunny South had done him wonders. His blond hair looked even brighter, and his skin had a hint of rich golden brown. Alex was envious but also relieved not to be sporting a wicked sunburn like some of the other guys.

"Heading straight to Heather's," he answered. "I shouldn't be long, though. Want to order dinner, and we can eat when I get back?"

Shawn bumped fists. "Gotcha."

He texted Heather as he got into an Uber, and she confirmed that she was home and ready for him. Then it was just a half-hour drive across the city, to the condo building and Heather's door.

Chapter Twenty-Six

I'm going to come right out and say that the fated mates plotline is one of my favorite tropes in romance. [I]t's mostly prevalent in Paranormal romances or any other subgenre of romance that deals with the fantastical.... But I also suppose that's part of the fun: physically powerful characters that are essentially powerless in the face of fate.
—Amanda Diehl, romance novel reviewer

"You're starving, aren't you?"

Alex jerked. "How did you know?" He shook his head before she could answer. "I don't know—I just fed on Sunday. It's only Saturday. Six days. And I'm—" He cut himself off with a growl.

"You're ravenous, as though you haven't fed in weeks." Heather spoke the words softly.

"Yeah." It was a constant throbbing through his entire body, every waking second. "What's going on?"

"You had sex with your Sasha."

The words made Alex lift his head in confusion. "Yeah, a few times. So what? You know about that. We've been together since 'Scades and Skates."

Heather sighed. "And that's the problem. At some point since then, you fell in love with him."

None of this was making any sense. "No, I didn't." He liked Sasha a lot, sure, but love? No way. He'd only been with Sasha for three weeks. *But you were attracted to him the moment you laid eyes on him just after the New Year.* And Sasha's scent had teased his senses even when they didn't get along.

I really like him. Alex frowned to himself. *Liked, past tense.* That wasn't true, either. Even right now, in the midst of fear and uncertainty and the threat of betrayal, he still liked Sasha. *He's handsome; he's kind and thoughtful. He has a sense of humor, and he was always trying to take care of me.*

Something settled in the back of his mind, a puzzle piece fitting into place.

Heather laughed. "Yes, you've figured it out."

Alex rubbed his eyes. "I'm not sure I *can* love him," he confessed. "He... I'm going to get outed, lose my spot on the team, and it's going to be his fault."

She hissed in a breath. "What?"

"He figured out that I'm a vampire. Told his friend and mentor, who... well, his friend doesn't like me. Thinks I'm a threat to his job. If he hasn't told Coach yet, he's going to, and it's going to be Sasha's fault."

"Oh, Alex." Heather rested a hand on his arm. "And yet, you do still love him, don't you?"

It was a bitter truth, but Alex couldn't deny it. "I think I do."

Heather nodded. "And that's the problem. That's why feeding from me is no longer satisfying you."

But that wasn't possible. Alex knew the lore as well as anyone; he might only be a half vampire, but his parents had made sure that he knew his human and Para backgrounds thoroughly. "Are you talking about... what? Bonding? That's something out of erotic vampire fiction and cheesy daytime soap operas."

"Sure," Heather said. "Except you're in love with a human and can't sate your hunger with anyone else. What would you call that?"

"A coincidence," Alex said firmly. "People don't actually bond, outside of, like, shifters who find mates or whatever. But vampires and fate? That's a romance novel, not reality."

Heather just stared at him, one eyebrow raised.

"There has to be some other explanation," Alex insisted. "Even if it *was* a thing, I'm not even a full vampire."

There was a glimmer in Heather's eyes that was most definitely amusement.

"Heather, I'm not forming a bond with Sasha. I'm *not*."

The amusement spread across the rest of her face, and Heather bit her lip as though trying to stop herself from laughing outright.

Alex sighed and fell back against the couch cushions. "You're wrong."

"Maybe," Heather said. "Or maybe I'm not. Are you really going to starve yourself trying to feed on me, though, when it's clearly not satisfying you anymore?"

The weight of the situation settled back on Alex's shoulders. "What choice do I have?" he asked softly. "You can joke about mates all you want, but the fact is that I couldn't drink from Sasha even if I wanted to."

"Can't or won't?"

"Both." Alex stared up at the ceiling, breathing in Heather's scent. Even now, he couldn't help but long for the woodsy, earthy scent that he'd grown so used to. "How can I trust him with something like this? He finds out I'm a vampire and can't even keep it to himself before he's telling someone about it. I can't ask to feed from him, can't be that… vulnerable, I guess."

Heather made a low sound, then shifted closer and leaned back as well. Her long hair tickled his arm, and she was warm and soft and exactly the opposite of who he wanted beside him.

"I guess you can't," she said. "But that leaves the question of what are you going to do?"

"No idea." Alex closed his eyes. "Keep feeding from you, if you'll let me. Hope it gets better. Hope this bond—or whatever it is—goes away. Hope I can keep playing hockey and keep living my life. That's all I *can* do."

Heather took his hand, lacing their fingers together. It was an intimate gesture, but it felt more like the closeness of siblings than lovers. "You know I'm here for you. And you have other friends as well."

Alex squeezed her hand. "Thanks. I mean it."

But even with Heather's nice words, he knew it wasn't going to be that easy. Already he could feel the toll it was taking on his body… and he didn't know how much longer he could last like this.

Ellen DeSmith (@EllenDeSmithESPN)
The Seattle Cascades could be this year's come-from-behind miracle story. With six games to go in the regular season, can this team defy all odds and make the post-season? My analysis: bit.ly/g44lR….

"You can't go to practice like this."

Alex peered up at Shawn, bleary-eyed and feeling like death. "Yeah, I can."

Shawn took a step to the side, moving between Alex and the coffee maker that he'd been stumbling toward. "No, Phantom, you can't. You look like shit; you're clearly exhausted. If you get on the ice in this state, you could really hurt yourself."

Alex closed his eyes and counted to ten. Then he opened them again and drew on every meager ounce of strength he could manage. "I have to go to practice, Shawn," he said slowly, "because I have to play tomorrow. Because I can't give them even the slightest hint of an idea that something is wrong or that I can't do my job."

Shawn stared at him, then moved aside silently.

With a sigh of relief, Alex stepped forward to fill his mug with coffee and try to get himself going for the day.

But as much as he hated to admit it, Shawn was probably right. He was lethargic and sore, like someone with the flu. He spent the car ride to the arena curled up in the passenger seat while Shawn hummed along to music and pretended like he didn't notice.

He'd fed only the day before, but his body sure as hell didn't seem to think so.

Thankfully, the cold, chemical-scented ice was enough to finish waking him up. He managed to summon enough energy for a full practice, even pulling out a few jokes and laughs when Bayer tried a fancy shoot-out move and failed epically. No one noticed that he was anything other than fine.

Except Shawn… and Sasha, who still kept watching and waiting.

The only time Alex made eye contact with Sasha, the other man looked worried. He mouthed the words *You okay?* at Alex, and Alex looked away without responding. But it spurred him to finish practice with as much normalcy as possible; if Sasha was looking and noticing, then it was possible someone else might as well.

After practice, a bunch of guys gathered around to make plans for a late lunch. Alex lumbered over to his stall, sat down, and closed his eyes for a second, listening to the chatter as restaurants were thrown around.

The next thing he knew, someone was sitting next to him and laughing.

"We wear you out so much that you can't keep your eyes open?" Alex blinked awake and looked over to see Mikhail, half-undressed and covered in sweat but smiling cheerfully. "You fall asleep in here, someone gonna draw a dick on your face, you know?"

Alex huffed a weak laugh. "Just didn't sleep well last night, I guess." The lunch crowd had moved on to the showers, and he hadn't noticed. "Thanks, I guess, for defending my face from Sharpies."

"Anytime." Mikhail grinned. "Hey, wanted to talk to you for a second, if it's okay?"

Alex opened his mouth to say sure, but was cut off by a growl before he could.

"Misha." Sasha's low voice carried easily across the room. "Что не так с тобой?" He continued on in Russian, sounding a mix between lecturing and furious, and Mikhail went still and tense as he listened.

Finally Mikhail nodded. "Простите, Sasha." He turned to Alex. "Sorry to bother you."

He vanished silently, fleeing to the showers.

Alex turned to Sasha, almost reluctantly. "What the hell was that?" *Did he not want Mikhail to talk to me because I'm Para?*

Sasha didn't look upset anymore, though. Instead, he looked apologetic. "He was bothering you, think he's helping. I tell him to go away. Him being a nosy old grandmother isn't going to make you talk to me."

That... was not what Alex had been expecting.

"I'm talking to you now," he said evenly.

Sasha smiled sadly. "Yes. And I'm thankful for this much. And maybe soon we can talk for real. I hope I can—" He cut himself off as a group of guys emerged from the showers. "But not here, and not now."

Then Sasha was following Mikhail to the showers, leaving Alex confused and alone in his stall.

What was all that?

"—Fanning just manages to get a glove out in time and deflects the puck up and out of play. The Seattle goaltender is slow to get up, but he doesn't look injured. He's been having a rough night, slow to start, but it looks like he has some energy in him now. Face-off will be to Fanning's left, and San Jose wins in. Looks like a set play, quick pass to the center and a shot on goal, but this time Fanning's able to catch it and hold on. Score at the halfway point in the second is 4-1 San Jose, and the

Cascades will have some work to do if they're going to dig themselves out of this hole."

—KTCP Radio 102.7, home of your Seattle Cascades

It was *so obvious* that something was wrong with Alex, but no one other than Sasha seemed to notice. Their goalie acted like he was sick, fatigue evident in every line of his body. Sure, he was still playing just fine in both games and practices, but he was also barely able to keep his eyes open when he wasn't on the ice.

So Sasha kept watching and hoped that whatever was wrong could be fixed soon, because he had much bigger problems to focus on right now.

They had another home game on the next night, then only four more games left to play—two away, in Colorado and Vegas, followed by two at home to close out the season. Alex was looking worse with every passing day, and Sasha had no idea what was wrong. Maybe he was stressed, wondering when his secret was going to be exposed to the world? But that didn't explain the way Carts always seemed to be hovering, worry clear on his face when he looked at his friend.

But Alex still wouldn't talk to Sasha, let alone look at him. And there were more pressing things to worry about... like what to do about Ed.

Ed's trial was only six days away, scheduled for the Monday after they got back from Vegas. So not only did he have to deal with trying to figure out how he was going to handle that, but the upcoming road trip only added another layer of pressure to the entire situation.

Помяни черта, Sasha thought as Ed appeared at his side, pulling him from his thoughts.

"Eddie." Sasha pasted on a smile, hoping it looked genuine. "Was just thinking about you. Feeling better?"

He didn't look any better, but he didn't look worse either. Sasha wondered what the trainers thought, if they'd even noticed the way Ed's appearance and mannerisms had changed.

"Doing good." Ed looked happy enough at least, sweaty like he'd recently finished a workout. His sling was gone, though there was a light brace visible on his arm and wrist. "I think I'll be back in the net to take some practice shots any day now; the coaches and trainers sound really optimistic."

This time Sasha knew his smile must look strained. "That's fantastic."

Thankfully, Ed didn't seem to notice Sasha's lack of enthusiasm. "You all keep going the way you are, and I'll be back for playoffs. You were right, Sasha, about the Para freak. We can use him to get the team to the post-season and then get rid of him when he's not needed anymore."

Ed wasn't even bothering to keep his voice down. Sasha glanced around furtively, hoping no one was close enough to overhear. "For sure, Eddie. But we gotta keep it a secret until then. Still five more games to play, and every point is gonna count."

"Sure, sure." Ed nodded easily enough. "And hey, trial is less than a week out. Soon all of this will be behind us, you know?"

"Yeah, I know."

"You'll be there, right?" Ed asked. "You know I need your support, brother."

The guilt that Sasha had felt over the last month was still there, but now it was mixed with new emotions: worry over Ed's obvious problems with alcohol, and anger because of what his best friend was planning to do to the man Sasha loved.

"Yeah, I'll be there," Sasha responded.

"Good man."

Ed kept talking, rambling easily about his training and the trial. But Sasha's thoughts had drifted back to Alex… and to how he was going to fix this problem with Ed.

What if I bribe Eddie? It was a distasteful solution, but it was also the only path forward he could see right now. *If I tell him that I'll testify on his behalf, but only if he doesn't reveal that Alex is a vampire.* It would mean lying under oath and almost certainly losing Eddie's friendship in the process, but… it would save Alex.

But Ed would never let him stay on this team. I'm certain of that much. He'd only agree to it as long as Alex requested a trade. So I could save Alex, but I'd lose him for sure.

Just thinking about it was painful.

But I'll do it. If that's what it takes, I'll do it for Alex.

Ed laughed at something he said, jolting Sasha back to the conversation. "Anyway, it'll be fine because I'll have you there with me, right?"

"Yeah, absolutely, Eddie."

"Great." Ed smiled. "We can go out for post-trial drinks when it's all done to celebrate!"

Sasha took a deep breath and held it, then let it out slowly. Ed obviously didn't see the irony in his statement, and Sasha wasn't about to point it out.

A flicker of movement out of the corner of his eye caught Sasha's attention. When he glanced over, Shawn was hovering… watching him.

Shawn hadn't said a word outside of practice to him in over a week. There was no reason for that to have changed either—unless whatever was wrong with Alex had just gotten worse. Sasha's heart began to race.

"Hey, Ed, sorry, but I gotta run. Looks like something's come up."

Ed glanced over and nodded when he spotted Shawn. "Defensemen bonding. I understand. I'll see you Monday at the trial… or maybe sooner."

"For sure. Later."

He waved goodbye to Ed, then hurried as quickly as he could to join Shawn.

Shawn didn't speak, though. Instead, he motioned for Sasha to follow him, glancing around as though someone might spot them. They wove through the back hallways of the arena, places Sasha rarely had any need to go, and finally stopped at a small conference room that was well off the beaten track.

"In here."

Sasha glanced inside. The level of dust said that even custodial staff often forgot that this room existed. It was the perfect place to talk about something in the arena if you didn't want to risk anyone overhearing you… which made it fairly obvious what this was about.

"How's Alex?"

The surprise that blossomed across Shawn's face told Sasha he hadn't expected that question.

"He's fine."

Sasha grimaced. "He's not. Something's wrong with him. I know you've noticed. He's sick, but I cannot understand how."

"No one else seems to have noticed anything."

Shawn wasn't wrong. If the rest of the team *had* picked up that Alex was exhausted, they probably would have assumed it was due to the higher-impact, faster-paced game that he was playing at the NHL level. But so far, none of their teammates had brought it up. Though Misha had definitely figured out that it was something more serious than just fatigue, if his quiet, solemn glances at Alex in the locker room were anything to go by.

But that was beside the point. "I noticed," Sasha said. "I watch him, and I can see that he's not okay."

The way Shawn simply pressed his lips together was confirmation enough for Sasha.

"What were you talking to Ed about just now?"

The sudden change in topic made Sasha straighten abruptly. "Why?"

Shawn glared. "Because if you're going to run back to Despres and report this entire conversation to him as soon as we're done, I need to know."

Oh.

"Carts, listen to me," Sasha said insistently. "I need to tell you what happened in Atlanta."

"I heard," Shawn said with a glare.

"No, you didn't." Talking in English was difficult enough when he was emotional, but he needed to make sure there were no further misunderstandings. "But I need to explain now."

Confusion and curiosity warred with distrust on Shawn's face before he nodded shortly. "All right, let's hear it."

For the second time in a week, Sasha found himself explaining what had happened between himself and Ed, including Ed's paranoia and irrational dislike of Alex and the way Sasha had carefully maneuvered Ed to buy them some time.

"I convinced him not to say anything for now. But when I ask Alex, trying to be sure what Ed says is truth, he reacted badly—he's so terrified, he cannot listen to me. And now he still won't listen, so I can't explain. But I only want to help him. I swear this."

By the end of it, Shawn's eyes were wide. "You need to tell him this."

"He won't even look at me, Carts." Pain laced Sasha's words. "I give him as much space as I can. There are a few options—distasteful, but I'll do them, if it keeps Alex safe. You have to believe this."

Shawn exhaled. "Do you love him?"

Sasha didn't hesitate. "Yes."

"Okay." Shawn dusted his hands off. "Okay."

"I'm going to help him," Sasha said, making sure every word was as clear as possible. "Even if he hates me, I will do everything I can. But I need to understand why he's sick."

For a long moment, Sasha thought maybe Carts wouldn't tell him. His partner looked weary and troubled. But finally he sighed and nodded once. "He can't feed anymore. I don't know the details, he won't tell me, but he feeds from Heather every other day it seems like, and it never helps."

That was bad... very, very bad. Sasha had spent hours online, poring over every website about vampires that he could find in English or Russian. Some of the things he'd read fit Alex perfectly and explained so many of his quirks and behavior over the last three months, while others clearly didn't apply. But all of the sites had agreed on one thing: vampires needed blood, and if they couldn't get it, then....

"Is he dying?" Three words, but Sasha felt physical pain simply thinking about them, let alone speaking them.

"Not yet."

It wasn't a no, but it was still enough that Sasha could breathe.

"How serious is it?"

Shawn bent over, resting his hands on his thighs and staring at the ground as he spoke. "He won't tell me, but it's obvious that it's pretty damn serious. He came home from seeing Heather on Sunday and looked almost worse than when he'd left. When I asked him if he needed another source, if I could help, he said no one could help him... except you."

"He said this?"

"His exact words were 'the only person who can help me is the only person I can't accept help from.'" Shawn scuffed his foot on the ground, then straightened back up. "Who else could it be?"

The words sliced Sasha open wide. *He thinks I can help him, but he would let himself grow sick and possibly die rather than come to me for help.*

"That's why I approached you today," Shawn continued. "I was going to beg you or threaten you, I don't actually know."

"No threats or begging needed." Sasha cracked a weak smile. "Help me talk to Alex. Let me explain, so I can help him with this too."

"Yeah, okay. I'll talk to him."

"Not tonight." When Shawn blinked up at him, Sasha shook his head and elaborated. "He's starting tomorrow against Washington. Alex won't want to listen until after the game because he'll be getting himself into the right headspace to play. Especially if he is this sick, trying to make him listen might make things worse."

Shawn's smile was a little lopsided, but his eyes were approving. "It's good that you care about him. And that you know how important hockey is to him."

Sasha waited.

"All right. Tomorrow after the game, if he's feeling up to it. Otherwise Thursday for sure. He's hanging in there for now, but I don't want to wait any longer than that. I'll do whatever I can to convince him to talk to you. But he's scared, Sasha. It's not going to be easy to make him hear reason."

"Yes, I know how stubborn he is." Sasha returned the smile. "Thank you, Carts."

Shawn held out his fist, and Sasha bumped it, feeling better for the first time in weeks.

Chapter Twenty-Seven

Seattle Cascades (@CascadesNHL)
The guys from Washington (city) manage an overtime win against the guys from Washington (state), as the Cascades fall to D.C. 5-4 in OT.

Mrs. Merkley… a girl can dream! (@MerkleyFan96)
is Fanning playing through an injury or something? :(Well, at least we got one point, better than none. #playoffsbaby #goscades

It was a relatively short plane ride into Colorado, and Shawn spent every minute of it twitching like he wanted to say something but was holding himself back.

Alex wasn't an idiot. He knew Shawn had spoken to Sasha; even if he couldn't smell the hint of earthiness on Shawn's clothes when they got back to the condo after the loss to Washington, it would have been obvious just from the weighted looks they exchanged every time they were in the same room. And whatever Sasha had said to Shawn, it was eating away at his best friend.

Part of him wanted to demand that Shawn spit it out; his friend was a human-shaped ball of frantic tension, and it was driving Alex crazy. But the other part of him was too worn-out, and he couldn't seem to find enough energy to ask.

The unsteady balance held as they got off the plane in Denver. Shawn didn't say anything, Alex didn't ask, and Sasha's gaze bored into Alex's back like a stick spearing him between the shoulder blades, waiting for one of them to break.

"You want to stay with me again?" Shawn asked. It was the first thing he'd said to Alex all day, and there was another layer to his question that Alex couldn't even begin to parse.

"Yeah, if that's okay."

"Sure, Phantom. Always." Shawn hesitated, like he was about to say something, then snapped his mouth shut. Alex gritted his teeth and dragged himself and his bag down the hall after his friend. Shawn wouldn't manage to hold out much longer, and he was honestly dreading whatever conversation they were preparing to have.

Coach had announced a mandatory team dinner-slash-bonding that evening at a restaurant across the road from their hotel. So while Alex wanted nothing more than to collapse on the other queen bed in the room and wrap himself up in a comforter, he changed into a pair of jeans and a dress shirt and let Shawn tug him outside and to the expensive Italian restaurant that had been selected.

"Let's sit down here," Shawn said, one hand on Alex's arm to guide him to the end of the table. Alex followed blindly, letting Shawn point him toward an empty chair.

And that's when he noticed the trap, because there, in the seat on his other side, was Sasha.

Alex went to stand back up, but Shawn's hand had moved to his shoulder and pushed him right back down into the chair.

"Carts," Alex bit off.

Shawn shook his head. "It's only dinner."

"This isn't the place for it." They were surrounded by teammates, and the last thing Alex wanted was to make a scene.

Shawn slid into his own seat on Alex's left. "Just hear him out."

But Alex couldn't. He was hungry—not for pasta, but for the rich scent that filled his mouth and nose. Even looking at Sasha on his right would be too much. As it was, just sitting this close to him was sheer torture.

He tried. Alex stared straight ahead at his plate, took tiny sips from his water glass with hands that shook and fingers that felt numb. The restaurant was loud, and he sank into the white noise of people talking and dishes clanking together.

It wasn't enough.

Sasha cleared his throat, and the soft sound cut through the din like someone tapping a glass with a knife. "Alex," he said softly.

Alex couldn't. He could smell Sasha, feel the heat coming off his body from so close. Every single atom in his body strained toward the person on his right, and Alex's resolve was crumbling with every lightly accented syllable that escaped Sasha's lips.

Chest heaving, he pushed back from the table and fled toward the bathroom.

It wasn't a surprise when Shawn followed him only a few seconds later. He pushed the bathroom door open tentatively, peering inside. "Phantom, you okay?"

Alex was slumped over the counter between the sinks, elbows resting on the surface while his head hung down between his hands. He glanced over at Shawn, but didn't speak, too busy trying to steady his breathing.

Shawn glanced over his shoulder, as though to make sure no one else had followed him, then slid into the bathroom and pushed the door shut firmly behind him. "I told the guys you ate something bad at lunch."

"Thanks."

"You can't keep going on like this, Alex."

So they were going to do this now. Alex closed his eyes and didn't move.

"Sasha is worried about you. So am I. And it's scaring us to see you this way, because it's obvious that you're really sick and getting sicker by the day, but neither of us can figure out why Heather isn't helping."

"Why?" Alex croaked.

Shawn took a step forward, shoes echoing in the small room. "Why what?" His hand rested tentatively on Alex's back and, when Alex didn't protest, settled more firmly.

"Why is he worried?" Alex's mouth was dry, and the words felt like sandpaper against his tongue.

"Because," Shawn said softly, "he loves you."

Alex jerked, a full-body shudder that knocked Shawn's hand loose and sent Alex reeling from the counter until his back hit the opposite wall.

He pressed himself against the surface, using it to hold himself up, as he gaped at Shawn. "He doesn't."

"He does." Shawn sounded so certain, and that insistence only made Alex ache even more. "He wanted to explain, but he didn't want to upset you when it was obvious you didn't want to speak with him."

The laughter that escaped Alex was harsh and humorless. "You know why I avoid him?" he asked. "Because I'm terrified of what I'll do to him if I let him get too close."

Shawn moved to his side. "What would you do to him?"

"God, Shawn. His scent drives me crazy, did you know?" Alex knew he wasn't making sense, that he wasn't answering the question, but now that he was talking it was like he couldn't stop the flood of words escaping him. "Every time he's near, it's all I can smell. Like the fresh scent of the air after it rains or the richness of dark chocolate on the back of your tongue. It's too much and not enough, and I'm *starving*, Shawn. I'm so fucking hungry, and he's the only person I can think about feeding from."

Alex looked up, eyes burning. "If I let him talk to me, if he gets too close, I'm not going to be able to stop myself from feeding off him. Do you understand?"

The silence in the bathroom was almost deafening. If he focused, he could just hear the faint roar of people eating outside in the restaurant, the rush of water through pipes, but otherwise the only noise he could hear was his own heartbeat pounding in his ears, and Shawn's soft breathing.

"No, I don't understand," Shawn said.

Of course he didn't. He was human, and he had no idea how Alex was being torn apart.

"Sasha already knows my biggest secret. Maybe he won't tell Coach or Dubois. He hasn't yet, or I wouldn't still be here. But he's already told Despres and god knows who else. And even knowing this, even with that awful fear surrounding every single moment of every single day, I love him." Alex exhaled, letting his head fall back against the wall. "Fuck, I love him. And apparently my vampire side won't feed from anyone but him."

It was such a horrible catch-22, and just thinking about it made Alex want to put his fist through the wall in rage and sorrow. Because he loved someone who he couldn't trust, and not being able to trust the man he loved was going to ruin him on two different fronts.

As he watched, comprehension filled Shawn's face. "Oh, Alex."

Yeah. Oh, Alex. "Now you get it."

But Shawn was shaking his head, and he was… smiling? "You need to talk to Sasha, Phantom."

"I agree with Carts," a new voice said. Alex's head whipped to the side, to see brilliant blue eyes watching him from the entrance to the bathroom. "We really need to talk, Alex."

Akseli Mäkelä (@AkseliMakela38)
Team selfie! Everyone eating lots of pasta so we have energy to destroy Colorado tomorrow. pic.twitter.com/9h2TRz....

Emma (@Cascadiac)
RT @AkseliMakela38: Uh, where's Cartier, Petrov, and Fanning?

SASHA HAD waited a minute or two after Alex had fled the table and Shawn had followed him toward the back of the restaurant. Once his teammates were again occupied with their menus, he'd made eye contact with Misha, then quietly slipped away from the table himself.

The only logical place for Alex to have disappeared to was the bathroom, so Sasha followed the signs down a hallway and to the marked door. It had quickly become clear that he was in the right place when Alex's and Shawn's voices had filtered out into the corridor.

He hadn't intended to eavesdrop, but curiosity kept him from announcing his presence. Instead, he leaned against the door, waiting like a guard to stop anyone from going in and interrupting.

And he listened.

"I'm terrified of what I'll do to him if I let him get too close." Alex's words were heartbreaking, so full of agony and hurt that Sasha brought a hand to his chest and clenched his shirt over his heart.

Alex, I'm sorry. He almost walked in right then and there, but something stopped him, made him listen in for another minute.

And then:

"Even with that awful fear surrounding every single moment of every single day, I love him."

"God, Alex," Sasha had murmured. He hadn't been able to resist any longer; he'd pushed the door open, and finally seen Alex there, looking broken and frightened and so, so strong that Sasha had felt tears burning in his eyes.

"We really need to talk, Alex," he said softly.

Alex was frozen across the room. Shawn glanced over his shoulder, nodded at Sasha, and took a step to the side.

"Alex, I know you're scared, but please, talk to me."

Alex wasn't a small man by normal standards, but in the shocking bright light of the bathroom, he looked tiny. He shook his head, clenching his fists against his thighs, and didn't move his back from the wall.

"I can't," Alex choked out. "Please, don't do this to me. Not right now."

"Phantom, please, hear him out."

Alex's expression was a combination of betrayal and dismay. "Shawn, you know why I can't."

Shawn nodded. "I know you're scared, man, but you know I wouldn't hurt you."

"I know." Alex took a long, ragged breath, and shook his head. "Not right now. I'm sorry, I can't."

And then he was gone, pushing past Shawn and Sasha and out the door before either of them could react.

Shawn shook his head sadly. "I've never seen him like this."

But Sasha understood. "He's sick, he's afraid, he does not understand what's going on. He worries he might lose everything that he loves." *Including me.* His heart was buoyed momentarily by the reminder of what he'd overheard. "Even someone as strong as Alex cannot handle this much at once."

"You gonna go after him, though?"

Sasha hesitated, but every inch of him was screaming to follow Alex back to the hotel. "Yeah."

"Good." Shawn smiled and dug a key card out of his pocket. "He's been sharing a room with me since Atlanta. Room 424. I'm gonna crash with Bayer tonight."

The key card was handed over, and Sasha tucked it into his pocket, fingers lingering over the fabric. "Thanks, Carts."

Chapter Twenty-Eight

The room was dark when Sasha pushed the door open. It only took a second for his eyes to adjust, though, and to spot the mound of blankets in the middle of one of the beds.

Sasha clicked one of the lamps on and gasped. In the dim light, Alex looked like death. He was curled beneath the blankets, pale, teeth chattering even though the room was comfortably warm. Bruise-like circles stood out in sharp relief beneath his eyes, and his hair looked limp, messy.

He'd been barely holding it together back in the restaurant, Sasha realized. But this was Alex without the pretenses, without the shaky disguise.

"Alex," he breathed.

Brown eyes opened heavily, and Alex drew a shaky breath. "I can't. Please don't do this to me."

"No." Sasha took a step forward as Alex's eyes fell shut once again. "Alex, солнышко, I must."

He took a seat on the other bed, facing Alex's huddled, shivering form. Alex curled in even tighter, eyes clenched and lips pale from being pressed together.

"I didn't tell Eddie about you being a vampire," he said, for lack of a better place to start. Alex didn't react. "He told me. I had no idea until he came to me, planning to use his discovery to have you kicked off the team. I convinced him not to tell anyone, for now—because I needed to know if what he said was true… and because I love you too much to let anyone hurt you even if it is."

That got a reaction. A tiny breath punched out of Alex, and his eyes snapped open.

Sasha continued before he could lose his nerve. "I love you, Alexander Fanning. I loved you before Ed came to me with this shocking accusation. And after, I had to research, to understand. It was scary—in Russia, being gay is bad enough but being Para is impossible. So I think, and I realize, *Yes, Sasha Petrov, you love this man because he's funny and beautiful and full of light. Why does it matter what he eats for dinner, as long as he loves you in return?"*

Alex had uncurled slightly and was watching Sasha with wide eyes.

"And then you got sick," Sasha said, "and you wouldn't speak to me. At first I'm thinking, give him space. He is scared and hurting and something is wrong. But now I know that giving you space is only hurting you more."

"I can't." Alex's words were so soft that Sasha wasn't sure he'd spoken at first. Then Alex repeated them.

Sasha leaned forward. "You can."

His hands were shaking the tiniest amount as he raised them to his shirt, fumbling the top button before it slipped free of its hole. The next one came easier, and the one after that, until the entire shirt was unbuttoned and he could shrug it off his shoulders.

Alex's eyes followed him intently as Sasha stood. He stepped out of his shoes, then pulled his undershirt off and tossed it on top of the abandoned dress shirt.

"Alex, let me help you."

Alex didn't protest. He didn't speak or even move as Sasha stepped between the beds and set one knee on the mattress beside Alex's blanket-covered form, then the other. Alex went easily when Sasha gently pushed his shoulder, rolling him onto his back, legs uncurling beneath the covers.

Sasha tugged the blankets away, revealing Alex's lanky form. He was dressed for a blizzard, heavy sweats and a thick hoodie, and his body trembled beneath Sasha's gaze.

"I told you that I researched," Sasha said. "You won't hurt me."

Alex licked his lips, pink tongue darting out. "It's—not all wounds are physical," he whispered. "Sasha, I love you, but—"

Sasha shook his head.

"But," Alex pushed on, "if I drink from you now, I'm not sure what will happen. It's possible that—I need to drink to survive. I can eat human food just fine, but I *need* blood. And if I drink from you, I might not be able to drink from anyone else ever again."

He'd said as much, back in the bathroom. Now, though, Sasha could see the fear in his eyes. "So?"

"So," Alex whispered, "I'd be dependent on you for the rest of my life. If you're traded, if you decide you don't want a Para boyfriend anymore, if I get kicked out of the NHL—"

"Alex." Sasha planted one hand on either side of Alex's head, leaning over him so he could look Alex straight in the eyes. Even weakened and ill, Alex was the most handsome man that he'd ever seen. "I love you. I've been drawn to you since the moment I first laid eyes on you. I thought I hated you, but I still couldn't stop thinking about you. Whatever is between us, it's not one-sided. I feel it too. I'm not going anywhere, and I'm not going to let you scare me with what-ifs." He grinned. "Besides, I have a no-trade clause in my contract."

Finally, some of the tension dropped from Alex's body, and a hint of a smile appeared. "Sasha."

Sasha hushed him. "There's more we need to talk about, I know. But right now you're sick, and you need to feed." He threw a leg over Alex's waist, straddling him, and saw the way Alex's chest hitched and his eyes darkened.

Lowering himself to cover Alex's body with his own made him realize just how bad things really were. Alex was still trembling beneath him, skin icy cold and body weak. Even through the thick cotton sweats, Sasha could feel his ribs and how thin he was. It was a wonder that he'd managed to play over the last week and a half, but it was obvious now that Alex wouldn't be able to go on like that for much longer.

Tilting his head to the side to bare his neck was the easiest decision that Sasha had ever made. "Come on, солнышко. Свет очей моих."

For a minute, Sasha thought that Alex was going to refuse. Then he felt Alex shift beneath him, felt the shaking body tense and arch up so Alex could press cool, soft lips to Sasha's neck.

"Sasha." Alex breathed the word against his skin. "You have to be sure. I can't do this unless you're sure."

Sasha closed his eyes. "The only things in life that I have ever been sure about are playing hockey and this," he said. "I love you."

"I love you too," Alex said, and then teeth pierced Sasha's neck.

ALEX HAD fed from dozens of people, human and Para both, in his lifetime. None had ever felt like this.

Sasha tasted exactly as he smelled, rich and brilliant, like the finest dark chocolate. He moaned as Alex drank from him, his body shaking above Alex's as his arms threatened to give out. Alex wrapped his hands around Sasha's neck and shoulders, pulling him closer, and sighed happily against Sasha's neck when the larger body finally settled on top of his own.

Like this, he could feel every vibration that passed through Sasha's body, the way his breathing hitched and the soft rumble of pleasure as he groaned deep in his chest. And Alex could feel Sasha's cock against his thigh, getting harder as he drank, until Sasha's hips were jerking forward in tiny, abortive thrusts.

He was feeling something else, though. Alex closed his eyes, trying to understand what it was. At first it was a sensation like a tickling in his mind, an awareness that he couldn't quite grasp. Then it shifted, becoming more defined—arousal, and languid pleasure, and love.

That's Sasha. Alex gripped the other man tighter. *I'm feeling Sasha, in my mind.*

A burst of surprise filtered through the new awareness, and Sasha gasped out Alex's name.

He feels it too. Alex latched on to the sensation—*the bond*, he realized, because that was exactly what was forming between them—and hoped Sasha could feel his happiness, his gratitude, and his own love in return.

"Yes, Alex." Sasha gasped the words. "Love you."

Alex drank less than he would have from Heather. Part of it was the fear of drinking from Sasha, the worry that a human wouldn't be able to handle it. But part of it was also his own body; while he wasn't physically starving, having continued to eat human food for the last few weeks, he wasn't sure he could handle drinking as much as he usually did. Sasha's blood was rich, powerful as it filled him, and Alex hesitated to overdo it.

When he finally pulled away, Alex was trembling once more, but this time from the pleasure and overwhelming sense of contentment. He was full for the first time in weeks—but more than that, he was warm and sated, and Sasha's arms were wrapped around him as though to keep him safe.

Alex pressed his lips to the bite marks on Sasha's neck, waiting for the tiny wounds to close before licking away the sweat and salt on

Sasha's skin, kissing his way up Sasha's neck and jaw. He kissed the corner of Sasha's lips, then paused.

"What?" Sasha's voice was thick, as though he was drugged, but the bond between them was clear and strong.

"I didn't want to kiss you if—" Alex pressed his lips together. He could still taste Sasha on the back of his tongue, mixed with the saltiness of his skin.

Sasha rolled his eyes, then yanked him forward. "Come here and kiss me."

Alex kissed him hard, unable to suppress his grin of joy and relief as Sasha kissed him back. He could *feel* Sasha, a spot in his mind that he'd never realized was empty, now filled with passion and arousal, hope and relief. And love. That was the most overwhelming sensation of all, the fiery heat of Sasha's love for him, radiating through the bond between them.

"I want you to smile like this," Sasha said between frantic kisses. "All the time. So beautiful." He lapsed into Russian, hands sliding beneath the thick hoodie that Alex was wearing.

And suddenly Alex realized how warm he was. He'd been frozen straight through before, fingers stiff with the cold and body shaking with it. Now he was burning up, both from the heat of the bond and from Sasha's blood running through his veins. He scrambled to slide out of the sweatshirt, Sasha helping to tug the heavy material off over his head.

"Oh, солнышко." Sasha voice was heartbroken. His hand trailed over Alex's chest a moment later, fingers bumping along the visible ribs. "I'm so sorry."

Alex blinked. "Sorry? Why?"

Sasha leaned forward, brushing his lips against the bottom of Alex's ribs. "For scaring you, for giving you so much fear, for making you hurt like this." He moved his mouth up with every word, pressing kisses up Alex's rib cage and sternum until he was hovering over Alex's heart.

"Sasha, no." Alex pushed him back, just enough that he could meet those bright blue eyes straight on. "You have nothing to apologize for. I should have trusted you. I should have at least listened. I let my fear overwhelm me."

He pushed Sasha down, with arms that were finally beginning to regain their former strength. Sasha went easily, falling onto his back and pulling Alex along with him.

"I never want to hurt you," Sasha said.

"You don't," Alex said. "You can't. I doubted before, but now I know it. You take care of me, comfort me…. You love me."

"Yes." Sasha pulled him down, kissing him deeply.

Alex spoke the next words against his lips. "You love me, and I love you, and right now I want to make you feel as good as you make me feel."

With that, he ground his hips down and back, sweatpants-clad ass dragging over Sasha's crotch.

And Sasha was hard. Alex could feel the heat and weight of him, and more than anything in the world he wanted to feel it against him, inside him.

"Fuck me," he said.

Sasha swallowed visibly. "Game tomorrow."

Alex leaned down until they were nose to nose. "I don't care, Sasha. Fuck me, make me feel it tomorrow while I'm in net against Colorado. I can feel you in my head… I want to feel you in my entire body too."

With a growl, Sasha launched himself up, tearing at Alex's clothes and his own. They laughed, hands tangling together as they rolled on the bed, trying to get to skin as quickly as possible. Alex went to work on Sasha's belt, working it free and tugging his slacks off, while Sasha fumbled at the drawstring on Alex's sweatpants before yanking them down and flinging them to the end of the bed.

They were both hard and sweating by the time they were skin to skin, flushed from the exertion. Sasha's eyes were shining, and he couldn't seem to stop smiling. Alex knew a matching grin was stretched across his own face.

"I love you," Alex said.

Laughter soon turned to moans of pleasure, and Alex closed his eyes as everything went hazy. He could feel Sasha's hands on his body, and he could sense Sasha's passion in his mind. The dual sensations only augmented his own arousal, until he couldn't tell what was his passion and what belonged to Sasha. They were tangled together, physically and mentally, and Alex never wanted to let go.

Sasha vanished for a moment, but Alex could still reach out to touch him while he was across the room, digging condoms and lube out of Alex's bag. Then Sasha was back, fingers slick as they pressed between Alex's legs, his large body forcing Alex's thighs wide.

It had been a while since Alex had done this. Sasha was a little clumsy as well, hands shaking as he pushed one finger into Alex. His nerves were obvious, and Alex closed his eyes and shoved every ounce of his pleasure and happiness through the bond.

When Sasha added a second finger, it was with a lot more confidence.

When he added a third, a few minutes later, it was with a wicked grin and a biting kiss. He curled his fingers, and Alex thrashed and moaned as the nerve endings inside him lit up.

"Sasha, babe." Alex licked his lips. "I need you. Now."

Sasha pulled away to fumble with the condom, and Alex took the opportunity to push the larger man down. He took the condom from Sasha's hands, tore it open with a teasing wink, then slid the condom over Sasha's hard cock, rubbing his hand along the shaft.

Then Alex straddled him, both hands pressing down on Sasha's chest. He absently ran a finger over one of Sasha's nipples and smirked as a shudder ran through the body beneath him.

"Sensitive?"

Sasha groaned, so Alex repeated the motion, flicking the edge of his nail over the hard nub again and again until Sasha was panting and watching him through hooded eyes.

"Please, Alex."

As much as Alex wanted to tease him, he wanted Sasha inside him even more. He slid his hands down Sasha's chest, then lifted himself up on his knees so he could guide Sasha's cock inside him. Sasha was big, hard, and Alex had to ease himself down carefully until Sasha was buried deep inside him. The defenseman didn't move, to his credit, though he twisted his hands in the sheets at his side the entire time, and his body trembled as Alex shifted and clenched above him.

Then Alex rolled his hips, and the cock inside him nudged over that bundle of nerves.

"Oh, fuck."

Sasha looked like he was about to snap. "Alex, please. Я так хочу тебя."

Judging by the need and desperation that saturated their bond, Alex could guess exactly what was being said. He rolled his hips again, then sighed and tilted his head back. "Yeah, Sasha. Fuck me."

In hindsight, Alex should have expected what came next. Yet, despite being aware of all the carefully coiled muscle beneath him and the tension in every line of Sasha's body, the first thrust of Sasha's hips still caught him off guard.

Sasha bent his knees to give himself more leverage, and his fingers curled around Alex's hips as he pushed himself up and pulled Alex down on top of him at the same time. Red-hot pleasure jolted through him, making Alex moan.

"Yeah, just like that."

With his legs spread wide across Sasha's hips, he couldn't get as much leverage as he wanted. But Alex did his best, riding Sasha's cock, lifting his hips up only to sink back down and let Sasha's cock fill him.

One second he was upright, and the next he was being tumbled upside down, Sasha's cock sliding free from his body. Alex's back hit the bed, and then Sasha was looming over him. He pressed their lips together and fucked his tongue into Alex's mouth. Alex didn't have a chance to feel disappointment, though, because only a moment later, Sasha lifted his hips and leaned over him before sliding back in with one long thrust. Alex arched his back off the bed and dug his fingers into Sasha's arms, urging him to do it again. With the new angle, Sasha's dick rubbed over his prostate, punching needy moans from Alex's chest every time he pressed inside.

There was no way either of them was going to last long. Between the emotions and the bond—which sent a feedback loop of pleasure through Alex's entire body, his own sensations amplified by Sasha's—Alex was honestly surprised they'd made it this long. Sasha felt so good inside him, over him, around him, until all he could feel and think was Sasha. Every time he sucked in another breath, Sasha's scent was there, and the bond throbbed and strengthened between them, filling Alex's entire awareness.

He became aware of Sasha chanting his name, *Alex, Alex, солнышко, please* breathed against his jaw as Alex kissed the soft skin there and fucked into Alex's tight hole over and over.

"Yeah," Alex exhaled. "Love you, Sasha, come on."

Sasha leaned up, and for a second Alex thought he was going to kiss him again, but then Sasha turned his head so his neck was in front of Alex's mouth.

"Alex." His voice was thick with desire. "Please."

Alex didn't need words or even the bond to know what Sasha was asking. He hesitated for only a second, then wrapped his fingers around

Sasha's shoulder, his other hand cupping Sasha's cheek. Then he reached up and slid his fangs into Sasha's neck again.

Sasha came like that, hips jerking as he buried himself deep inside Alex's body, and Alex drank from him and felt his own orgasm wash over him like a building inferno until he was utterly consumed by it.

This time, he pulled back from Sasha easily, helping the bite to close while Sasha shuddered above him as aftershocks rumbled through his body. He lowered himself unsteadily to the bed beside Alex, eyes closed and dark eyelashes fanned on his cheekbones, looking so peaceful and content that Alex couldn't resist leaning forward to kiss him gently.

"Thank you."

Sasha hummed, eyes fluttering open to reveal bright blue eyes staring back at him softly. "Это было изумительно," he said. "Я тебя люблю."

Alex didn't speak Russian, but he recognized the last word, the Ls tripping over one another. He smiled, then said teasingly, "You know I don't speak asshole."

Sasha laughed, rolling onto his side to face Alex, and pulled him in for another kiss. "Going to have to teach you. You repeat after me. Ya."

"Ya," Alex parroted back, trying and failing to keep a straight face.

"Tebya."

Alex's grin escaped as he repeated the word.

"Lyublyu."

"Lyublyu." Alex kissed him again. "Pretty sure I know what that means. I love you."

"Yes." Sasha returned the kiss, then settled Alex against him and exhaled in contentment. "I say, that was amazing. You are amazing, and I love you."

They still needed to talk and clean up, and there was a strange bond between them that needed to be explored... but it could wait.

Alex closed his eyes, let happiness wash over him, and knew he was loved.

Avocados and Avs (@avocolorado)

guys, I know my team is great, and I love them... but after just the first period of this game tonight I feel pretty confident in saying we are well and truly screwed. daaaaaaaamn, seattle is playing lights-out tonight.

Emma (@Cascadiac)
Wowwww. So, uh, Seattle really wants that playoff spot, huh? Why can't they play like this ALL THE TIME?!

SASHA COULD feel Alex on the ice.

It wasn't instinct, the way he often knew when Shawn was out of position or when one of the forwards was going to drop-pass to him just before the blue line. Instead, it was a sense like sight or smell, a newly awoken part of his brain that told him where Alex was and how he was feeling.

He was battling along the boards for a puck when he felt a thread of alarm race up the back of his mind. Sasha glanced up just in time to avoid being hit hard by one of the Colorado defensemen.

"Did you know?" he asked during a TV timeout, skating past Alex's net. "Did you know it would be like this?"

Alex lit up, joy and warmth and the simple pleasure of playing good hockey tangled together. "No, but I'm not complaining."

Sasha tapped him with his stick blade. "Neither am I."

The game was an easy win, the kind that felt effortless. Alex was practically glowing, and he looked a hundred times better than he had the night before. He was still clearly recovering from weeks of physical and mental stress, but he seemed intent on proving himself, and the team fed off his energy.

They sat beside each other on the bus, whispering low as their teammates celebrated the win on the way back to the hotel.

"I always thought bonds were only fiction, y'know?" Alex tilted his head against Sasha's shoulder, a physical and mental bundle of warmth. "Heather was the one who realized what was happening, and I didn't believe her at first because I've never heard of anything like this actually occurring outside of a movie."

Sasha hummed, turning his head to press a kiss to Alex's hair. He could hear their teammates behind them, a few guys talking about hitting the hotel bar when they got back, others playing cards or video games and shouting playful insults.

"It's a good thing," he said softly. "I'm glad, because it means I know when you are happy, that you are safe."

Alex smiled, but there was a twinge along the bond. "Not safe yet. Not entirely."

Sasha snuck a hand behind Alex's back, where any passing teammates wouldn't see it. Right now it looked like two tired teammates grabbing a few minutes of sleep on the bus ride, but anything more and the rest of the team would definitely notice.

"Ed's trial is in three days." He rubbed his thumb in tiny circles along Alex's back, trying to massage away some of the tension there. "I can make him back down, leave you alone, but I'm certain it would mean having to trade you to another team."

The sound Alex made was part pain, part bitter amusement. "That asshole." He rested his hand on Sasha's thigh briefly, an apologetic rub. "I know he's your best friend, but I can't forgive him for what he's doing to you, and to me."

It was more complicated than that for Sasha, and he could feel the understanding and sympathy from Alex as he tried to process his own complex emotions. If he didn't use his testimony as blackmail, it meant he'd have to tell the truth—and that would mean helping to convict Ed for sure, and send him to jail most likely. It wasn't the potential sentence that made Sasha hesitate, though; instead, it was the knowledge of what would happen to Alex if and when Ed revealed Alex's secret.

"I trust you, babe," Alex murmured. He did sound exhausted, still not back to 100 percent even after feeding the night before. Sasha wanted to offer again, but he knew Alex would never accept more blood this soon. "You'll do the right thing, whatever it may be. I trust that, and I love you no matter what."

Sasha could feel Alex drift off, and hugged him closer while resting his cheek on the top of Alex's head.

I'm thankful that he believes in me this much, Sasha thought, *but I wish I could believe in myself enough to know what the best option is.*

Chapter Twenty-Nine

Eduard Despres will appear today in court on charges of DUI and damage of city property. If convicted, he faces a maximum punishment of up to a year in jail and a fine of at least $5,000, though more could be assessed given the damage. Despres previously entered a plea of Not Guilty and is expected to fight a blood test that was performed, which his lawyers call "inconclusive." Despres is best known as the starting goaltender for the Seattle Cascades, the local NHL team. Sources say the team may take further action, depending on the outcome of today's trial.
—Jamie Morgenstern, Seattle Daily News

Sasha took a deep breath and glanced around the courtroom. He wore suits most days as part of his job, but today the tie around his neck felt like a noose.

Warm comfort trickled over his spine, and Sasha smiled. Alex had offered to come to court with him and sit in the audience, but Sasha had declined. It would be hard enough to face Ed today as he knew he had to, but it would be even harder with Alex there.

"Alexander Petrov, if you could raise your right hand."

Sasha was sworn in and took the seat he was directed to. The court room was small but filled with observers and a few media members who had managed to sneak in the back. Ed had opted for a jury trial, and Sasha glanced over the twelve individuals who would be deciding his best friend's fate by the end of the day.

Will he still be my best friend, after this? It wasn't likely, and Sasha ached at that realization. But what Ed was asking him to do was even more painful.

"Mr. Petrov, can you please describe for the court the events of January 3rd and 4th?" The defense lawyer who Ed had hired was calm, handsome in his expensive suit, and incredibly competent, if the news was to be believed. He seemed somewhat bored as he walked Sasha through the initial phone call and Sasha's quick rush to the scene of the accident.

He thinks he knows what answers I'm going to give, Sasha realized, *because Eddie has told him what he believes I'm going to say.*

"And when you finally saw Mr. Despres, what did you notice?"

Sasha let out a long breath and looked away from Ed and the lawyer. "The first thing I noticed was that Ed looked badly injured. There was blood on his face and shirt, and the EMTs had wrapped his arm in a splint. His eyes were unfocused too. At first I thought maybe he had a concussion, but then—" Sasha paused. *Moment of truth.* "Then I smelled the alcohol."

There was a buzz in the audience, and the jurors shifted uncomfortably.

Ed's lawyer had been pacing, but now he stuttered to a halt. "You believe you smelled alcohol?"

"I know I did. Beer and whiskey. It was strong, but even more noticeable when he spoke."

Sasha would give the lawyer credit for one thing: he thought quickly to try to recover. "It's possible, however, that what you smelled was simply alcohol that had been spilled on Mr. Despres earlier that evening?"

"It's possible," Sasha had to admit. "But I've seen Eddie drunk many times before, and I am certain he was very drunk that night."

The lawyer glanced over at Ed, then back at the judge. "No further questions, your honor."

And then the prosecution, seeing a golden opportunity, jumped up for their own questions.

Sasha could feel Ed's gaze burning into him as he spoke, and only Alex's steady strength in the back of his mind kept him from caving beneath the intensity of it.

I'm sorry, Eddie, he thought, when the last question had been asked. *I just want you to get better, and I think this is the only way you're going to.* Maybe their friendship would never recover from this, but Sasha hoped that someday, at least, Ed would recognize that Sasha loved him.

The court adjourned so the jury could deliberate, and Sasha slipped out of the courtroom to find a bottle of water and somewhere quiet to wait.

Ed found him at the vending machine.

"How could you?"

Sasha's back went stiff, and he turned around cautiously with his bottle in hand. "Eddie."

But it was clear that Ed didn't really want an answer to his question. "I thought you were my brother," he said. "And you betrayed me like this?"

"I told the truth." Sasha shifted the bottle between his hands but didn't open it. "You need help, Ed. You drink too much. You *are* my brother, and because of that I can't just stand by and let you destroy yourself."

"Trou d'cul, tu m'as trahi!"

Rage flashed across Ed's features. It made him look even older, emphasized every line in his face and the way his skin seemed sallow and aged. Sasha closed his eyes against the onslaught of French Canadian cursing, then opened them again when Ed lapsed back into English to lay into him.

"How many times have you been to the bar in the last three months, Sasha? How many? And you're going to judge me for having a drink every now and then, when I know you like to go out with the boys after a game? You're going to ruin my life because you think you're better than me? Décâlisse avec ton hypocrisie. How dare you?"

Watching Ed get even angrier, seeing five years of friendship and brotherhood crack down the center, was genuinely agonizing. Alex sent a pulse of sunshine through his chest, as though to say *I'm here. I love you.*

It wasn't enough to override the pain, but it helped Sasha find strength to take a breath and say, "Enough, Eddie."

Ed's mouth snapped shut.

"You are my brother, whether you hate me after today or not. But I can't ignore what I've seen these last few months, and what I noticed before and dismissed." Sasha met his eyes, trying to push every ounce of worry he could into the gaze. "Yes, we go out with the guys and we drink. But that's not what you do, Ed. You drink too much. Last May you drive drunk. Now again in January. You went out alone the night before a game, and you drank so much that you totaled your car."

"That was the ice," Ed interrupted.

Sasha shook his head. "That was the amount of alcohol I could smell on you," he said calmly. "You kept drinking, even after you were released from the hospital. I saw your house. I watched you pour yourself a drink in the middle of day. You've withdrawn from the team, from *me*. And you've grown paranoid."

Ed's silence was so cold that Sasha half expected the bottle in his hands to freeze over.

"The team has noticed," Sasha continued. "Your mood swings and your paranoia are causing problems in the locker room. And others have noticed too, the way you threaten Alex, your insistence that he's there to steal your job."

"Alex?" Ed's eyebrow went up. "Is that what this is about? You've not only replaced me as a goalie, but you've replaced me as a friend, eh? That's why you're doing this…. You don't need me anymore, because you have *Alex* around." He sneered the name, as though it were a particularly foul word.

"Alex is my friend," Sasha said. "And the rest of the team likes him. He's a good goalie. But he is not your replacement."

But again it was clear that Ed was set in his train of thought, and nothing Sasha could say would make him deviate. "You've been on his side since the beginning. Have you been planning this from the start? My god, Sasha, what's next? You have a new goalie, a new friend. Is Fanning to be your new brother, as well? Or maybe," he spit, "you want to skip right over that and fuck the boy, just so you can fuck me over entirely."

Sasha looked away. It was only for a second, but it was more than enough for Ed, who knew him so well, to read the truth in the small gesture.

"You are," Ed breathed. "You're fucking him. Fanning."

Maybe Alex could pick up on his panic, because he sent a sharp, bright burst of concern along the connection. Sasha, feeling like he was about to topple over, latched on to it, using the bond with Alex as a safety net.

"Yeah," he said. "I'm with Alex. But it has nothing to do with you, Eddie."

Ed's lips went flat. "It has everything to do with me."

Sasha finally uncapped his bottle of water, taking a sip to calm his racing heart. When he looked back down, Ed's stare was devastating and furious. "Eddie, I love you. You are and will always be my brother. And Alex can never replace that, because the love I have for him isn't remotely the same."

Too late, he realized his mistake. Ed's glare went from angry to triumphant. "You love him. The little Para freak. That's what this is all about, then." He laughed, a low, ugly sound. "It makes sense now."

Fear gripped Sasha's lungs. Before he could speak, though, an announcement came over the intercom, calling them back into the courtroom.

The jury had reached a verdict.

"Eddie, don't do this," he pleaded.

Ed just turned away. "If I lose this, your little Para boyfriend is done."

Sasha watched him walk back into the courtroom, dread pooling in his gut.

Seattle Sports News (@SeattleSportsNews)

BREAKING! Cascades goaltender Eduard Despres found guilty of DUI, a gross misdemeanor carrying a penalty of up to one year in prison + fine.

Emma (@Cascadiac)

Ho. Ly. Shit. Saw a tweet from someone who was there that Petrov testified *against* Despres? This is nuts y'all. Will the Cascades even let Despres play again after this?

ALEX WAS sitting on the couch at Sasha's house with his tablet when the front door opened. The TV was on in the background, but it was muted, a local news station flashing a banner about the trial and Despres's guilty verdict. Alex flipped it off when Sasha trudged in, exhaustion hanging off him, and held his arms open.

Sasha collapsed into them with a groan, his large form covering Alex's on the couch. He made a soft, sad noise and snuggled his head down onto Alex's chest, burying his nose in the T-shirt and pressing his ear against Alex's heartbeat.

"You did great, babe." Alex set the tablet down so he could card his fingers through Sasha's hair. "I'm really proud of you."

He'd followed the trial through a combination of social media and Sasha's emotional impressions, sending back his own silent support whenever he could. It was impossible to imagine what Sasha was going through; Alex couldn't begin to fathom what he'd do if it was Shawn on trial, in need of his help and so adamantly unwilling to accept it.

"He will never forgive me," Sasha mumbled. "And I don't blame him."

"If the judge is any good, he'll require counseling and treatment for addiction. Maybe, someday, Eduard will understand why you did what you did."

Sasha turned his head so he could look up at Alex. With a gentle smile, Alex curled forward so he could kiss Sasha, letting it deepen naturally as he poured as much love and support as he could through both the bond and the action.

When the kiss ended, Sasha settled back against Alex's chest. "Even if he forgives me, it won't be soon enough. He's going to tell Coach Henrique... probably tomorrow, if not sooner."

Alex sucked in a breath, panic clawing at his chest briefly before Sasha's tenderness and calm smothered it like a fire blanket over a flame. "We knew this would happen." Even to his own ears, his words didn't sound convincing.

"We did." Sasha wasn't freaking out, at least. "And this will be okay. I promise you."

It had been a surprise when Sasha sat him down to discuss the trial—with Shawn, who he expected... and Volkov, who he did not. Sasha had explained that he'd had two options: he could lie on the stand and bribe Despres with that support in exchange for not telling anyone about Alex's Para heritage. Or he could tell the truth... and get Eddie the help he needed while also putting Alex straight in the crosshairs.

Alex hadn't hesitated, even with the fear lurking beneath the surface. Shawn and Sasha had voiced their immediate support: if the Cascades chose to discard their best goaltender, they would lose their two best defensemen as well.

And then Volkov had added his support. Mikhail had looked fiercely brave as he revealed that he was also Paranormal, and that he'd rather leave the NHL and the Cascades with the three of them than sit around and wait for the genetic testing vote to go through.

With three of their best players and their rising-star rookie threatening to go, they could only hope that it would be enough to stop the Cascades from making the wrong decision.

"I hear Sweden is nice in April," Alex said, fingers once more ruffling through Sasha's hair, tone light.

"Hush, солнышко. We're staying in Seattle. Even old frightened men in the NHL offices will not be so stupid as to lose all four of us."

Alex could only hope that he was right.

Chapter Thirty

Seattle Cascades (@CascadesNHL)
Two more games to go, and it's going to be a tight race to win the last wildcard spot in the Western Conference. We're taking on Detroit tomorrow for two must-win points!

Practice the next day was the strangest that Alex had ever attended.

The four of them—Shawn, Mikhail, Sasha, and Alex—seemed to exist in a bubble of tension and weighted looks that none of their teammates could notice or breach. Every time Coach walked into the room or blew his whistle on the ice, Alex's shoulders would go up and his head would jerk around to look, just waiting to hear his name called out. He knew Sasha was the same, though Shawn and Mikhail seemed intent on channeling their own stress into a kind of frantic energy, working so hard that an assistant coach had to tell them to relax before they wore themselves out ahead of that night's game.

At one point Alex skated to the bench to grab a drink of water. When he flipped his mask up, he caught sight of Dubois leaning over the railing of one of the balconies that overlooked the practice rink. His face was difficult to read from that distance, but Alex was sure that Dubois was staring directly at him.

Sasha skated up behind him and grabbed his own bottle.

"Nothing so far."

Alex sprayed down his face, closing his eyes for a minute against the blast of water. When he opened them again, Dubois was turned to look at the other end of the rink—where Shawn was practicing a drill with Otter.

"Dubois is here."

Sasha's gaze went up at once. "Not looking at you."

No, he's looking at us. All of us, I'm sure of it. "He was a minute ago."

"Ach." Sasha said something under his breath in Russian that sounded like a curse, given his tone. "I just wish this was over one way or another, you know? The waiting, the anticipation of something bad happening, it feels like a weight pressing down on me."

The sensation was one that Alex could relate to. "I think Dubois knows that something is up. At least, he suspects."

Sasha raised an eyebrow. "Because of one look?"

Alex shook his head, but he wasn't sure he could explain. It wasn't just Dubois, but Coach Henrique also. He'd split Shawn and Sasha up for drills, something he rarely did. And he'd kept Alex working down at the other end with a group of forwards, instead of with either of them.

In fact, Alex was surprised they'd gotten away with standing at the bench for the last minute chatting.

A whistle sounded. "Petrov, you're up!"

Ah, there it is. Sure enough, Henrique was watching them, his own expression inscrutable. *They know Shawn and I are friends. Everyone knows that. And Rico himself made sure Sasha and I would be friends after that road trip in January.*

All he had to go on was a suspicion. It might have been simple paranoia, compounded by the stress of having a metaphorical sword hanging over his head... but Alex didn't think he was wrong about this.

"Go, before Rico starts yelling. We'll talk after practice."

The Western Conference playoff berths are pretty much all locked up, but there's one wildcard spot still up for grabs. The Cascades can take it, but to do so they have to win both games against Detroit and Kansas City AND Arizona has to beat Colorado in regulation on Wednesday AND Los Angeles has to lose on Thursday in regulation or OT.

u/cascadingstatistics on r/hockey

AT FIRST he'd assumed that Alex was seeing things or that his nerves were getting the best of him. But with every hour that passed without a word from Henrique or Dubois, Sasha started to wonder... and he started to watch.

He found Shawn in the locker room before the game against Detroit and stole a roll of tape from his partner as an excuse to sit down beside him and duck his head. "Still nothing?"

"No. Alex is freaking out."

Freaking out might have been an exaggeration, but Sasha could feel his lover's tension and worry, a tangled web in the back of his mind. He looked over at Alex, who glanced up immediately and smiled tightly when he met Sasha's gaze.

When Sasha looked away, his eyes danced over his teammates, all of whom were getting ready for the game ahead, and Coach Henrique—who was standing just inside the locker room doors and watching him. Rico met his eyes and held them for a second, then glanced away unhurriedly.

And Sasha might have been able to dismiss it, except Misha skated up to him during warmups and bumped their shoulders together before saying, "Dubois is watching us. He's not in the media box like usual; he's in one of the VIP suites."

When Sasha glanced up, he quickly found the familiar form of the Cascades GM, leaning at the railing in the box suite level and watching the far end of the ice—*watching Alex*.

So as much as Sasha wanted to dismiss Alex's paranoia as such, it was becoming evident that Dubois and Henrique knew something—and that they were watching, waiting.

"I wish they'd just make up their mind," he said to Alex during a stoppage in play, halfway through the first period.

Alex used his stick to clear some ice shavings from his crease. "Me too. It's hard enough to focus on the game, but the anxiety is making it even more difficult."

But nothing happened, and nothing kept happening. They defeated Detroit, and Alex accepted his hugs and head taps from their teammates with a tight smile on his face. They showered, changed back into their suits, and said good night. No one stopped them as they left the arena for the night; there were no calls from Dubois to come to his office and no announcement from Henrique to bench Alex in the final home game.

Sasha followed Alex and Shawn home, ate leftovers with them standing around the kitchen island while each of them did their best not to talk about whatever was happening.

And then Sasha and Alex went up to his room, where Sasha pushed him down onto the bed face-first and opened him up without any teasing or flirting. Alex writhed beneath him, burying his face in the pillow to keep noises from escaping as Sasha used two fingers, then three, spreading him open and getting him wet.

They fucked face-to-face, Alex on his back with his legs wrapped around Sasha's waist, digging the heel of his foot into the base of Sasha's spine to get him to go harder, faster. And when Sasha jerked forward, burying himself deep into Alex's body as he came, Alex dug his fangs into Sasha's neck and fed, his moans muffled against Sasha's skin.

Afterward, they curled up around each other, both exhausted but too nervous to fall asleep.

"Maybe this is a good thing." Alex pressed his lips to Sasha's clavicle and inhaled deeply.

"Maybe." Sasha ran one hand lazily up and down Alex's back, wishing he could relax the stiff lines of tension there.

Eventually they fell asleep, gripping each other tight and refusing to let go.

Oliver Marks (@OliverMarksESPN)
Still unconfirmed, but hearing initial reports that Cascades goaltender Eduard Despres will not be offered a new contract with the team. Despres was convicted Monday of DUI and is currently awaiting sentencing.

Seattle Sports News (@SeattleSportsNews)
#BREAKING Cascades part ways with G Eduard Despres. Despres has been with the team for the last eight years and will be UFA on July 1.

THE NEWS broke while practice was winding up on Wednesday, which was why Sasha didn't know anything about it until he was walking out of the showers with a towel around his waist and realized the entire locker room had ground to a halt.

"What's going on?" he asked Mo, who had stopped halfway through getting dressed and was currently reading something on his phone with his jeans hanging open and a T-shirt thrown over one shoulder.

Mo glanced up, noticed it was Sasha standing there, and his eyes went wide. "Uh." He shook his head. "I'm probably not the best one to tell you, man."

Looking around the room didn't reveal any other clues. Confused, Sasha headed for his stall. Most of the team was either showering, finishing up on the ice still, or stuck doing media, but there were about half a dozen guys scattered around at their lockers.

And no one would look at him.

Confusion gave way to fear. Everyone was glued to their phones or talking in hushed whispers among themselves, but they'd occasionally pause and look over into the corner of the room—no, Sasha realized, at Alex's stall.

Alex, who was on the ice still, determined to prove that he wasn't giving up on the team regardless of whatever Henrique and Dubois eventually decided. Ice flooded Sasha's veins. *Did the news break, then? Did Eddie go to the press?*

But when Alex finally did come into the locker room a moment later, sweating and still fully dressed in his goalie pads, he didn't seem scared at all. In fact, his eyes were bright, startled but cautiously happy, and he made a beeline straight for Sasha without bothering to get out of his gear or skates.

"Did you hear?"

"Hear what?" Sasha looked around the room once again. "No one is telling me anything. Just got out of the shower and everyone's acting like NHL is canceling postseason."

Alex shucked his glove and blocker, set them down in Sasha's stall, and fumbled through the shelf above Sasha's locker. "You need to see this." He made a small triumphant noise when he found what he was looking for: Sasha's phone. "I only heard about it from Ogilve, who sounded pretty shocked, so I don't know the full thing either."

He entered Sasha's passcode—because that was something Alex knew now, because Alex was his boyfriend, and it gave Sasha a moment of warmth and delight to realize that—and opened Twitter, then passed the phone over.

Sasha didn't use Twitter often, though he followed a few local beat reporters, the team account, and his teammates. But he didn't need to scroll to figure out what was going on, because *all* of them were talking about it.

Eduard Despres, goaltender for the Seattle Cascades, will be allowed to walk as of July 1. The Cascades in a public statement this afternoon said they do not plan to offer Despres a new contract.

"I don't understand."

Alex shook his head, apparently just as baffled as Sasha was. "I don't either. But it sounds like he's gone. Maybe another team will pick him up, but he's off the 'Scades for sure."

By now the rest of the team were filtering back into the locker room, most of them from the showers, and conversation was picking up around them as teammates filled one another in on the news.

"This doesn't make any sense," Merkley said.

Klausman shrugged. "Second DUI, almost certain jail time. I figure it's a PR issue for the team if they re-sign him, especially if he might not even be able to play next year."

Merkley seemed dismayed. "Why not suspend him then? Or wait until the sentencing to know for sure?"

On Sasha's other side, Bayer was whispering with Rager, though whispering for them was the equivalent of talking in a normal voice for just about anyone else.

"I bet it's because of the booze," Seth said.

Braiden hushed him. "We don't know that."

"I mean, everyone could smell it on him," Bayer insisted. "It's not like—"

But Braiden caught sight of Sasha watching them and quickly silenced Bayer, dragging him away to gossip somewhere else.

Alex had clearly overheard too, and was giving him a sympathetic grimace. "Look, I need to get out of this gear and shower. Coach will probably be in soon to go over stuff for the game tonight, and I can't miss that. Just...." He glanced around quickly and lowered his voice. "I love you, and I'm sorry this is happening to your friend. But you can't blame yourself for his own behavior, okay?"

Sasha managed a weak smile. "I know."

And he did know, logically. There had been little doubt in Sasha's mind that Eddie would face some serious repercussions for what he'd done back in January, and even preceding that. And Ed had threatened his lover, had tried to get Alex kicked off the team because he was jealous and petty and cruel.

But he was still Sasha's brother, and all the wrongdoings in the world couldn't change that.

It was the right thing to do, he told himself. And it wasn't impossible for Ed to get his life back in order, if he truly wanted to. If he got treatment for his alcohol addiction, if he served his sentence, maybe he'd be back on the ice soon. It wouldn't be in Seattle, but he wouldn't lose everything.

Of course, there's still a chance that Alex does lose everything. Sasha had no idea what the Cascades management was thinking by essentially firing Ed like this. Cautious optimism made him hope that Ed hadn't told them about Alex being Para after all—though if he hadn't yet, he absolutely would now. And if he had told them? *Maybe they don't care. Or maybe they're just waiting for the vote this weekend to decide.*

Conflict raged in Sasha as he dressed automatically, keeping his head down as whispers and theories continued to fly around him. Whatever happened, they still had one more game to play this season. And no matter what went down after that, he'd still have Alex, at least.

Chapter Thirty-One

Seattle Cascades (@CascadesNHL)
Game day! Our last matchup of the regular season is versus Kansas City, and it's do or die for the Cascades tonight.

MARTIN DUBOIS was the most intimidating man Alex had ever met. His office was all dark wood and gleaming chrome, and the man himself an imposing figure behind an equally imposing desk. He glanced up when Alex appeared in his door and motioned him inside but didn't hang up the call that he was in the middle of.

"Absolutely, George. But I don't think you will get the votes you need for this. Go ahead with the proposal if you'd like, but I have spoken with several other managers and I believe the majority of us are in agreement."

Alex closed the door behind him and slid into one of the stiff leather chairs intended for visitors. Dubois was intent on his call, a stack of paperwork in front of him. He lapsed into French briefly, sounding annoyed, but didn't acknowledge Alex or seem to care that he was present.

Finally, Dubois made a scoffing noise at the back of his throat. "George, I have only respect for you and for what you are trying to do with this league, but I think you will find that your proposition has some very unexpected consequences." He paused, and Alex tried not to move or breathe for fear of being noticed. *Is he talking to George Heatly? The commissioner of the NHL?* "Oui, bien. We will talk more this weekend, then."

Dubois disconnected the call and set his phone down, then picked up a pen and wrote something carefully on the sheet before him.

And then, finally, he straightened and looked up at Alex.

"Apologies, an unexpected call that I needed to take."

"Uh, sure." Alex twisted his fingers in the fabric of his slacks, nervous. It was scary enough sitting across from Dubois and knowing he was in the presence of a living legend. There were photos on the walls around them, all tastefully framed, showing a younger Dubois hoisting the Stanley Cup, wearing gleaming medals, shaking hands with other famous people.

But it was even worse knowing that Dubois was his boss. And being summoned to the boss's office on the last day of the regular season was like being sent to see the principal back in school... though, if Alex was being frank, about a million times worse.

"There are a few things we need to discuss before the season ends," Dubois began, "first and foremost of which is your performance over the last three months. Daniel Henrique and I have both been very impressed with your play and your ability to adapt to an NHL pace. I think it's safe to say that without you stepping up and performing as well as you did, this team would not be in the position it is right now, on the verge of making a postseason appearance."

Alex grimaced. He couldn't help it, but the way Dubois said it made him react instinctively.

Dubois noticed, however. But instead of getting upset, he simply laughed. "I know, superstition. But I do believe in you, Alexander, and I believe that you'll win this game tonight and bring us the two points we need. Whether Los Angeles wins... well, that's outside our control. But I have faith in your ability to help this team succeed."

That was comforting, at least. *I can sense a* but *coming on, though.*

As though reading his mind, Dubois's good mood vanished. "But," he said, "there are some... other factors, shall we say, which I believe need to be addressed."

The words were innocent enough, but Dubois's tone was weighted and careful, and his eyes were fixed on Alex as though he were studying a specimen in a glass jar. It was enough to make Alex want to squirm, or at least yank his eyes away from Dubois's intimidating stare.

Heat burst at the base of his neck, spreading down his spine. *Sasha.* The sensation of support and love was enough to help Alex find courage. He straightened in his chair and took a deep breath.

"I'm not sure what factors you want to address here," he said carefully. "I think my play speaks for itself. Any problems that might have existed in the locker room have been resolved, and I think I bring a lot to the team and the locker room. But I also believe I'm good enough to play anywhere in the NHL... or in other leagues, if a situation were to arise that would prevent me from playing in the NHL. As my teammates Sasha and Shawn pointed out, the Swedish league is excellent."

Because he was watching for it, he could see the moment understanding passed over Dubois's face. It was a slight widening of the eyes and then a calculated stare that was equal parts surprise and approval.

"I thought that might be the case." Dubois picked up his pen and shuffled through the stack of papers in front of him, finally retrieving a few pages that were clipped together. "The NHL has changed since I was a player. It's gotten faster, more centered on skill than size. I've seen rules come and go, and had the genuine privilege of helping to shape this team and the league around it as the game evolved. But there are also some things about the sport that I believe shouldn't change and shouldn't be allowed."

Alex's courage, which had been rock solid at the beginning of his speech, began to fracture. He dug his nails into the palms of his hands, waiting, and not even Sasha's soothing warmth could make him relax. Dubois paused, glancing over the pages in front of him.

"Mr. Dubois," Alex said. "I'm not sure what Ed Despres told you, but—"

Dubois held one hand up, the universal sign for *wait*. "Mr. Despres is no longer affiliated with this franchise. And what he may or may not have told me before we parted ways is irrelevant. However, you *are* still affiliated with the Cascades, and that's a state we'd like to maintain for next season."

It took Alex far longer than he'd like to admit to understand what Dubois had just said. "Wait, what? Are you saying I'm not fired?"

To his credit, Dubois looked genuinely startled by the question. "Fired? Why would we fire the best goalie this team has? We've worked to develop you in Portland for the last three years, and I think all of our scouting and coaching staff will agree that you're a vital piece to the future of this team."

"But.... Despres...."

"As I said before, there is no reason for Mr. Despres to be brought up in this conversation. We evaluated all of the options for our team and determined that you represent our best chance for success." Dubois set the papers down and slid them across the desk. "We'd like you to join the Cascades full-time next season. And for this postseason as well, of course."

Alex opened his mouth, glanced down at the papers before him, and closed it.

It was a contract. A standard contract with the usual boilerplate language, like he'd seen half a dozen times before in his career. But this was a one-way deal, one year, a chance to prove himself in the NHL and show them what he could really do. And the number listed had… a *lot* of zeroes on it.

"Obviously you'll want to talk to your agent," Dubois continued, "but I think this is a more than generous option for a trial contract. Matthias has expressed an interest in finishing his career here in Seattle, and we think his veteran presence will help you grow over the next year as he backs you up."

As he backs me *up?* Alex froze. "You want me as the starter?"

"For most of the season, yes. Obviously Coach Henrique will evaluate as he sees fit, and it may be closer to a 50-50 or 60-40 split, at least to start." Dubois settled back in his chair. "No need to decide now, of course. We have one more game to get through and then hopefully playoffs as well, but—"

"Yes."

Dubois looked a little put out over the interruption, and Alex flushed.

"Sorry, sir," he said. "I just meant—well, yes. I'm honored that you're giving me this opportunity, and I, um, am definitely interested."

Once the surprise had worn off, Dubois looked more amused than anything else. "Excellent. We'll talk again soon, then, Alexander. Thank you."

Alex shook his hand when it was offered, collected the paperwork, and stood to head to the door.

Dubois's voice stopped him. "Alex."

Alex turned around, one hand on the doorknob.

"The league has changed a lot since I was a player, but some things haven't changed at all. I'm really pleased to welcome you to this team."

He tilted his head, eyes gleaming strangely in the light of his desk lamp, and smiled when their gaze met.

"Thank you, sir," Alex said, nodding, and slipped out of the office.

Ellen DeSmith (@EllenDeSmithESPN)

Word trickling down the grapevine that several team managers are now opposed to Saturday's vote on introducing genetic testing for all players. Hearing that tensions are rising as GMs call for the vote to be removed from the agenda.

"Holy shit, Sasha."

Sasha glanced down at the man burrowed into his arms, apparently uncaring that they were both covered in sweat and thick layers of padding. Forty minutes down, twenty minutes to go, and the Cascades were up 1-0 on Kansas City. And Alex was trembling against him, part adrenaline and part excitement.

"That goal, oh my god," Alex said.

Sasha laughed, grabbing Alex's mask from where it was perched on top of his head and pulling it away so he could tilt the younger man's face up and kiss him.

They were in a back hallway, but the rumble of the crowd was still audible... as was the sound of their teammates only just around the corner, heading back to the locker room for the intermission. It was probably stupid to be here, where anyone could walk by and find them, but Sasha couldn't bring himself to care right then.

Alex kissed him back, hard and energetic, more a tangle of lips and tongue than anything elegant enough to really be called a proper kiss. He was laughing too, and his eyes were shining.

When Sasha had found him before the game, Alex had been glowing with excitement. The weight of the last couple of weeks had been gone entirely, replaced by a combination of relief, joy, and optimism. It was the same look he still had now, hours later, and Sasha couldn't resist kissing him again and again, feeding off their shared happiness.

"Hey, losers." Shawn turned the corner, laughing as they jerked apart. "This is why I volunteered to find you. You guys couldn't even wait until the game was over?"

Sasha tucked Alex's head beneath his chin so he could glare at his line mate. "What do you want?"

"Coach wants a meeting."

It was early enough in the intermission to be unusual, but Shawn didn't seem concerned. Normally the team had about half of the fifteen or so minutes in the locker room to change clothes, hydrate, do whatever they might need to do. Then Coach Rico would come out and go over strategy for the rest of the game. But Sasha had been tracking the time in the back of his head since the moment he and Alex slipped away, and he knew it had only been a couple of minutes that they'd been gone.

Still….

Alex gave him another kiss without prompting, still smiling brightly, then pulled back to walk over to Shawn—who dragged him over and ruffled his sweaty hair.

The rest of the team was loosely gathered around when they walked in, and Coach launched right into it.

"LA was playing in Colorado tonight," he said. "Their game just ended. They lost."

Excitement filled the room like a dull roar. Everyone knew what that meant: Los Angeles had been the only team standing between Seattle and the last remaining wildcard spot. With tonight's loss, they were one point ahead of the Cascades in the standings… unless Seattle could capture a win, and the two points necessary to pass them and take the last playoff spot.

Coach waited them out, then continued. "The last two periods were good, but I think we can do better. Thanks to Petrov, we have a narrow lead right now, but Kansas City's defense is cutting us off in the neutral zone."

Sasha accepted the shouts of support and high-fives directed his way, then glanced to Alex. Alex's eyes were narrowed, his lips quirked into a teasing smile that clearly said he was going to reward Sasha with more than a high-five later that night.

"So here's what we're going to do in the third."

Using a whiteboard, Coach diagramed a couple of plays, some weaknesses in the Kansas defense that he thought they could work around, ways to keep the puck out of their own zone as much as possible.

"Any questions?"

No one answered.

"All right." Rico capped his marker, then crossed his arms and looked out across the room. "However tonight ends, I want you to know that I'm proud of each and every one of you. The second half of the season wasn't what we expected, but we managed to hang in there, thanks to Matty's and Alex's hard work. And I know some troubling news may have come out yesterday, but I heard from Martin earlier today that we have a new goalie to welcome to the team next season."

Alex ducked his head when Carts and Bayer piled on him.

Coach nodded approvingly. "So I want you to go out there and give it everything you've got. Let's win this!"

Shouts and cheers filled the room as everyone jumped to their feet. There were twenty minutes left to play, and it was obvious that Kansas City had no idea how much determination and desperation they were about to go up against. Everywhere he looked, Sasha could see excitement building, and pride.

This is my team.

There would always be an empty spot in the room where Eddie should have been, but it wasn't as sharp and painful as it had been in January, when he'd first walked into the locker room and felt that gaping hole keenly. Now, when he looked at the goalie stall in the corner, the ache was buried beneath feelings of love and joy.

As though sensing Sasha's eyes on him, Alex glanced up from where he was retying a leg pad. Sasha grinned at Alex, channeling every bit of pride and love that he could into the look, and felt it returned to him with a burst of sunshine.

There was no way to know if they were going to make playoffs or win the Stanley Cup. Hell, they didn't even know how Saturday's vote was going to go—though Alex seemed hopeful enough. But whatever happened, he had his team, and he had Alex, and that was everything he could ever hope for.

ELYSE SPRINGER is an author and world traveler whose unique life experiences have helped to shape the stories she wants to tell. She writes romances with LGBTQIA+ characters and relationships, and believes that every person deserves a Happily Ever After. Her asexual F/F romance *Thaw* was an Amazon #1 Bestseller. When she's not staring futilely at her computer screen, Elyse spends her time adding stamps to her passport, catching up on her terrifying TBR list, and learning to be a better adult.

You can find Elyse online at:
Website: elspringer.com
Twitter: @ElyseSpringer
Facebook: www.facebook.com/elysespringerwrites

WORLD TURNED UPSIDE DOWN
ELYSE SPRINGER

WORLD OF LOVE

After three winters in Antarctica, Simon Bancroft is an old hand on the ice. The harsh weather and extreme isolation aren't for everyone, but he enjoys the tight-knit community at McMurdo Station… and lately he's enjoyed watching the hot new researcher, Asher Delaney, who's recently arrived to study the aurora. But Simon's just a janitor. Asher doesn't even know he exists.

When Simon's friends propose a wager, he gets a chance to introduce himself to Asher at last. But Asher defies all of Simon's assumptions, and suddenly he finds himself reevaluating everything he thought he knew about Asher, himself, and falling in love at the bottom of the world.

www.dreamspinnerpress.com

Also from Dreamspinner Press

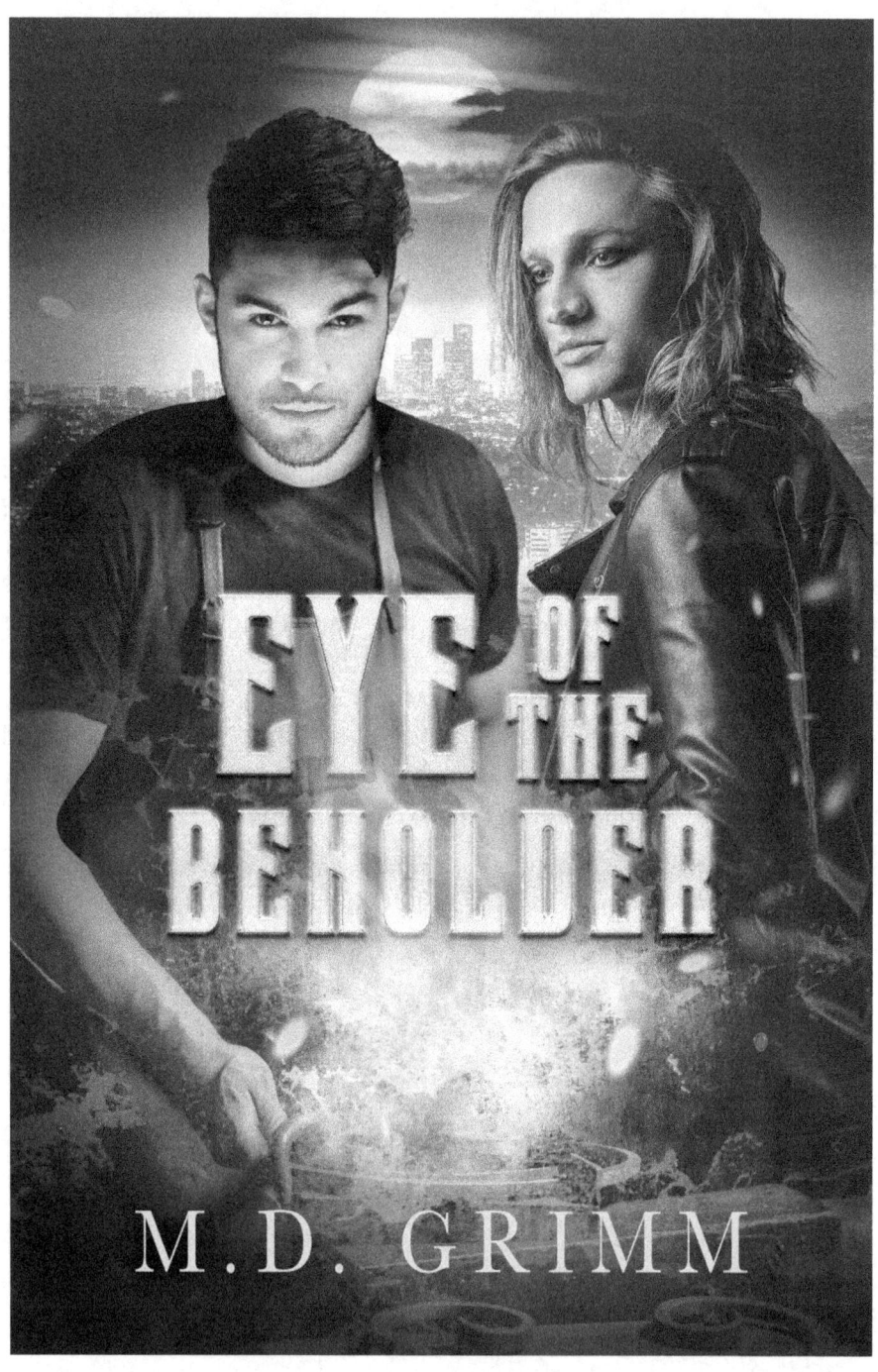

www.dreamspinnerpress.com

Also from Dreamspinner Press

www.dreamspinnerpress.com

 FOR **MORE** OF THE **BEST GAY ROMANCE**

dreamspinnerpress.com